MW00616592

Preface

These fact-based events with fictitious characters take place in the years before the second world war to some years thereafter, a unique period in the history of Norwegian immigration to the United States of America.

Norwegian immigrants settled in several places in the United States over a 50-year period, with a large colony in the New York area.

Encyclopedias describe the word *vision* as images, dreams, hopes, aspirations.

This book is released simultaneously in the Norwegian language under the title *Visjoner*.

Human beings are like small boats adrift on an ocean. It takes determination and courage to alter a predictable drift.

Most immigrants followed in the footsteps of the ones who had gone before them. However, some managed to chart their own course.

© 2006 Oswald I. Glibertson
All rights reserved, including right
of reproduction in whole or in part.

Print:
www.PrintmediaBooks.com
Anaheim, CA USA

Cover Design:
Carol Kerr Graphic Design
www.carolkerr.com
San Diego, CA USA

Cover Photograph: author

ISBN-10: 0-9788447-5-0
ISBN-13: 978-0-9788447-5-2

FIRST EDITION

Contents

VISIONS

A Norwegian Immigration Story

Oswald I. Gilbertson

Flaten family

Tor was the youngest of the four children in the Flaten family. He had lived at home until his father had to be moved to a home for the elderly and his oldest brother, Martin and his family, had taken over the house with the attached grocery store. Tor had rented a small apartment closer to the center of the community. The second oldest brother had left the family home to study and had eventually settled in the nearest town. Their mother had passed away several years ago.

The only girl in the family was Signe, and she got married at quite a young age. Her husband, Adolf Bakken, was an only child who had lived alone for some time on the small family farm that he had taken over after his parents. His father had been unable to manage the farm due to failing health and his parents had therefore taken up residence in a centrally located apartment. As soon as Adolf and Signe were married, they moved to the Bakken farm and started their lives together in quite comfortable surroundings.

Tor had always had a good relationship with his sister and this continued after she married and had children. He had known Adolf before he married Signe, and the three of them had many good times when they got together.

Tor had always been a bright and capable boy, well liked by his peers and the elderly alike. He was handy and not afraid to start up on one thing or another. As he matured, he had tried being a carpenter in construction, a furniture maker during the winter months, an electrician and a plumber. He had become familiar with the various tools used in these occupations, and he actually liked all of these trades. He had taken a woodworking class one winter and a couple of correspondence courses in commercial subjects. The local educational opportunities were rather limited. Early on he realized that he needed advice on educational possibilities if he was to achieve a career in a particular profession. He knew that if he was to seek additional education, he would have to leave his native district.

Little by little it became evident as the population and size of the rural community grew that technical assistance was needed in several areas. An older man had been hired on a part-time basis by the municipal leaders to act as technical advisor, and it did not take long before he realized that he needed an assistant. When this became known to Tor, he presented himself at the proper office and explained that he was interested in the position. The mayor had his office in the same building and gave his full support when he learned of Tor's request. He could do this because he had known the Flaten family for many years and knew Tor to be a capable young man. The mayor was certain that Tor would soon develop into a valuable employee for the municipality. He did not see a problem with the fact that Tor had limited formal education. The mayor had his answer ready when that question came up: "What the boy lacks in education, he more than makes up for with his experience and practical sense." The older man who had been employed temporarily would be retiring in a couple of years, and the mayor could not think of a better successor to this position than Tor.

Thus it was that Tor became assistant technical manager at quite a young age. He was given the opportunity to participate in some educational courses that were arranged by the municipality and the state, and his expertise and respect grew rapidly in the district. He was totally engaged in his work and liked his responsibilities. He became involved in things like maintenance of official buildings, roads, bridges, new construction, water supply and sewer systems. He took on all assignments with the same enthusiasm and became a busy man as he worked himself into the position. Tor was well liked and the mayor was proud on behalf of the district because, after all, it was primarily he who was responsible for getting Tor the position.

Tor visited his sister and her family often in his spare time, and he was a popular uncle to the children of that household. He spent time with friends and participated in various activities as often as his free time permitted. He was skilled on skis, played soccer and liked to take long walks. He went to movies and dances with his friends. It happened quite often that he would see a girl home after an evening of dancing, but he had not developed a serious relationship with any girl. Signe was the one who had taught him to dance, or maybe she had just been practicing her own skills with him. In any event, he managed well on the dance floor and had many pleasant evenings at the local dance hall.

Gradually several of his friends from his early youth moved away from the rural district. Some left for cities in different parts of the country and a few had traveled as far as America. He received letters from some that had left the area, and when they returned for a visit it was a matter of course that they would pay a visit to Tor's office, where they would find him buried in stacks of work. What they described to Tor was for the most part positive experiences. The ones who had left the area had managed well and found good jobs. Several of them told Tor that they had reasoned that even though they often longed for the place where they grew up, they could manage in some other place for a while and adjust to a new way of life. Maybe they would move back home someday. Tor noted especially the ones who had left for America. He corresponded with two of his childhood friends who had settled in different places there and had asked them many questions in his letters. He had contemplated the possibilities and concluded that a trip away from the local area would probably be advantageous for him also, as appeared to be the case for most who had left. What he was told by the ones who had left sounded exciting and made him restless. What could he do to satisfy this restlessness? If he decided to leave for America and if he left his present job properly, he assumed that it would be possible for him to get a job again in the municipality, if that should be necessary. He could possibly get a leave of absence for a long period, because if he acquired new experiences, these would surely also benefit the local municipality when he returned. On the other hand, why in the world would he even consider leaving his beloved home area where he had a very satisfying job? He had much to ponder.

Urge to emigrate

When Tor presented his plans for the future to his superior and leaders of the district, they almost went into shock. They shook their heads in disbelief and looked at him with questionable expressions and stammered, "Did we hear you correctly? We thought that you liked your position. Why? Has anything happened to you that we should know about?" Tor explained as best he could how and why he had arrived at the decision of emigrating to America. He told them that he did not see this as a permanent move and that he wished to apply for a leave of absence for a year. In this year he expected to gain much experience that would be beneficial to the district. He would get a chance to experience another part of the world and after a year, he figured that he would return because he would have satisfied his urge for America by then, or he would be too homesick to remain there any longer. He understood all too well those in the district who expressed loudly, "Have you heard that Tor wants to leave for America? He who has such a good position! He could surely hold on to that job for the rest of his life. Who has put these silly ideas into his head?"

The district considered his application thoroughly and objectively, and had concluded in a just way that a leave of absence could not be granted. The district could in no way see how it could defend holding the position open for such a long time in anticipation of his possible return. It was explained that the position was so important that it had to be filled as soon as possible. Tor registered some disappointment after having read through the response for the first time, but after a while he understood the reasoning from the leaders of the district and agreed with their decision. In the letter he received, the district leaders expressed their best wishes in every way and stated that if he should decide to return one day, they would do their best to get him employed again. The letter also contained a testimonial, and much to his surprise they had included this in two versions, one copy in Norwegian and the other in English. This was considerate of the district and he really appreciated this gesture. The attestation presented the bare administrative facts plus a few lines at the bottom, with the mayor's signature, where the district expressed its complete satisfaction with Tor. It was stressed that they were completely confident that Tor's next employer would also be completely satisfied with him.

Tor had three weeks' notice that he used to complete several cases in the office and additionally he had to wrap up some different private matters. He talked to someone in the district who had been to America and he had studied the conditions "over there" in books that he found at the library. The three weeks came to an end much too soon, but Tor was satisfied with all that he had managed to do and was ready when the day for departure came. He had packed only a few of his possessions and had been able to store the few pieces of furniture that he had acquired at his brother's place.

Tor had purchased passage on a ship that traveled between a Norwegian west coast port and New York City and had been told that the voyage was scheduled to take eight days. The agent had also told him that the Norwegian America Line ship was fully booked. Tor's experience with the sea was limited to a few fishing trips off the coast in an open boat. He was looking forward to experiencing the activities on a large ship for several days. He had some misgivings at times about his resignation from a secure position in familiar surroundings that surely would have lasted through his lifetime. But he had made his decision and had a positive outlook for prospects in the New York area.

Europe was in an uneasy period at this moment in time with bleak assertions from several sources to the effect that the policies conducted by Germany could result in tragic consequences. Tor had not had much time or serious interest in engaging in news from foreign countries. During the crossing of the Atlantic Ocean it was not possible to avoid the worldwide news that was posted on bulletin boards and the discussions that could be heard all over the ship. Germany had provoked and made difficult demands of its neighbors. The big question that occupied the world was, would it be possible for countries in Europe to avoid a war.

~

His friend, Anders Dalen, with whom he had corresponded for some time, met Tor when he came to America in 1938. Anders was also the person who had arranged for the necessary guarantees for Tor to get permission to immigrate. The routines from the arrival in the harbor of New York to the examinations of his papers by the health and immigration authorities took place without difficulties. The clearance had still taken several hours, but that was probably caused by the fact that two ships from Europe arrived on the same day, which resulted in long lines in front of each inspector.

Ellis Island was the place where millions of immigrants got their first exposure to America. The activity at this clearance center, on a small island in the harbor area of New York, was at its height in the years 1892-1924, when thousands of immigrants were cleared every day. The immigrant flood tapered off at the end of the 1920's, when stricter immigration laws were established with the adoption of the so-called National Origins Act. It is said that more than 100 million Americans can trace their family tree back to someone who got their name registered by the authorities at Ellis Island. The place was closed in 1954.

Anders brought Tor to his home and offered him a small room containing a bed and some furniture in which he could store his few belongings. He was told that he was welcome to stay with him and his wife for as long as needed to get himself acquainted and established in the new land.

Anders and his wife had settled on First Place in the center of Brooklyn when they first came to the country. They had changed apartments a couple of times and had an extra room that they used to rent to newcomers. The Norwegian Seamen's Church was active from 1928 to 1984 in this area. This became a natural place for immigrants to meet until the end of the 1920's, when Bay Ridge gradually became the place where immigrants settled. Not far from the Seamen's Church a poor quarter was built up in the depression of the 1930's. People of many nationalities lived there, including Norwegians. These people found themselves without means of support, without work, and without any form for federal or state support. They had to fend for themselves as best they could. Among things that became popular, to bring in small amounts of money, was for grown men who were out of work to walk the streets and try to sell an apple or two to passers by. A famous painting from that period portrays a girl selling flowers while resting on a stairway with her basket. Even as difficult as the situation is for the girl, the painting shows that she is willing to share her sandwich with a begging dog seated by her side.

Tor was at work as a carpenter after only three days in Brooklyn. He was working as partner to Anders and had him to thank for getting started so quickly. He soon learned that many experienced craftsmen were without work at that time. Tor had not done any physically demanding work in a long time and the first days were therefore hard on him. He took in the experiences that he was exposed to every day, and it was not long before he had a suggestion for his friend.

Tor was excited when he explained to Anders that some of the work they were doing was suitable work for a subcontractor, and he was of the opinion that he would be able to do the administrative part of such work himself without difficulty. He was confident that he had seen and experienced sufficiently to have a very good idea for how that kind of work was done. It was his opinion that if he only had a better understanding of how to find information on where future projects were planned, who had been awarded the contract, and how one should proceed to become a contractor, they would be able to take on projects as subcontractors. Anders, who had worked for some years on framing, explained that he had been led to believe that it was not quite that simple. A firm had to be created and duly registered. They would have to present their experience to the larger contractors and maybe also to architectural firms. They would have to offer competitive prices, and quite possibly they would have to go to the trade union and be prepared to answer many questions there. Anders was especially troubled about how they would be able to develop offers and present attractive bids. Prices would have to be competitive and still afford them profitability. Tor detected a somewhat negative tone from his friend and swept it aside by simply saying, "Let us get started." He went on to say that, "We are not going to get all the jobs we bid on and while we are waiting for a contract from a builder or a contractor, we can continue to work as we do now." He looked directly at his friend when he said this, and when he did not meet a negative reaction, he continued, "We need a name for our firm, what do you like?"

Quite a few suggestions for a firm name were discussed in the next several days between them, and they told no one about their plans. On Sunday evening, about a week later, they were in agreement, the firm was to be called Norse Builders. Scandinavians in the building trades were well liked in the area, and they felt that the word "Norse" in the name reflected favorably on their backgrounds. They had considered Viking Builders and had selected this name as an alternate in case the first name was already registered by others. They set out on Monday morning to the administrative offices and arranged for documentation to establish a firm and registered the name to get a business license. The process took some time, but it was not difficult. The friendly and helpful personnel at the different offices made the experience easy.

Tor had also told Anders, when they were discussing the name for their firm, that he planned on taking some evening courses to improve his English and to learn more about the building trades. Anders agreed that this was a good idea and said that he had been thinking along the same lines himself.

The war in Europe, which developed into the Second World

War, put a brutal stop to their plans. Both had received letters to register for military service. The examinations by the military doctors found Tor to be in good health. He was mustered and was offered options for different branches of the military that needed recruits. He selected the engineering and construction arm of the marines, the so-called Seabees. Anders was rejected because of a knee injury that he sustained several years ago and because his eyesight was not satisfactory. He received a lower draft classification, which meant that he could possibly be called upon at a later time. In this way the two friends were separated. Tor was sent off to a military post in another state for basic training and Anders had to find himself a new carpenter partner.

Occupation

The politics that Germany had pursued resulted in a war that caused enormous loss of human life, vast property damage and untold horror and suffering for people in most European countries. The German army had advanced rapidly on several fronts and felt superior. The army leaders had in a short period of time conquered large land areas with minimal losses of their own personnel and equipment. England and France joined forces and declared war on Germany. With that the Second World War was under way on September 3, 1939.

The unbelievable, unthinkable, yes, inconceivable, also happened during the darkness of April 9, 1940, when German forces slipped in on the Norwegian coastline and had all of Norway occupied after only a short time. The attack came so suddenly and unexpectedly that the Norwegian military did not have time to call up all of its conscripts. The few units that were organized fought hopelessly against the superior German forces for a couple of months. The small innocent country that had tried its best to remain neutral was not prepared to withstand a military attack, especially not of the magnitude that Germany could muster. Suddenly the country was occupied and drawn into the Second World War. Norway had been surprised by a major power and the Norwegian people had to submit to orders from the German occupiers.

Conscripts had been ordered to meet for bus departures at specified locations that had been organized in great haste in some parts of the country. The plan was that the conscripts were to be taken to the nearest military bases where weapons and further orders would be issued. Signe said good-bye to her two brothers when they entered the bus with other young men their age. It was in the late afternoon and the tears flowed from the many family members that had showed up. The conscripts received so much unaccustomed attention that they became embarrassed in their confused state of mind. The young men reacted as if they were in a dream, and the family members who took their farewells with them was a gathering of crying parents, young relatives, neighbors and friends. Neither the young men nor their relatives had any inkling of what the future would hold for them, and to a man they had only the vaguest understanding of what modern warfare really involved.

The bus trip for Signe's brothers became a short one. They all returned after they had been gone for a few hours, and in the early morning they were all back in their homes. The bus had been met by some high-ranking Norwegian military officers long before they reached the military base and they were told that they arrived too late. The enemy had simply taken the area in a surprise attack. The men were to return to their homes by the fastest possible means and they were told to act as if nothing had happened. Later on it was revealed that the statements expressed by some of the Norwegian officers were incorrect. A few officers sympathized with the Germans and formulated their decisions from that point of view.

Hitler indicated in his book *Mein Kampf* that propaganda during warfare was to be considered as a weapon. The German propaganda ministries had become experts in this field. They knew how to explain to the Norwegian population that the action Germany had initiated was not to be perceived as an occupation. It was explained that the proper way to understand this action was to appreciate that this was a defensive measure that they simply had to initiate. They used the case of the Jøssingfjord incident as an example, which took place less than two months before the German troops came to Norway, when the English broke the Norwegian declaration of neutrality by storming into the fjord with the cruiser *Cossack*. The German ship *Altmark* had been pursued by the British navy in open seas and had fled for safety to the innermost end of the Jøssingfjord. The *Altmark* had 299 shipwrecked British seamen aboard, from different ships that the Germans had plucked up after their ships had been torpedoed. Naturally this side of the story was not mentioned by the Germans. The British navy decided to enter the Jøssingfjord on February 16, 1940, to board the German ship that it had shadowed for weeks against Norwegian protests. The *Altmark* was a 17,000-ton ship with a top speed of 25 knots. The British succeeded in freeing all the prisoners. Six German soldiers were killed in the ensuing exchange of gunfire.

For many of the prisoners aboard the *Altmark* the torpedoing had been caused by the large German battleship *Admiral Graf Spee*. The battleship had operated relatively unhindered in the North and Atlantic seas for a long time. When the Allies finally were able to neutralize the battleship's action radius, the captain realized that the ship was isolated and Hitler ordered the ship to be sunk. The battleship was sunk with explosive charges outside Montevideo, Uruguay, on

December 17, 1939. Several historians will claim that the Jøssingfjord episode caused Hitler to accelerate his attack plans for Norway.

The Germans justified the attack on Norway of April 9, 1940, by making reference to the minefields that British and French navies had deployed in strategic locations along the west coast of Norway as late as the day before. This was done to stop exports from going out of Norwegian ports to Germany, primarily to prevent Swedish ore from being shipped from Narvik. They also blamed Norway for not maintaining neutrality toward England by allowing the warship *Cossack* to enter the Jøssingfjord. The Germans explained an additional reason for having come to Norway: since the Norwegians and the Germans are of the same race it was only natural that they should stand together as friends and support each other against common enemies. The Norwegian population ought to be grateful for the German assistance, and ought to do their best to assist the occupation force and the German troops. This was reasoning that many Norwegians accepted and that gave Germany friends in Norway. People who sympathized with the occupation forces helped the enemy on several occasions both deliberately and in quite innocent ways as the occupation developed. This contributed to disastrous consequences for the Norwegians who had a different view of the occupation and the German forces.

The transition from peace to war, that took place over a few hours, was incomprehensible for the population. From a peaceful daily existence, life was suddenly complicated by the invasion of armed soldiers who spoke a strange language. The initial and inevitable curiosity among the people was in a relatively short time replaced by uncomfortable feelings when they were within reach of the soldiers, and these feelings turned little by little to fear and hate. The German army was powerful. It behaved arrogantly and orders from it were to be accepted and obeyed without reservation. Many Norwegians had not seen people from other countries close up before, they had not heard people who spoke a foreign language, and they had never seen or heard loud and armed soldiers in activity. Contact with the outside world had for most of the people been limited to some information over the radio, movies, newspapers, periodicals, and stories told by returning seamen. The German soldiers had plenty of Norwegian currency when they arrived and they were eager buyers in the shops. They had been without different types of goods for a while, and sweets were especially popular. They bought all kinds of chocolate and ate butter directly from the package or put huge portions of it onto the dark bread that they seemed to eat often.

The Flaten and Bakken farms were located some distance from the center of the community and it could take days before the farmers there got an understanding of what was going on there. They were generally better informed about national and international news because of their radios. And, of course, they followed the weather forecast, especially as it might affect the running of the farm. Radios were bulky and expensive before the war. They were fabricated as a piece of furniture and treated as such, and their wooden exterior would often match the furniture of a living room. Not every household had a radio because of the expense or the poor listening conditions that limited the number of broadcasts that could be heard. Particularly in rural areas it was necessary to install external antennas to enable even minimal reception of both domestic and foreign broadcasts. Before the radios were confiscated, the occupation force had told the population over the national radio station what it wanted them to know as provided by its censored information service. Better equipped and favorably located radios were able to receive BBC London.

All radios were listed in a national registry before the war due to the collection of an annual fee, the so-called listening fee. On August 12, 1941, the authorities ordered that all radios were to be turned in. It was simply a matter of following the licensing list to ensure that no radios remained with the population and truckloads of radios were brought to storage places. However, some unregistered radios remained with the population and additional radios found their way into the country. Illegal radios could have been smuggled into the country by returning sailors or overseas travelers to avoid the listening fee, built in radio shops from spare parts or air dropped as part of military equipment for the resistance movement. Ownership of radios was illegal and listening to one had to be done in total secrecy. But people took the risk. As illegal radios were exposed, often by a slip of the tongue or by a tip from a traitor, the owner was arrested. The violators would be sentenced to serve time in jail, or in a concentration camp.

The Norwegian population was to get all the news from their friends, the occupation force, after the radios had been confiscated. News was distributed through a heavily censored newspaper and with a large map of Europe mounted in a glass-covered bulletin board. This was posted centrally and locked securely. The military front lines were shown on this map with colored thread strung between pins. The German military updated the front lines diligently every day as long as their armies made advances. However, when withdrawals started on several fronts, the updating of the front lines on this map was often neglected.

People heard in secrecy through BBC radio in London that His Majesty King Haakon and members of the Parliament had managed to escape from Norway and had arrived safely in England. They had announced that the Norwegian struggle against the occupation force would continue from there. Radio programs from BBC in the

Norwegian language started to contain coded messages at the end of the transmissions, messages that meant nothing to outsiders but were of great value to those who were active in the underground. The messages could, for example, be a go-ahead signal for actions, information for the necessity of certain units of the underground to go into hiding, give information for the need to monitor movement of warships along the coast, troop movements, prisoner transports, and so on.

Life on the farms had to go on as before, caring for and managing the crops and the animals. But it was not easy for the Bakken family with three small children that had to be protected and sent off to school. Everyone did their share and little by little a routine developed in everyday life. The routine was often interrupted by people who stopped by and could tell stories of one thing or another that had happened in other parts of the county, country or in foreign countries. These were often rumors of events that were impossible to verify. It was not possible to trust everything that was heard, and one had to be especially skeptical with what was heard from certain sources. If you passed on what had been heard, you could risk that it would be used against you if you were arrested. Rumors told of arrests, and the newspaper carried stories about what would happen if the occupation forces were not obeyed. The newspaper reported from time to time that Norwegian saboteurs had been arrested and that the death penalty had been carried out. The "traitors" had been shot, and usually this had taken place outside the old Akershus fortress in Oslo.

After Japan's surprise attack on the naval base at Pearl Harbor, Hawaii, on December 7, 1941, and when Germany declared war with America four days later, America entered the war. Not many days would pass before rumors about these incidents circulated among Norwegians. People believed that the war would soon be over with

America's help. The rumors also told about where the war was ravaging and that the German army had suffered heavy losses. The German army had experienced rapid advances initially when it attacked Russia. But the Russians, with help from America and others, were able to mobilize such a strong resistance that Hitler was never able to reach his goal of capturing Moscow.

The occupation force explained that it was unlawful for small groups to engage in discussions and it was ordered that such groups would be disbanded. People whispered between themselves and in public places they would congregate for only short periods of time, always looking around for military patrols or possible German sympathizers. Children had to be shielded from discussions about the war. They could easily make a slip of the tongue to strangers and thereby place the entire family in jeopardy.

The shops had less to sell and eventually most groceries were rationed. Scarcity of goods and rationing brought forth resourcefulness among people. The service life of clothing and footwear was extended with repairs such that it was common to see clothing with multiple patches of material that could even be of a different color. Gradually it became customary to trade, and it became common for merchandise to be sold on the black market. Even if the food producers were closely monitored by the authorities, some things always escaped the inspectors.

Soap, for personal use, was produced in a process where fat, caustic soda and salt were cooked for a long period and the soap was skimmed off over time. It was a smelly process that gave usable soap that was best suited for doing the laundry. The scarcity of tobacco and coffee was difficult for many. Some households cultivated tobacco plants. It became a passable smoke after the tobacco leaves had been marinated in different ingredients and dried carefully in an oven. A coffee substitute was produced by roasting green peas. Razor blades were sharpened by rubbing them back and forth inside a regular drinking glass. The word “substitute” became well used both in conversation and in print.

Different sizes of the official emblem of the Nazi party, with eagle and swastika, became a common sight, as on buildings, flags, pennants, uniforms and vehicles. Even the Norwegian postage stamps were stamped over with a swastika. It became customary to observe German soldiers while they performed their military duties and they usually marched to and from these assignments. Often they marched from their billeting, which could be a requisitioned schoolhouse or a house of prayer[1], with a view to impress the local population and the need to uphold the discipline of their soldiers. They would sing a great deal and often while they marched, surely to maintain cadence and keep up their spirits. The songs were inspiring and contained promises of victory in coming battles. The point of one song that was popular for a long time described the capture of England. The refrain of this song, "denn wir fahren, denn wir fahren, denn wir fahren gegen Engeland " (then we depart, then we depart, then we depart for England), was sung loudly while the soldiers marched in perfect unison. The sound of marching soldiers, amplified by the steel-studded heels on their boots, carried a long distance and had an intimidating and revolting effect on the occupied population. Soldiers were seldom alone in their spare time, and when they had patrolling duties, they operated in pairs and were equipped with helmets and loaded rifles. One could see prisoners from countries like Yugoslavia and Russia that sometime were put to different types of manual labor while guarded by German soldiers. The prisoners were poorly dressed and they appeared malnourished.

The German soldiers operated many types of military vehicles that were of great curiosity for both young and old. They often used motorcycles that had a sidecar, a vehicle that few had seen before. All vehicles were painted in the German army's green camouflage colors. The standard German gasoline cans could be seen all over. These solid cans became popular and were also copied by other countries. The British called them jerrycans. Gasoline was available for the German army, but it was severely rationed for private use by Norwegians. Practically all private cars had been confiscated by the Germans. Official vehicles used gas from charcoal that was generated in units attached to the buses and cars. The Germans also used horses, and sometimes large Ardennes horses would pull cannons and heavy equipment. Norwegian Fjord horses that had been confiscated by the army or purchased from local farmers were also used.

When darkness fell and lights had to be lit, whether electric or kerosene lamps, people had to isolate themselves from the outside world. All places that were to be lighted had to have all windows covered with black shades. Light had to be blocked completely from the outside and there was no mercy given to anyone not satisfying this demand. Hinged moldings had to be installed on the side of the windows such that they could be folded back over the pulled shades to ensure that no light would filter through. On a dark fall or winter night it was therefore pitch dark outside and the result was that people spent most of their time indoors. The Germans considered the blackout a serious matter because Allied planes were dependent on lights or terrain to orient themselves. If someone ventured out for a quick trip, for example to visit the privy or a neighbor, they could use a small flashlight. That is to say if they had been fortunate enough to obtain a battery. Flashlights were used sparingly and the life of the batteries was extended by heating the batteries on the stove. Anyone surprised by a patrol while outside, would hear the order "halt." Interrogation would follow: "Where have you been and why? Where are you going and why? Where do you live? Show me your identification papers." If the patrol did not receive the proper answers or if irregularities were suspected, detention would follow. Such an experience, or just to have heard of such an experience, contributed to tension and considerable anxiety among the population. If a brutal knock on the door was heard, the light inside had to be shut off before the door was opened. It was quite shocking and frightening when seeing police personnel outside; often there would be one or more gestapo, or members of its police troopers in the attire that oftentimes was a full-length skin coat, assisted by German soldiers with full military equipment. Typically it could be four to five men that demanded that all rooms were to be examined, including all drawers and cabinets. The intruders carried on the search on their own once inside the house, and it was not possible for the surprised family to follow them everywhere and to see what was examined and what was possibly removed.

Uncle Martin visited the people at Bakken often and he always brought something from the store that he shared with them. This could, for example, be some dried codfish, a few salted herring, a can of fish balls or a couple of sardine cans. Martin also had a good deal of detailed information about the war that sounded authentic and Signe suspected his source. She knew that Martin had many contacts and what he told her came without doubt from illegal listening to a radio somewhere. Signe did not question Martin, she only cautioned him and begged him to be careful. Both knew that to cross the stringent occupation rules against illegal radio listening would result in arrest and possible prison camp. Martin understood her concerns and assured her that he would be very careful.

Adolf became busy in the evening hours by taking trips to friends and neighbors. When he came home and bedded down next to

Signe, he told little of what he had done during the evening and night. He only told enough for her to understand that he had been listening to the news from an illegal radio but not where he had been. He was eager to tell what he had heard, how the war was developing and how the Allied forces now resisted Hitler's mighty armies on several fronts. Adolf knew that Signe was deadly afraid when he was out on these secret errands in the evenings, she was afraid for her children, her husband, herself, and her other family members. They had heard about how the Germans had conducted raids in the dark of night and how they had demanded that everything was to be made available for inspection. If they found something that did not suit them, it would lead to arrests. What would happen if such a raid should come in the night when Adolf was not at home? How would she be able to explain why her husband was not at home in the middle of the night? If a person wanted to join with the underground or flee to Sweden, he or she would be placing the rest of the family in grave danger. A family member would be taken as a hostage and incarcerated in a prison camp in Norway or in Germany. Signe did not dare to think this thought through.

Adolf often brought something with him when he returned from these nightly trips. If it was 10-12 pounds of fresh meat, then Signe knew that he had participated in illegal slaughtering. It was possible for the farmers to fool the inspectors if a sheep or lamb was missing. It had simply vanished in the mountains. Most likely it is the wolf that is ravaging again, it was said. It happened that sheep and lamb fell over a cliff. Yes, it is unfortunate that these animals are not so easy to keep in check, explained the owners with sadness to the inspectors. Pigs and bulls that had been raised in secrecy were slaughtered. The fresh meat could not be stored for long by the owner and was therefore shared between neighbors and friends as it became available.

Housewives became clever over time at canning; meatballs, cutlets, sausages, fish cakes, and vegetables that were stored in glass jars, so-called Norway jars.

Once in a while Adolf would bring home four or five pounds of white flour. That meant that he had been milling wheat with his friends at the old mill on the brook. This was quite risky because the sudden increase in the water flow due to the opening of the dam could reveal what was going on. But it was a proud housewife who once in a while could present a newly baked layer cake. They all enjoyed it and this was a joyous change from the routine foodstuffs that gradually became monotonous. The bread from the baker got only worse as the war progressed. It looked nice and had a nice crust. However it was so doughy in the middle that it stuck to the knife when a slice was cut off. During the first world war it was customary to add wood fibers to bread. The additive to bread during this second world war was probably similar.

There were times when one or more planes would fly over the valley during daylight and people assumed that these were German. One time it happened that two planes flew so low that people could see the German markings clearly on the sides, and for a short while they were even able to see the pilot. People at the Bakken farm had also seen Allied planes that came flying in formation from the ocean. These had attacked German warships in the fjord and bombed strategic targets further inland that supported the German war industries. Attacks like these were not publicized because of the stringent censoring. The only people privileged to this information were the local population from personal experience or from information provided by firsthand knowledgeable people. Information about occurrences of this type became known by the population as the story was related from person to person. The accuracy of these stories would often diminish in proportion to the distance from where the incident had taken place.

One pleasant moonlit evening Signe remained motionless after she came out of the privy. She listened and believed she heard a murmur of motors in the distance, in the direction of the mountains. She concluded that she was hearing airplane motors. She was listening intensely where she was standing and was definitely hearing a distant sound once in a while. After a few moments the total stillness returned and she went back into the house. She assumed that it had to have been Allied planes she had heard because it was unusual for German planes to be active after daylight. Adolf was not at home that evening so Signe did not get to tell him about it until the next morning. Adolf listened politely to her story and said that he could not contribute with comments beyond what she had deduced. Or maybe he did not want to?

It is possible that the sound of airplanes that Signe had heard was from Allied planes that were engaged in parachute drops of military and communication equipment to designated locations that had been packaged in special containers. Members of the resistance were in place in the drop zones. They collected all the equipment quickly and placed it in one or more secure hiding places. Distribution to credible persons would be made later.

Young people who had managed to escape to England, by boat over the North Sea or through Sweden, received, among other things, education in the use of explosives and radio transmitters. People with such expertise were returned to Norway in all secrecy via parachutes with Allied planes or by landing along the coastline from small boats. Their objective was to instruct members of the resistance in the use of the military equipment and plan and manage raids. After the war ended, Signe was told that Adolf had participated several times with a resistance group that had received the air-dropped equipment from Allied planes and had helped in bringing it to safety.

Households also took advantage of what nature had to offer. They picked many different types of berries that were boiled into jams, syrups, and juice. The whole family would take off on these berry picking trips, and the children were proficient and made their contributions. There were plenty of berries and fruit trees at the Bakken farm, currants, black currants, gooseberries, strawberries, apples, pears, and plums. A couple of large cherry trees usually gave a good crop. The children were allowed to climb these trees and they picked many quarts of nice berries. Berries that they had collected beyond what they could use could be sold easily. Signe kept a neat house and she baked willingly providing flour was available. She baked large stacks of *lefse*[2] and *flatbrød* and she had baked for other households several times in the fall after the potatoes were harvested. She liked that kind of work, was skilled at it, and it gave her a good supplemental income.

The boys of the household were responsible for snaring fowl and small animals as an important contribution to the food supply. From an early age they were taught the art of making traps and how best to place them in the terrain. The first traps were the so-called rocker traps that were excellent for catching fowl. These traps were placed in the birch forest and it was often that several grey hens, grouse, and even blackcocks were brought home. Larger animals such as hare and fox were caught in traps. A hare gave them several meals and the fox skins were sold. Before the war it was customary that elders, who had firearms, would go hunting and the youngsters were allowed to participate as chasers. Adolf had grown up with firearms and had participated on several hunting trips. However, during the war all firearms had been confiscated by the occupation authorities such that no hunting parties could be arranged for reindeer, elk, or deer.

The boys at the Bakken farm had acquired a large collection of homemade arrows, bows, and slingshots. Fishing poles of thin and straight small birch or alder, were arranged in rows in the outhouse. They usually brought some of this equipment along when they went to check on their snares. The boys were to shoot fowl with their bows, but the result was dismal. The exception was once when the youngest son, Ole, had managed to sneak up on a grouse. He had managed to fire off an arrow with his longbow and had killed the grouse instantly.

As a rule the boys on the farms did the freshwater fishing. They fished in mountain lakes or small rivers and could come home with nice rainbow trout. A problem with all the catch was the preservation. They had their ways of smoking and salting the fish. Pork meat could be preserved by salting and smoking. Sheep meat could be salted and dried, but fowl was more difficult to preserve. It had to be consumed as soon as possible after it was caught or be sold. It was important for the family to know at all times how much of the different kinds of provisions they had on hand, what types they needed to acquire, and how much excess they could manage. All of this activity to keep body and soul together demanded considerable effort by large and small members of the household.

Severe winter

It was in the middle of winter during the first year of the occupation and no one could remember a worse winter. It had been snowing day after day such that forests and fields had a snow cover of three or more feet. Roads were practically impassable for the few cars that traveled the main roads. The visibility for the drivers was difficult after dark, when the light beams of the headlights were reduced on orders of the occupation forces. The lamp lenses were painted over with black paint so that only a small horizontal opening remained clear on each lamp lens. What remained of civilian vehicles was a few trucks and buses. Most of these were fueled by gas that was generated on a charcoal burning unit mounted on the back of the vehicles. These vehicles did not move fast, but they served their purpose. Military vehicles were gasoline driven and were seen mostly when they were driven in columns. They also had problems with the snow, as many of the military drivers were not trained to drive on narrow and slippery roads and quite often they slid off the roads. Snow plows were mounted on regular trucks with limited horsepower engines. They did their best to keep the roads open, but they were few in number and their capacity was severely reduced by the large amounts of snow. Road clearing crews, consisting of men with shovels, were required to open the worst stretches of roads that were blocked by large snowdrifts.

When the intense cold came, the snow luckily helped as insulation, but this was still not adequate for several households that had installed tap water. The tap water froze and water had to be transported to the house from a brook, river, or lake. This could involve long and difficult transport for some households. It was difficult enough to find water for a household, but it became a serious problem if there was also a barn with several animals that needed water. Households gathered what they had of large containers and pulled these on sleds back and forth to the water source, which had to be a river or a lake. The ones who had a horse could pull large wooden tubs on their sleds. The water holes in the ice had to be chopped open every day and little by little a ring of ice would build up around the hole. Water would splash from the containers during transport so that the path and the road after the many trips would become a sheet of ice. Sand had to be located and spread over the worst areas. With the onset of the cold and with snow on the ground, the otherwise dark winter nights became quite bright on a night with a full moon. People were then able to see the northern lights dance in several colors high in the sky behind the north facing mountains.

When the cold gave way, the wind arrived and the loose snow would whirl all over and create large snowdrifts. People had to get out and shovel a path from the house to the most important places, like the main road, the outhouse, and the barn. The following day they would have to be prepared to do the same job again. When the cold subsided, it was assured that the overcast weather would bring more snow. Yes, this was indeed a hard and difficult winter that brought on additional chores and responsibilities for the household.

The children frolicked in the snow. They would be cross-country skiing, ski jumping, racing with their sleds, and sliding on their kick sleds[3]. They built igloos and created a cozy atmosphere when they were able to get hold of one or two pieces of candle ends. They built fortresses in the snow and friendly snowball fights took place many a time. The ones who were lucky enough to have ice skates had many frozen lakes and rivers to play on. When they came back to the house at dusk with rose-colored cheeks, the children were full of snow, partially wet, tired, and hungry. That is when mothers had to help them remove their clothing and organize places to hang it near the stove in order for them to be dry the next morning.

At the Bakken farm they had lost the running water to the barn, but they were lucky to still have water in the kitchen faucet. It had been possible for them to maintain a small hole in the ice of the brook where they had collected buckets of water for the barn when they cared for their few sheep and horse. When the water flow of the brook became small and the ice froze solidly there, they brought water to the barn in buckets from the kitchen faucet. They had sold most of the animals shortly after Adolf died. The oldest son, Per, had asked that the horse be spared, because with it he could get day work now and then, and he would be paid the going rate for an adult with horse. As they still had hay, it had been possible to keep the horse. The horse had been rented to nearby farmers once in a while and had thereby earned some money. Per had several times received work with the horse to do seasonal farmwork and had been employed a few times on road work with his horse. He had liked to get together with other workers and had always received advice that was useful in the maintenance of a farm. It had been easy to move about with the horse and sled in the snow, and Per would often take neighbors along when he took necessary trips to the stores. Neighbors were very appreciative for getting goods brought home by him and they always rewarded the Bakken family with one thing or another. This could be some clothing for the children or some home – baked items.

The winter cold had been so severe that they often found frozen potatoes in the bin. Signe had remembered how they had a similar problem earlier one time, but that had been several years ago. The frozen potatoes tasted sweeter than the ordinary but no one could eat them. They also had some carrots, turnips, and rutabagas packed in sawdust and saved in a bin. Practically all the carrots had frozen and were given to the animals, while the turnips and rutabagas had fared better.

The Bakken farm had been leased to a farmer. This had worked out well, because he was a man they knew and one they could depend on. The agreement was for a lease on an annual basis. The farmer saw to it that the Bakken family received parts of the harvest each fall, like potatoes, turnips, rutabagas and carrots. The Bakken children lent a hand whenever they could. It would not be too long before Per could take over the chores totally, but first he would have to complete school and he needed more experience in running a farm.

It was in the third year of occupation that Adolf became ill. He finally had to seek a doctor for his cough and weakness and had been diagnosed with tuberculosis. They had heard that this illness was rampant but had never thought that it would strike them. When all members of the family had been examined, it turned out that Adolf was the only one to be infected. Unfortunately there was little the doctors could do for him and Adolf died after a short time.

It had been a terrible time for all after Adolf died, especially for

Signe. Here she was, a widow on a small farm with three children, in a country that was occupied by a large military power – it was simply as bad as it could get. The only thing positive was that no one else in the family had been infected by the tuberculosis, and that they had quite a bit of family nearby that could lend a helping hand. Signe's brothers had been exceptional in this way, and the neighbors had also been helpful. The times had changed of late such that now they lived every day in a certain degree of fear. They heard about people who had been arrested in the middle of the night, and they had read about people in the local newspaper who had been condemned to death for having committed an offence against the occupation force. A newspaper report of this type often concluded with the words "judgment carried out."

Signe knew that America had also come into the war and she often thought about her brother Tor who lived there. Because of his age, she assumed that he had been drafted for military service. "I wonder how he is managing," she thought. She knew from the newspaper that Japan and America had declared war against each other and that Japan had occupied several islands in the Pacific Ocean. She missed the letters from Tor that had come regularly until the war started. She had talked to several who had family and friends in America and all were worried about them. This war would have to end one day, and she took pleasure in thinking about how Tor would resume contact with her. He just had to survive the war!

Bakken family

The Bakken farm had been inherited through many generations. It was a small farm with some acres of land suitable for different types of crops and some outlying fields that were well suited for grazing. The farm had a few pine and spruce trees and a good number of birch and aspen trees. The birch and aspen were used as firewood and to make articles for everyday use, like furniture, braided baskets, wooden boxes[4], and dishes. Every generation had worked diligently to enlarge and improve the crop land, the barn, and the main house. As soon as the children came of age, they would help as best they could in the many tasks that a small farm required. Just to provide sufficient amounts of water and firewood required much time and effort.

The outlying fields had plenty of fine birch trees that were easily accessible. These and some aspen trees were well suited for firewood. Adolf and one of the boys could take off early in the morning and be away all day, busily cutting down trees, sawing to stove lengths, chopping and piling up the wood in stacks. They would stack the wood in the fields, often between trunks of a couple of birch trees, and put corrugated sheet metal with big rocks on top. Tree trunks that were suitable for cutting into planks and boards were placed in a separate stack and covered. When the snow came, they would harness the horse to the sled and bring home the air-dried firewood as needed. In the wood bin at home they could only store two or three cord feet of wood and they would need ten to twenty cord feet of wood each winter. If they had any extra wood stacked in the field, it could always be sold for a good price. And as they had a horse, they could deliver the firewood directly to most customers.

The first wildflower that appeared was the white anemone, it was found on bare spots between patches of snow that would still cover the ground in many places. Every year it was customary that the children would compete for being the first to find and bring home these delicate white flowers that were immediately placed in a vase with water. As other flowers appeared in the fields, quite an assortment of flowers could be seen and smelled in the house. There were plenty of lilies of the valley flowers in the fields and the children brought home large bouquets. Vases of these could be found in many places in the house and the wonderful scent could not be avoided.

Later on in the fall, when the first wild berries were ripening, there would be a contest to see who could find the first ones. Blueberries were the first to ripen, and the very first to be found could amount to just a few berries that were collected in a cup. The finder would choose how he or she would eat them: as they were, crushed with sprinkled sugar on top, and/or if they were to be shared with others. Necklaces and bracelets were made with berries strung onto a grass straw. Everyone in the household had to help locate and pick the various berries that eventually ripened in the field, like blueberries, raspberries, cloudberries[5], lingonberries[6], and blackberries. The berries were turned into juices and jams and would add flavor to meals for many months. Often they would sell various berries that they had picked to provide extra income for the household.

As soon as the children came of age, they would have to start school. Luckily the schoolhouse was not far away and the children could walk to and from on their own. It was a bit difficult when they were going to the school for the very first time – then it was comforting to hold on to mother's or father's hand to and from school. However, this was not much of a problem. Their timidity subsided and soon the children got into the school routine. The children knew most of the pupils in the class beforehand and the friendship between them developed further in school. They attended school every other day in primary school and got quite a lot of homework that they would struggle with under the lamplight in the family room. The homework was probably hardest for the oldest child because the younger ones would be helped by the oldest. The parents did their best to help even if their own schooling might have been inferior to what the children received.

The barn was located a short distance from the main house, and before died, they had two cows, twelve sheep, a dozen chickens, and the horse. The barn was quite full with this many animals and they demanded much attention. The distance to the brook, where all the water for the household and barn had been collected for generations, was not far. The laundry was done near the brook, where the clothing was boiled in an iron kettle over the outdoor fireplace and the rinsing was done in the brook. The little pond that they had created with a dam provided a nice bathing place for the family in the summertime. The brook had been a good source of water over many years and even if they had long periods without rain, they would still have water in their brook. It had been a great relief to the household when Adolf had managed to install water pipes to the barn and the kitchen from a covered water storage that he had built in the brook.

In the spring they would let the sheep and the cows roam inside the fenced in area of the field, where there was a small lake that the animals could drink from, and where it was possible to fish for beautiful rainbow trout. Oh, how the animals did run and leap every spring when they escaped the barn after a winter. Every morning and evening someone had to take off for the field with a couple of pails to milk the cows. They kept the calves until fall, when they were usually sold with a couple of sheep and some lambs. At times they would keep a calf and sell off an adult cow instead. Adolf had taken various jobs away from the home whenever he could justify leaving the farm. In this way generations had managed. They had enjoyed a good life even if it could be difficult at times.

Shortly after Adolf died, they agreed to sell off the cows because the work in the barn became just too much for Signe and the children. Little by little they had also reduced their flock of sheep. The next animal to be considered for sale was the horse, but that was a decision that Per was reluctant to make. He knew with certainty that he would keep the horse until he finished the trench in the new crop field, and he needed a horse to transport the firewood home when the snow came. He needed to find out soon if he could possibly rent his neighbor's horse once in a while, if he should decide to sell his own. Rental of a horse as needed would be a good solution because the work in the barn would be much easier and the operating expenses would be reduced without the horse.

~

Evening was approaching after a long and hard day. The sun had set some time ago and he started with long strides toward the home and the warmth. Per was looking forward to getting out of his dirty clothes. They were wet with sweat and mud, and he needed to get washed. Thereafter he looked forward to something warm to drink and eat in the company of his sister, brother, and mother. He was well satisfied with what he had accomplished this day, and he smiled as he walked, because he felt that he had come up with the solution to a major problem that had pestered him for a long time. Even if the decision would mean much hard work for a while in the immediate future, he still felt relieved. The struggle to arrive at this decision had in fact been a big burden on him, but now he had a solution for this problem. He longed to get back to his family and the warm house and decided that he would think through his plans for a couple of more days before telling the others. With this thought his gait became only faster.

From early in the morning he had been on the new crop field and had been digging a drainage trench that was needed before one could expect good harvest from the field. He had put in two weeks of labor so far and had most likely just as much time left before the trench would be completed. He had set as a goal to dig the trench knee-deep, and that was hard labor with considerable rock that had to be dug out. There was quite a bit of water in the trench after all the rain they had received lately. This was most likely only an advantage because then it was easier to dig and loosen the rocks. He had started to dig at the lowest end of the field so that the water ran off gradually. He would often be standing in mud and it was impossible to avoid having cold and wet feet. He had to dig around the rocks and get one or more ropes attached around the largest and harness the horse to it. As a rule he had to assist by using an iron bar to loosen the rocks. Fortunately it was adequate to pull the rocks only a short distance to the edge of the field. From there he tipped the rocks into the scree and they rolled down with thunder and crashing sounds until they settled among all the rocks that were there from before. The soil that he dug out was for the most part good topsoil and he piled it on the side of the trench. In the spring he would fabricate a conduit in the trench, and he knew of a place not far away where he could find sufficient amounts of slate for this purpose. He would wait until the snow came before transporting the slate to the trench because this was the easiest way to get them there. In the spring he would backfill the trench and smooth it out such that the field would be ready well ahead of when they had to start with the spring farming.

Per left the field with the horse, his loyal helper, who without doubt also longed for food and rest after a long day. The horse leaned its head against Per's shoulder while he scrubbed its mane. He placed the horse in its stall and made sure that he had oats, hay, and water. When he petted the horse and thanked him for being a good helper, the horse turned its head and neighed as if it were saying: "Don't mention it and thank you for a nice day."

His father had started to work on clearing this new crop field and had managed to get it to yield just about enough hay for one cow before he died two years ago. Per was only a teenager when he had to assume the man's role on the little farm. His father had often talked to him about finding time to install a drainage ditch that he felt would increase the harvest considerably. It happened frequently that the ground would be submerged in rainwater for long periods of time and that the harvest would rot. Per had known for a long time that it would be his responsibility to get a drainage ditch dug, and he started as soon as the haying was completed in the late summer. He managed to dig approximately six feet of trench a day whenever he had time to work on it, and he expected to be finished in about two week's time.

He had helped his father on the farm for some years and on this new field, and he was well acquainted with the conditions. In the middle of the field there was a large boulder that had been a nuisance to him and his father for a long time. It was higher than the terrain as if it were a large skull, and it always appeared to be in the way. Both had bumped into it with their scythes. If the plow was worked to close to it, the point of it would be bent or, what would be far worse, broken off. Many years ago he had been told the story of how his grandfather had tried to get rid of this boulder. His grandfather had dug around the boulder to ascertain if it would be possible to get the boulder lifted sufficiently to get it tipped over and down into the scree below. He had to give in after several days of toil. The boulder was much too large. It was positioned rather flat, and in several places it was barely visible above the surface. His grandfather had covered the boulder with topsoil that he had brought from other places on the farm to get some grass to grow there. That is why the field was a little higher where the boulder was than the rest of the field. Per had made his decision. He would make the necessary arrangements to rid the field of the boulder once and for all. He simply would not tolerate that this bothersome, partially submerged boulder was to remain in the field any longer.

His mother caught sight of him from the living room window. Twilight had fallen and she had lit the lights in the living room. Signe admired the young boy who now worked as an adult. It was a shame that he had to toil so hard, but there was nothing she could do about it. He had the same spirit as his father, and he would soon gain the same proficiencies as his father. She was proud of her oldest son.

It had not been easy for Signe after her husband died. Her parents lived some miles away and she saw them only a couple of times a year. The oldest of her brothers was married and ran the shop that he had taken over from their parents. The next to the oldest brother was not married and he had left for America five years before Adolf died. If Per had not been able to take on the manly chores on the small farm when his father died, they would not have managed. She often thought about how she was going to continue on. She tore herself from these thoughts and went to the kitchen to see to the fire in the stove and make sure that there was enough warm water for Per in the pot on the stove. She had found clean clothing for him as usual, and the food would soon be ready for the evening meal. The two other children, ten-year-old Helga and eight-year-old Ole, were struggling with their homework.

That awful world war lasted two years after Adolf died. The peace, and thereby the end to the occupation, came in the month of May. Even though Germany had capitulated unconditionally on May 7, 1945, at 14:41 in Europe, the German divisions in Norway were not prepared to surrender immediately. But, it was only a matter of time. The jubilation among the people increased. All church bells in the country rang for one hour starting at 15:00 on May 8, and the resistance forces began to appear from their hiding places. The Norwegian flag flew at high mast from the Akershus Fortress on May 11 at 14:35 after the uniformed German commander turned over the fortress to a representative for the resistance forces, who was dressed in a windbreaker and knickers. The country was in an enormous victory celebration the entire month of May.

After the evening meal was over and the dishes washed and put in their proper places, Signe came from the kitchen with a sly smile and a paper sack that she extended and said that she had a surprise for them. Signe had been to the store and had bought this surprise that was available in the shop already, only a couple of months after the peace came. The children wanted to know what she had in the bag, but Signe said that first they had to listen to a rather funny and innocent story about its contents. She explained that she had been to the store and had seen that they had received the first shipment of bananas after the war. She opened the bag and gave one to each of them. "Do any of you remember having eaten a banana before?" she asked. Per was the only one who was old enough to remember bananas, but he could not recall how they tasted. "Let me tell you what happened in the store today," Signe said. There had been three children there aged of six to seven who had received one banana each that they were encouraged to eat right away. The children had been more than willing to taste, and they bit directly into the banana. They had no way of knowing that the skin had to be removed first. This had led to much laughter among the elders who saw what took place. The store had also received another type of fruit, and a young man of about twenty years of age gave one of these to each of the same children and asked them to eat it. He explained that it was an orange they had been given and that it had to be peeled before they could eat it. He was not about to fool them like they had been fooled with the bananas, he said. The children peeled and when they had removed some peel, they bit into the fruit. It resulted in screaming and spitting because it was so sour, and the elders got themselves another good laugh. The children had not seen a lemon or an orange before, and were fooled again. It was not nice to joke with the children in this way, but it was done in a friendly manner and no one intended to be mean.

"Now, please enjoy your banana," Signe said. "Next time I go to the store there might be oranges. If so, I will buy some for you to enjoy."

Manhood test

Per greeted his mother, sister, and brother enthusiastically a few days after he had made his decision, as he removed his muddy boots outside the back entrance to the house. They understood right away from his tone of voice that he had experienced something exciting, and they competed in asking him what had taken place. Per admitted that he had something important to tell them, but he apologized for not wanting to start a discussion before he had cleaned himself and changed into different clothes. They understood all too well, even if his sister had only a tiny question about something in her homework that she was burning to get help with.

It did not take many minutes before Per had removed all his clothing and piled it in a heap on the floor. It was muddy and smelled of sweat, and the outer garments were quite moist. His mother would see to it that all would be washed and made ready for another day. The warm water felt especially good on his back that had become sore today. It was enjoyable to just relax in the tub. But he was very dirty and started to wash himself. He had used several hours today to clean the trench, and he was without question dirty from top to bottom. He washed the black topsoil out of his hair, face, and hands. He had also gotten the topsoil into his boots and his legs and feet were muddy up to his knees. He stepped out of the large bath tub that was placed behind a curtain in the kitchen. He knew that the others were waiting for him and he hurried in order to delay the evening meal as little as possible. He put on the clothing that his mother had found for him before he took his bath and was soon ready to participate in a good meal. He had come home not only dirty today, but he was also hungry as a bear. While he was taking the bath and dressing himself, his sister had cleared the schoolbooks off the table and put on the tableware. His mother brought in the smoking hot food that Per had smelled while he was drying himself, and he took his place at the table as soon as possible.

Table prayer was said and the meal started. His sister was first to pose her question about the homework, his mother was eager to know if the new shirt she had sewn would fit him, and his brother wanted to know when he would be allowed to help with the ditch digging. Per helped himself to a large portion of stew[7] and devoured it with relish as he answered the questions in turn. Toward the end of the meal it became his turn to tell the others what he had decided.

Per explained that he was making good progress with the drainage ditch. He said that after he had started on it, he had considered changing his mind several times because he feared that the job would last too long, and become too strenuous, too difficult, and boring. The job would not have been possible without the help from the horse, he explained. What motivated him was the knowledge that the little field would be so much better when he was finally finished one day. They would no longer have to experience the harvest rotting there again.

He reminded them of the large boulder in the middle of the field that had been such a nuisance for years and explained that he had arrived at a solution for getting rid of it once and for all. The others reacted with surprise and questioned: "If you thought that the drainage ditch was a big undertaking, how in the world can you even consider tackling that boulder?" they all wanted to know. Per asked them to wait with their comments until he had presented his plan in detail. He ensured them that this was a problem that he had considered thoroughly over a long time. Per continued by explaining that he intended to ask his friend and neighbor for help with this undertaking. His friend, who was a few years older, was also a good friend of a man who worked for the road administration. If Per could get these two men to help him, he estimated that it would only take two to three weeks before the boulder could be blasted away. He assumed that a permit for using dynamite could be obtained because the purpose was to increase the harvest on the farm. As compensation, Per would offer his friend help to repair the roof of his barn that had sprung a leak, something that he had been told a few days ago. He assumed that he, together with his friend, could in one way or another reciprocate with a favor to the man from the road administration. Per had to admit that even if the boulder was removed, it would not have a drastic influence on the harvest. Maybe the improvement would amount to enough hay for a couple of sheep over the winter. But, oh my, how irritating that boulder was and had always been! His mother thought this sounded like a good idea, even if she was a little skeptical. Could these three fellows really tackle such a difficult job? She hinted that they possibly should continue to accept the boulder as so many of their generations had done before them. She also wondered if it would be possible for this man, who was employed in the road administration, to borrow tools for private use. Per reminded the others that equipment and tools were much better than had been the case in earlier times and that it therefore was not a major problem to get a boulder like this removed. He was of the opinion that if his grandfather had ever had similar plans, a job like this would have been practically impossible for him. Per was so enthusiastic that his mother did not in any way want to sound too skeptical. She remembered well how irritated her husband had been with this boulder many a time and therefore gave Per support to propose the plans to his friend. Per talked eagerly about how nice the field would be without the boulder, how much easier it would be to manage, and how the harvest would be greater. In addition the field would be much better when it would be draining with the new trench. Per expected to talk to his neighbor about this the very next day.

Per said further, with a sly smile, that as this boulder looked like a very large skull, it was possible that it once had been a troll. Maybe something similar to the folktale in which the boy had tricked the troll into the sunshine, had happened here also? Or, a troll could have strayed into sunlight and thereby been petrified. The skull had remained in the new field and the rest of the body parts of the troll had been scattered about when the troll cracked. Who knows, since there are plenty of rocks down in the scree, he said.

Signe reminded them about the fact that this boulder had been used for many pleasant outings over the years, and that the children's grandmother, her mother-in-law, had always liked to go to the boulder in the spring, as soon as weather permitted. Signe felt certain that this was a custom that went back several generations. Even they had gone on outings to the boulder. They had brought the coffeepot and had cooked coffee between some stones that they had arranged under the kettle. Another custom was to boil eggs at Easter at the same location, and the family had also celebrated Midsummer Eve there. The place had a good view, they could sit and see when the Midsummer Night's bonfires were lighted over a wide area. They had also had a bonfire, and had enjoyed storytelling and singing as they sat or danced around the fire. Something home baked had been prepared and brought for these occasions and the children had selected their own favorite homemade syrup or juice that they brought to the boulder. They used the water in the brook to make a tasty drink of juice and water[8] by diluting the syrup or juice until it achieved suitable strength and taste. Outings to the boulder were reduced considerably during the occupation, when bonfires in the evenings were prohibited. The occupation army would have considered such fires to be signaling devices.

The first white anemones were found in the grazing field only a short distance away, and it was handy to have the boulder as a place to arrange the flowers into bouquets. Later on the lilies of the valley appeared and they had to be arranged to make fine bouquets. In the fall when the first blueberries were found, it was again the boulder that was often used as the place to pick over the berries before they were taken into the house. Later on the lingonberries were picked over on the boulder. Everyone would participate in this work and together they had enjoyable times with the telling of stories that brought out much laughter, and often they would strike up a song that they had learned in school. The boulder was a place for meetings on several occasions, and they would most certainly miss it if Per should succeed in his quest to get rid of it.

They would lie on their blankets on the boulder that had been warmed by the sun. It felt as if they were on a boat in the landscape when they looked up at the sky. It did not take much fantasy to imagine that they were sailing on a big ocean. The whole family could be spread out on their blankets and be looking at the clouds sailing by against the blue sky. The smells from the field were so refreshing and clean. It would be green by that time and the field would be filled with many types of flowers that swayed in the breeze. The migrating birds had started to return and were busy building their nests. The cuckoo was heard often, and they saw larger birds such as eagles and hawks sailing so elegantly and effortlessly while they scouted for smaller animals on the ground. If the children remained completely still, they could at times see a hare run by, and on a couple of occasions that had even seen deer.

Signe also reminded them how the farm animals had a habit of visiting the boulder when they were let out in the spring. The sheep liked to rest on the boulder and especially the horse liked to stand on the boulder and look around. Every so often he would neigh and toss his head as if he were saying, "It is I who rule the animals on this farm." When the grass in the fields grew higher, both the horse and the other animals had to be tethered or fenced in to save the grass from being trampled.

And now Per wanted to put an end to all of these old traditions! He had made up his mind and had provided detailed information on the advantages of getting rid of the boulder. He had assured his mother that he would be able to carry out the task, had promised that he would not exceed his limits, and that he would use all the help that he could obtain. To get rid of the boulder was sad in a way because it had always been like an icon on the farm, and it would most likely be missed. However, the loss would eventually be accepted. They would just have to find another place in the field where they could have their outings.

Per had made his decision and Signe knew that he was in many ways as stubborn as his father. In a case like this it would not be possible for her to get him to change his mind. Nor would it help to discuss with him how small the addition to the field would be with the boulder removed. He had his reasons, the field was to be nice and without hindrances for the seasonal work that had to be performed year after year. He reminded his mother of all the boulders and rocks that had been tossed over the cliff for years by generations who had cleared the land here before him. Now it was his turn to make his contribution, and he knew how to tackle the problem. With the boulder removed and with the drainage ditch in place, he would have contributed to ensuring that the harvest would be good and reliable, and he would have done his share of what could be expected from one generation. So that was that.

All participated in clearing of the table, and the dishwashing was completed quickly. Per helped Helga with her homework, and he promised Ole that he would be permitted to assist the very next time he went into the field. The shirt that mother had made was a perfect fit and it came in handy because the previous best shirt had started to show wear. There was time for some stories and a couple of songs before the youngest had to get ready for bed. Per was tired, and it did not take him long before he also was under his *dyne.*[9] After a short while, Signe also felt tired and prepared to go to bed. But first she peeked in, as was customary, on her sleeping children and praised herself fortunate because they were healthy, able, and affectionate. They were doing well at Bakken. She did not feel old in any way, but she admitted to herself that she missed someone her own age that she could share her pleasures and problems with. Signe missed her husband.

The troll skull

Two to three days after Per had presented his plans for removal of the boulder to the family he had been promised assistance by his friend. The working plan became that Per was to continue digging on the drainage ditch until the others showed up after their normal working hours, at which time they would start to drill holes in the boulder that were required to get it blasted. His friends had also promised to help as much as possible on their days off. Peder, who worked for the road administration, was familiar with this type of work. It was therefore he who decided how many holes had to be drilled, how deep they had to be, and where they should be placed in order to get the most effective blasting. Egil was a friend of Per who lived only a good mile away and was practically his closest neighbor. These two farmers had been friends for many years and they were always ready to help each other. But, many holes were required and it was to take a long time before the drilling was completed.

The drilling was done whereby one man held the bit and the other two struck the bit alternately with a large sledgehammer. They exchanged their roles regularly and little by little the bit sank deeper and deeper into the boulder. It was time-consuming and many blows were needed with the heavy sledgehammers before a sufficient number of holes were drilled to required depths. They had jury-rigged a wooden tool to hold the bit so that the person holding the bit did not have to hold his hands directly on the bit. This was a good idea because once in a while one of the fellows with the sledgehammer would miss with his blow. A hand would have been severely damaged from such a hard blow. They put a birch peg into each completed hole to keep them clean. After a while it looked as if a type of hair brush was growing on the troll skull with the many pegs that were sticking out of it

Peder had not had any problems with the loan of the tools from the road administration, the only reminder he had been given from there was that the tools were to be kept in good shape. At the end of the day he would bring the bits back to the workshop for sharpening for the following day. The weather had been quite good while they were drilling, and Peder had been able to work a couple of hours after his normal work day practically every other day.

Finally the big day arrived when the blasting was to take place. Peder arrived early Saturday morning and had brought dynamite, blasting caps, and fuses. He explained to the others how to make the preparations and kept a watchful eye on everything to make sure that things were done the way he wanted. One or more sticks of dynamite were placed in each hole and carefully poked into place with a broom handle. Any space above the dynamite in the hole was filled with fine sand. This would give the dynamite better effect inward and reduce spray from the hole. The blasting cap, and equal lengths of fuses, was attached to the last stick of dynamite in the hole. From the point were the fuses from the individual holes were joined, a main fuse was attached and brought in the direction of a safe location that they had selected. On the top of the troll skull they had placed some birch trees that they had cut down and placed crisscross over the area to reduce the spray.

Peder walked around, looking at everything to ensure that all was in order, before he shouted with an authoritative and loud voice, "Heads up!" He turned in two other directions and repeated the warning. He waited just a little bit before he lit the main fuse. As he straightened himself, he shouted three times: "Heads up, the fuse is lit, fire in the hole," and walked with firm steps toward the others who had sought shelter behind a large boulder at the edge of the forest, some three hundred feet away. Peder assumed that it would take four minutes before the blast would take place. The main fuse was ten feet long and the individual fuses were about the same length. Per had tied the horse to a tree nearby where it was grazing, not suspecting what was about to happen.

The wait became extremely long. They dared to peek from behind the boulder, they saw the smoke from the fuse and waited and waited. Suddenly Per saw what looked like the troll skull trying to shake free from the ground, shortly after he heard the bang and felt a vibration in the ground. They saw that rocks were thrown high into the air over a large cloud of dust. Luckily no rocks came their way. The horse became restless. Per went to it and soon had it calmed down with some gentle stroking and soft talk. The large dust cloud moved slowly from the blasting area.

Peder explained that they should use caution and remain where they were for a few minutes before going to the skull site. While they waited, he explained that it was possible that some charges had not gone off. This could happen if a charge went off before the charge in the neighboring hole, which then could have caused the fuse to be pulled away from the blasting cap there. If this had happened, the easiest solution was just to put on a new fuse and light the individual charges separately. After a while they walked slowly toward the spot, Peder in front. What a sight that greeted them! What some minutes ago had been a slick, large boulder was just a large pile of rocks with lots of birch trunks and branches mixed in. Peder looked around carefully for any hole containing dynamite without a fuse. He found two such holes and explained to the others that he would make ready for blasting again. Peder put on individual fuses and lit them. He walked again toward the boulder for safety where the others already had sought shelter and shouted again, "Heads up, the fuse is lit, fire in the hole," three times. While they waited for the blast, they exchanged congratulations because it looked as if the blasting had been completely successful. It blasted again, much less this time, with two separate blasts, and they waited again for some minutes before they approached what once had been a partially buried troll skull. They all looked around thoroughly for the possibility of additional untouched drilling holes. They admired what was now just a pile of rock of sizes that would be easy to handle. Peder was satisfied with what he saw and again with his hands formed like a megaphone, he shouted three times, "All clear," while he turned about. Signe and Helga, who had waited indoors for the all clear signal, came running to see what was left of the troll skull. The small group of five that stood around the place smiled and declared all as one that this was a major event. The good result had to be celebrated and Signe invited all for coffee and fresh waffles.

Per paid Peder for the cost of the dynamite, blasting caps, and fuses during the coffee break, and they collected all the tools that belonged to the road administration after the break. Peder said that he had to get going, and Per thanked him for his help. Per did not feel like working anymore that day either. The blasting had been very successful and with that part of his project done, he had completed a large and difficult portion of it. Per's friend Egil remained for a while and they made plans for how to get rid of all the rock. With the help of the horse and the sled they felt that it would not be too difficult to get the area cleaned up.

It took several days and many trips with the special *stubbslede*[10] before all the remains of the troll skull were removed. All the rocks had been tipped over into the large scree where they had come to rest after having rolled down with rumbling and crashing. Maybe the rocks of the skull got united with the body parts of the troll down in the scree!

When the ground around the hole was cleaned out of rocks and birch trunks, a wide hole remained with a depth of three or more feet where the skull had been. What once had been a troll skull that had penetrated the ground had now become a crater in the new crop field.

Per knew where he could find sand to fill the hole, before he filled in the top soil that he already had ready nearby. Several loads of sand and thereafter of topsoil were needed before the hole in the new crop field was filled in. He saddled the horse to a dipper. After a few turns back and forth with it, he followed up with a few turns with the harrow, and with that he had succeeded in getting a good-looking crop field. He had completed the trench earlier and the drainage worked perfectly. Per had always felt that each generation had an obligation to improve on what was transferred between generations. His main contribution to the farm was with this completed, and he assumed that this accomplishment would follow the history of the farm.

Deliberation

Signe put a couple of sticks of wood in the multilevel stove. She rearranged the lap rug, which hung over the back of the rocking chair, pulled the chair closer to the furnace, and adjusted herself comfortably with her feet resting on the hearthstone. The cold winter was loosening its grip every day as the spring sun became stronger. Snow could still be seen on the ground, but it had slid off the roofs some time ago, and it was no longer necessary to keep a fire going in both wood-burning stoves night and day. She had placed kindling wood next to the stove in the kitchen to get a fire started as fast as possible in the morning when she was to prepare something hot to eat and drink. They all liked oatmeal for breakfast and she had placed the rolled oats in water. She liked a good cup of coffee for breakfast and Per had also grown accustomed to it, but the youngest children drank milk. The cat jumped into her lap and purred with well-being while she stroked the soft fur. The last of the children had gone to bed, the house was quiet, and she felt like doing some thinking in peace and quiet. She had done this on several occasions, and she knew instinctively that she had problems that needed to be solved regarding her and the children. Seven years had already passed since her husband had died. It was the tuberculosis that took him away from her and it had happened so fast. Luckily no one else in the house had been infected, and they had all had regular medical checkups. Good grief, how much easier life had been while her husband was alive.

They had managed well on the small farm that they had received from her husband's parents. Adolf had always managed to find work during the different seasons when the farm did not need much attention every day. The extra income made it possible for them to manage well, and they had a happy life with many enjoyable moments. The children that arrived little by little were of great pleasure, and they had grown up to be fine youths. She had loved her husband and missed him a lot. She knew that if she had a man again of her age as a life partner, her life would be much easier. But, could she fall in love again, and how would the children react to such thoughts? She said to herself, "You are not old, only 37, and you should therefore still have the possibility of spending many years together with a man." She blushed at the thought that she could still get pregnant. Quite simply stated, she was a good-looking woman and she recognized that men often gave her extra glances and smiles. She was not shy and contributed often to conversations in mixed company. She was an eager reader and had an understanding for many of the matters being discussed. It happened in such gatherings that she would be asked how she was able to manage the farm, about her children, and if she felt lonesome. Yes, being lonesome is probably what she was. But that was something she could not and would not admit. She took great pleasure in being with the children, is what she used to respond to such questions. She wondered if she could really associate herself with a man again. She wondered if there was a decent man in the neighborhood who would be willing to become her life partner from here on. She decided that she would not resist immediately if a suitable man should approach her. She could at least have a go at it, and let fate decide. The conditions in the local area were open, but something along the lines of a suitor could not be kept secret for long. But, one thing was certain. She was going to have a talk with the children about this as soon as possible.

After the five-year-long world war finally ended, Signe was often in contact with her brother who had left for America before the war, and now lived there. The relationship between them had always been good and so open that she could tell him what was bothering her and keep him informed about her plans. Tor wrote regularly, and often he sent her a five- or a ten-dollar bill and he instructed her to buy something for herself with it. The currency notes were welcome gifts, and the package with clothing that her brother had sent would be put to good use. Her brother had on several occasions suggested that she and the children ought to come to America. Tor felt that they would be able to settle in after only a short while and he believed that obtaining work would not be a problem for any one of them. He offered to help them find a place to stay at the start. As tempting as this sounded, she still had misgivings. On the other hand, maybe a new start in America was what she needed to get her future in order. A suitable man could surely be found there? She was pleased that she had been able to arrange for a lease on the farm a couple of years ago. They managed with that income, what she earned from some domestic helper jobs that she took on once in a while, with what the oldest boy earned as a carpenter, and what they sold of different crops. The children were able, they were intelligent, and she had decided long ago that she would do her best to get them advanced education.

It would soon be four years since the oldest boy had come home from the new field and explained how he would complete the drainage ditch that his father had talked about so often. His father had planned where the ditch should be dug to be most effective and how deep it needed to be. They had considered the possibility several times, but his father had just not gotten around to start the work. Good grief, how hard Per had worked, and she remembered the filthy clothing when he came back to the house after a day in the trench. He had been soaked by rain and sweat, and several times he was so tired that he had gone to bed for the night right after having had his evening meal.

She smiled when she remembered how eager the boy had been when he had decided to remove the large boulder in the new field once and for all. Per had been so young to take on such adult chores and from time to time she had really been concerned for him. Luckily she had not attempted to tone down his eagerness too much. He had really been adamant and had completed both of these challenging projects without difficulty, installation of the drainage ditch and the elimination of the annoying boulder. He alone had arranged for help to get the boulder blasted and removed. They had now obtained a fine meadow that a proud Per had shown to his mother after he had it plowed and harrowed for the first time. Signe had become so enthusiastic and proud of her son that she had hugged and kissed him on both cheeks so much that Per had become embarrassed.

The new field had become a model for a small field, they had alternated between oats and potatoes every other year and had always had a good crop. The leaseholder had planted potatoes this year and they would receive sufficiently of that crop from him to last them over the winter. But now the oldest boy had become an adult and before too long he would find a sweetheart. Signe would eventually have to get used to sharing him with another and this would most likely lead to marriage and children. How would they then all manage at the farm? She saw this as a potential problem. They might have to consider a different approach. Poor Per, he deserved a better life than what he could get here with a need for much hard work that barely would reward him adequately to support himself and his family. Her brother had tempted her so many times with America – could this be something for Per? Would it be an idea for him to take a trip? Could he not try his luck in the strange country as so many others had done before him? He could always come back! On the other hand if it turned out well for him, would it not be possible for her and the other two children also to take the trip across the big "pond"? Her brother had said that well-paying jobs could be had for a man with Per's experiences. He could enroll in a school in the evenings a couple of times a week to improve his English and to learn a trade, Tor had written. Yes, these were possibilities that could be good for them. "I wonder if Per has given any thought to America himself?" Signe speculated. This was to be expected, as she knew that Per had friends and acquaintances who had left that he most certainly would have heard from. Signe realized that she could not wait too long before she presented her proposal and decision for the children.

Proposal

It was on a Sunday afternoon that Signe invited her children to a discussion about their future. It was windy and raining outside, or was it a bit of sleet that was hitting the window panes that were facing toward the west? They were all gathered around the table, coffee and freshly baked cake was being served. The dry birch firewood crackled in the multilevel wood burning stove that stood in a corner of the living room. It was still adequate for heating the whole house. If the heat was to be maintained in the entire house when winter started in earnest, they would have to maintain heat from the stove in the kitchen also. The youngest wanted to play a card game as soon as they finished their meal. Signe had interrupted and said that after the dishes had been washed and put away, she wanted to speak about something very important, namely, their future. She promised that there would be plenty of time for games and card playing before bedtime.

She received help as usual from Helga with clearing and washing the dishes so that it did not take long before the dishes and the linen were properly stored. Signe and Helga took their places at the cleared and cleaned table and Per and Ole did the same at the urging of Helga. Signe began with a short summary of how they were doing now, regarding finances and accommodations in the house, and said that she was concerned for how they would manage onward. Ole, as the youngest boy, had received his confirmation a short while ago, Helga was in high school and had ambitions for further studies. Per worked as a carpenter and had been lucky to be fully employed in a small carpentry shop. When fall came it would be more difficult for him to be able to work every day because the sale of windows, doors, and stairways for new construction would fall off. Signe worked for a couple of days a week in a shop that sold needlework, handwork, and handmade items. They had leased the farm to the same man for some years now. The income from that lease was helpful and the relationship between herself and the lessee was good. But with the plans that they had for the future, she was concerned for how they would be able to finance it all, she said.

Signe addressed the children in turn and started with the oldest. "Per, you have been able and worked hard. As the oldest you have the right of inheritance to everything here at the farm. You can look forward to a life as a combination of carpenter or cabinetmaker and a small farmer. One day you will find a girl and it will lead to a happy wedding. Children will arrive and the pleasures in the house will only increase. You will be safe and comfortable in this house, but without excesses of any kind." Finally she said that "you must also realize that when that time comes, it will be difficult for Helga, Ole, and me to fit in here any longer."

"Ole, you who were confirmed recently and taking the trade school during the winter months, have to think seriously about the future. Do you want to find a job, continue with additional schooling, or what? I am not terribly concerned about your future; you have ability and if you apply yourself, you will be able to handle just about anything."

"Helga, you have been smart in school and have indicated that you would like to continue with studies. You will manage well in the future with whatever profession you will eventually select. You will be exposed to many large temptations; among others, you will be meeting boys who would love to be your life companion. If you are not strong enough to withstand the many temptations that will come, you can risk that your future will be changed totally, such that continuation with studies will not be possible. You could end up being married to a farm boy and then you will be forced to stay on the farm to help with the daily obligations there. It is not possible for a man to manage all the responsibilities on a farm alone," she said. "But," she continued, "you still have many years ahead of you before you come to this important crossroad in your life." Fortunately, Signe thought to herself.

"We have managed fairly well," Signe continued, "and we have not suffered any hardships. But, the future that I have outlined for you will require higher income than we have now. We have the maintenance of the house to consider and we might possibly have to knock down a wall to expand for an additional room if we all continue to live at home. We need to repair the roof on the barn before we get serious problems with it. In addition we will have the added expense when any of you decide to apply to continue your studies. You know that my brother, Tor, often writes from America, that he is fine with lots of steady work, and is making good money. I know that Tor is thinking about us often and that it would be a pleasure for him to help us to a life in America. "Is his offer not to be considered thoroughly and seriously?" She let the question hang in the air for a long time before she continued. "For example, how would it be if you, Per, left to try your luck? From Tor's letters it sounds like most of the new arrivals over there are doing some kind of carpenter work and since you have good experience with that, I would think you ought to fit in easily and quickly. What are your thoughts about this, Per?"

Per had to admit that he had given some thought to America, and that he knew of the offer from Uncle Tor. Little by little he had become acquainted with someone who had departed and he had heard from others that they were doing fine. They worked very hard, but were not complaining. Per said that he had given this some thought, but as he felt an obligation to his mother and the farm, he had decided that it would be best to forget such thoughts. How did his mother believe she could manage without him? "Yes, we would miss you, but as long as we knew that you were fine and we received regular letters from you, we would also manage here," said Signe. "After you had been there for a year or so, we would have to evaluate your recommendations and decide what we should do." This became much food for thought and as a decision was so difficult to arrive at, they decided to sleep on it. Per wanted to talk to the brothers of someone who had left for America and a man who had returned from there recently to get their reactions. When returnees told of their experiences "over there," they always found eager listeners among the local population. Per promised to discuss this matter again in a few days because it was easy for him to understand how important a decision like this was for all of them.

Signe fetched the deck of Old Maid cards, and they played several merry rounds before they made ready to go to bed.

Fate

When Tor presented himself during the enrollment for military service, he had impressed the personnel with his education and experience. It was recommended that he should apply for the engineering corps and officer training school as well. But first he had to complete basic training. This did not pose any problem for Tor because he was in good physical shape. He was an excellent marksman, received medals for his marksmanship, and was also certified as a machine gunner. All soldiers, no matter what position they held, had to know how to use weapons. Tor left for officer training school after completing basic training and became an officer with a Colt revolver as part of his uniform. After the basic training and the officer training, he received special training suitable for the engineering corps, the so-called Seabees. He was trained to build and blow up bridges. He was trained to clear land in a short time to build landing sites for military transports that flew in reinforcements and supplies for the troops that fought on the different islands. This training became valuable when he came to islands in the Pacific and participated in several landings there. Tor had been given a list of islands that were candidates for troop landings and had studied these for the possible need of establishing airbases. He had to collect data for typography, wind conditions, temperature, and tides. Tor and his staff put their prepared plans into action shortly after troops were landed and established. It was important to get supplies out to the troops that were fighting on the front lines against a well-protected enemy. As an officer he was responsible for about one hundred men and women. He became popular, liked the demanding assignments, and carried out his responsibilities well.

Anders had managed to keep the firm name while Tor was away, but he had not started up the firm on his own. While he waited, and hoped that Tor would come back, he had collected information that would be useful for them when they finally could start up their own firm. He had even attended evening classes and taken courses in English and accounting.

Japan surrendered unconditionally on August 15, 1945. The date became known as V-J Day for Victory over Japan, similar to the earlier victory in Europe that had become known as V-E Day. Tor had returned from the war in the Pacific with many horrible war memories that he did his best to forget. He also returned with valuable experiences: he spoke English fluently, had become an US citizen, and was entitled to free education. He had not waited long after his return before he enrolled at a major university to get a degree in architecture, something that had always been his big dream.

~

Ten years had passed since Tor Flaten and Anders Dalen had their important discussions about their future. Now they were pleased that they had started out on their own, because they had experienced success with the firm and in their private lives.

Not long after Tor started at the university, he managed to study at the same time as they started up the firm. From the beginning they had overlooked many details that they had to correct over time. One thing that they had underestimated was the need for starting capital, but it had not been difficult to arrange for a loan because of Tor's military service. They liked the work and both had worked hard with long days and little time off. After Tor received his degree in final architecture, he engaged himself even more in the firm.

As activity and income increased, they had to hire help for the office. They needed help to take care of the payroll for up to fifty men and women, they needed a person with expertise in taxation, they needed people that could keep track of what types of projects were proposed and approved for the area, for both pubic and private purposes. With time they also needed persons that could keep up with and become experts in buying favorable lots that they could possibly develop. They had concentrated their activities in an area of the territory that made it possible for them to drive home every night after work. They had long since been well acquainted with the trade union offices, the city's engineering and architecture offices, and subcontractors of different types. They now had an office staffed by twelve persons that worked on the many duties, and the owners of the firm were still the two same friends that had started the firm. The relationship between them was good and they each had their primary responsibility. When major decisions had to be made, they were made jointly after the problem had been discussed using their own expertise and after consulting experts.

Establishment of the firm had demanded big efforts from both owners. So many inquiries were received that many times some had to be declined. This also meant that they had arrived at a position where they could select projects that they were best qualified for, were most comfortable with, and that would give the best return. Their work ethic had always been to give customers good service and to keep promises. The firm that had been a construction firm initially had also developed into an architectural firm, and with increasing income from that side, they felt the need for a new firm name. The partners had sat down and talked through several suggestions as they had done when they first started out together. They tried to come up with something that was easy to remember and pronounce in English. They were not able to come up with anything using Flaten, nor were they able to come up with anything using a combination of Flaten and Dalen names. At last they agreed to use a part of the Dalen name, and with that the new firm name became Dale Architects and Builders, Inc.

Tor had always liked to take in the sights of the city once in a while, and he had also looked at the ladies. An innocent incident, which was to lead to major consequences, happened to him a year or so after he was discharged from the military. He was in his favorite delicatessen shop to make some purchases. With the grocery bag in one hand and the wallet in the other, ready to return it to the back pocket of his pants, he had his back toward the entry door as he answered a last question from the owner. He had become well acquainted in this shop and often had conversations with the owner on such things as the stock market and sports results. He answered the owner's last comment and as he turned somewhat rapidly toward the door, he bumped against the arm of a customer who was receiving her change over the high counter from one of the shop ladies. The customer lost her shopping bag and its contents, which included a bottle of milk, were smashed with a bang. The result was that broken glass was spread over the floor together with the rest of the contents of the bag, and the spilled milk flowed outward. Customers nearby had moved away quickly from the area and a couple of them had gotten some milk splashed onto their shoes. As Tor straightened himself, he stood face-to-face with the unfortunate customer, who also was straightening, and there she stood in front of him. He was as though paralyzed, he had never seen anything as beautiful, anything as lovely. He was able to stutter an excuse while the shop personnel arrived with brooms and mops to wipe the floor. The woman took the incident calmly and accepted his apology with a smile while she wiped her shoes with a towel that she had been given by a shop worker. Tor indicated that he wanted to replace the contents of the bag without any of them making an attempt to discuss what this had been. They talked with rather awkward gestures, and Tor finally was able to propose they should go to a small establishment nearby where they could continue their talk while they had lunch. She accepted the invitation and they remained at the restaurant for a long time. It turned out that she was visiting her parents, who lived nearby, and was going back there after her meeting with Tor. They separated after they had exchanged names, telephone numbers and addresses, and with an agreement of meeting again soon. Both of them had completely forgotten to replace the milk bottle and the other ingredients of the shopping bag.

Tor drove the short distance to his home as if in a dream. He had without question met his life partner. He did not know why he could think like that after such a short meeting. He was just sure that she was the one. He knew only a little about her, she was roughly the same age as he, was as pure an American as it is possible to be, and lived only a good hour's drive away. She lived in the neighboring state where she had started to work in a law firm directly after having received her degree from a large university. She had advanced rapidly in the few years that had passed since she started to work and now had a demanding position. Tor intended to learn much more about her and would give this matter high priority. Good grief, how easy she was to be with! Her name was Susan Langer and Tor could not wait until they were to meet again.

Leaving home

Almost two weeks would pass before Per took up the discussion about their future again. As the custom was in the house, he waited until all had finished their meal and until the dishes were washed and put away, before he said that he wanted to talk about their plans for the future. He started by saying that he agreed with his mother when she had said that they were at a difficult period in their lives when hard decisions had to be made. Per said that he had thought about this a lot and had discussed the possibility of emigrating to America with someone who had been there and others who had family and friends there. He simply said that he had come to the conclusion that he had to take the trip to America. The opportunity was offered to him, and he had to give it a try. His reasoning was basically the same as what his mother had given earlier, his age and his experience with carpentry, and with the assurance that the three of them would be able to manage the farm without him. He had also investigated with a travel agency and had learned what the ticket price would be and when the next ship was leaving from the nearest port city. He assured them that this had not been an easy decision for him. Uncle Tor had several times promised to help with money for the ticket, but they determined that they had saved enough money to manage the ticket for Per. The next ship was to depart in only three weeks, but that would be too soon because this would not give sufficient time to notify Tor. Per had learned that there was another man in the area who was to take the ship that was to depart in about six weeks. This man had family who would meet him on the dock in Manhattan, and he wanted very much to have Per as his traveling companion.

Thus it was that Per made ready to leave for America in only six weeks' time, with big expectations, hopes, and a good deal of nervousness. His mother, brother, and sister, who had participated in the discussions and had been so in agreement with the conclusion, could only hope for the best for him. Uncle Tor had put up the necessary security for the American authorities.

The day that Per and his acquaintance took off was a difficult day for all. Signe tried as best as she could to assure Per that they would be fine and she wished him a nice trip and all the best. Helga cried and said in between gasps that she would miss him. Also Ole pulled himself together and said with body language and words that he was prepared to take over the male responsibilities on the farm, so that was one thing he did not want Per to worry about. All three told him several times that they would be waiting anxiously for his first letter, which they assumed, would arrive with the returning ship in four to five weeks.

They took their leave at the local bus terminal. Per noticed other families who were there to say good-bye to their loved ones. Maybe they were saying farewell to someone who was about to take the same trip as he? A small waving group of people, with tears in their eyes, remained standing when the bus left. The bus passengers waived back and sat in silence for some time, each with their own thoughts. Per had traveled the road to the big city twice before when he had accompanied his father. He had difficulty concentrating on the places they passed. He knew the names of some of the places and even knew some people who lived there. Someone on the bus told about strange events that had happened in places they passed, but such statements were more often than not commented on with a semi-polite "Oh" or "I see." Per and most of the others on the bus wanted to be left alone with their thoughts.

When the bus came to the outskirts of the city, the passengers saw an impressive sight. They saw a large white ship with two smokestacks at anchor some distance from the dock. This was without question the ship that many of the bus passengers were to board. Boy, oh boy, how big it was! It was so big that the large city dock was too small for it. All passengers who were to board the big ship were taken from the dock in a small boat together with their hand luggage. Larger items and cargo were checked on the dock and brought to the ship on a barge. Those who had assembled on the dock to take their good-byes with their family and friends had to do it there, and Per heard some crying and whimpering from both old and young. Their documents were checked before they entered the small boat and again when they came aboard the big *Stavangerfjord.*

When they were safely aboard the ship, they were shown their cabins. It turned out that he had been assigned to the lower birth of a four-man cabin and his friend had been assigned to the next door cabin, also a four-man cabin. One of his traveling companions had already taken his berth above Per. He was a twenty-year-old fellow who was about to embark on his first voyage. The man who had been assigned to the upper berth on the opposite side came into the cabin shortly after Per. He had taken the trip to New York once before and offered to help the newcomers with whatever they might need. They would have plenty of time to talk in the next days, but now it was important to go up on deck to observe when the ship started out the fjord on this fine afternoon. A number of people had gathered on the dock to witness the departure but it was not possible to recognize anyone due to the distance between the ship and the dock. One man who was standing near Per announced loudly that he could see his wife because it was she who was waving with the white head scarf.

As the ship gained speed, it became cold on deck and people started to move into the lounges. The smoke from the stacks was black and heavy and hung as a veil behind the ship. On their way out of the fjord they passed a couple of small fishing boats with fishermen who waved, otherwise there was no life to be seen along the shorelines. Per saw many small islands and skerries beyond the mainland and further ahead he saw the open sea. A number of seagulls flew shrieking behind the ship and snatched tidbits tossed to them. He became aware of the three passenger classes that existed aboard, first class, cabin class, and tourist class. Little by little he noticed many posted signs that directed people to their respective cabin classes. For example, he saw signs that informed the reader that to continue further in the direction indicated on the sign was only for passengers with first-class tickets. He had to descend several stairways before he arrived at his lounge in tourist class. He examined the lounge and oriented himself for the way to the dining room, where the doors would open in a matter of minutes. His appetite had not been the best before he left home. He had not eaten for several hours and had become really hungry. He had not eaten anything on the bus trip to the city, while waiting before being transported to the ship, or during the orientation onboard. He had heard about all the tasty and varied food that was served on this ship and was eager to experience it for himself.

Auto accident

The relationship between Tor and Susan developed rapidly from a relationship as acquaintances, to friends, to good friends, to lovers, to an engaged couple, and to having a date set for the wedding. Tor had designed their home that was under construction, with completion expected well before the wedding. They had discussed the wedding guest list, a little about their future, and had agreed that Susan was to continue in her position for the time being. They expected to continue to drive between their current homes, a trip that could take a long time when traffic was heavy.

Four months before the wedding was to take place, Tor received a message one evening while he was still in the office. The message was short and brutal, Susan had been in a terrible traffic accident on the way home from her office and had been killed instantly. Tor refused to believe what he heard – it could not be true, it had to be a mistake. It could not be Susan. He had been told which hospital she had been brought to and drove there immediately. Luckily Anders had accompanied him to the hospital. Tor was escorted to the hospital mortuary to identify the woman that had been brought in earlier. It was Susan that he found there and his whole world collapsed. He had seen dreadful things during the war with dying and dead soldiers that he had become quite friendly with. He had been in the war zone several times and it is natural to assume that one could get used to all of the horrible sights. That is not possible; one only gets filled up with emotions that will surface in quiet moments at a later time. This was much worse. His feelings wanted to crush him, the whole thing was so unbelievable, so unjust. He had been told that Susan had died instantly because she had received massive head injuries. Anders did his best to help his friend and the doctors at the hospital had also been most helpful. Her parents had arrived and they comforted each other.

Susan's parents were often together with Tor after the accident, and they had tried to console each other as best they could. Tor had his job that he tried to concentrate on, and the parents tried to travel a bit to get new impressions that would possibly help them in their sorrow. As time passed, the contact between them became less frequent. None of them mentioned that their meetings, as nice, friendly and helpful they could be toward each other, were still quite difficult, because it was natural that the subject of every conversation was Susan. The memories that they all tried to suppress came back so clearly every time. Each one of them had to struggle for several days before they could get back to their respective routines after a meeting.

Memories of the accident were also brought back the day the legal proceedings started. It was Susan's insurance firm that had brought the case to court. It turned out that the accident had occurred as a large truck had passed Susan on her left side on a dark evening. This was fully permitted, but the problem arose when the truck suddenly cut back again to the right so that it blocked the road for Susan. She had been unable to stop or move out of the way in time. Her car was pinned against the side of the truck and it was pressed toward the right and forced off the road. This became very clear from the police investigators who had examined the location right after the accident. Why the truck had suddenly cut to the right was not clear, but for Susan's insurance firm it did not have any bearing for the outcome of the case. It was speculated that Susan could possibly have been in the truck driver's blind zone, but that sounded less plausible because all the cars were driving with their lights on at that time. The case lasted two days and the verdict was in favor of Susan's insurance company. This had been two difficult days for Tor and Susan's parents.

Tor had not been the same man since the day of the accident. He had always worked hard, but after that day he sacrificed himself completely for his work. Now he was grateful for all the work the firm had, and he was not one to turn down new challenges if he only could find the time. Every time he came into a conversation with a woman, he would measure her against Susan and no one could compare with her. The house that he had designed and built had been sold some time ago. Now he lived in a large apartment in a building that he owned in the city proper.

Now and then Tor thought of the days in the rural district in Norway when he worked in the small technical department there. He had learned a lot there and much more since. He spoke fluent English, had graduated as an architect, and sat as a member of the board of an architectural organization in town. He had good contacts in his line of work and the firm had built several homes and office buildings. His friend Anders was an excellent person to collaborate with, and he had what it took to be a daily leader on a project. As he liked that type of work, it had become his primary role in the firm. Tor worked more with the administrative part of activities and their many important contacts that had to be maintained. He also developed designs for new construction projects and had won a couple of architectural competitions. With his work routines and the many assignments that he had taken on, he did not have much time to spend in his apartment.

He had maintained contact with the "old country" over the years. Contact with earlier friends was reduced with time, but with Signe he had regular contact, except for the five years that Norway was occupied during the second world war. He felt that Signe could somehow understand him better than any other person. They had always had a good relationship as they were growing up. She had lost her husband at a young age and he had lost his chosen life companion. Tor was surprised and saddened when he learned of Adolf's death in the first letter from Signe in five years. Poor Signe. Both had lost their dear ones, and the letters between had provided comfort.

To a foreign land

There was time for a quick trip around the ship before dinner was served, and Per and one of the men he shared the cabin with took a trip from end to end of the ship on the promenade deck. They also climbed the stairs to the uppermost deck and took in the many sights that were strange to a landlubber. This was a large ship in their judgment, and none of them had seen or been near anything as fantastic as this. The ship was simply very big, and everything was so magnificent that they were unable to express their feelings. They had been informed that the ship was fully booked with approximately twelve hundred passengers. These were divided into three classes, with by far the most on third class, where they were. Both of them were mighty impressed after the fast tour.

Eventually they found their way to the dining room, where a small line had formed outside the locked doors. These were opened precisely according to the designated time. They entered the large room, noted all the tables, and were directed to the table that was assigned for their cabin. The table had room for twelve passengers, and they introduced themselves to each other as they arrived. Most were young men on their first voyage, all had the same purpose for the trip, and by far the greatest number of them came from the same area of the country as Per. The table had a white tablecloth and on the tableware they noticed the initials NAL for the Norwegian America Line. The amount of tableware that was set for each person was impressive. Efficient waiters brought them the different dishes.

The menu for the first dinner was fish soup followed by roast pork. Chocolate pudding with vanilla sauce was served for dessert, followed by coffee and cookies. Oh, how wonderful it all tasted. They were all hungry after a trying day and they ate heartily. The discussions dealt with such subjects as who would be meeting the individual when they arrived at the New York dock, if they had a job to go to, if they had family nearby, and if they had marketable job skills. None had applicable job experience and none been on as large and magnificent a ship as this. Four young men at the table had been fishing off the Norwegian coast for one season and they were not concerned about the voyage. The others indicated that they had heard of people who had become very seasick on this trip. It was not easy for anyone to predict how the crossing of the Atlantic Ocean would be; that depended on the time of the year, among other things. They were all anxious for what kind of a journey they would experience with the crossing of the large Atlantic Ocean. They agreed that this would become clear to them in due time. They just had to take one day at a time.

They all retreated to the lounge after having concluded the meal. A three-piece orchestra was playing dance music and the floor became filled with happy couples. Per was not much of a dancer. He and his friend from the same rural district were watching the dancers for a while. There were indeed many girls their age and they thought that they had seen a couple of these before at a rural event back home. But evening was approaching after a long day and they decided to take a stroll on the deck before turning in for the night. They were standing at the railing watching the lights from land sliding farther and farther into the distance. They were quiet, and each in his own way wondered if he would see these shores again. Before they turned in for the night, they studied the map with the drawn-in route of travel that hung centrally located in the corridor together with information about the ship. Among other things there were also pictures of the different decks with information as to which deck was accessible for the different ticket classes.

Separate and well-marked toilets and showers for men and women were located at the end of the corridor for the third-class passengers. Per oriented himself regarding the toilet location in relation to his four-man cabin before he entered it. Each person had been allocated two drawers and a small space for their hand luggage. The larger luggage pieces had been placed in the common aboard baggage compartment and was available during the crossing for one hour each day. Luggage pieces that had been assigned to the cargo hold were not accessible during the crossing. Per lay down in the bunk and found it to be quite comfortable. He saw the other three come into the cabin. They found their bunks quickly and after the last man to turn in had turned off the light, it suddenly became quiet in the cabin. Before Per fell asleep, he heard the thump-thump sound of the engines and the sea hitting the side of the ship. The ship rocked slightly, just enough to bring about a rapid and deep sleep.

~

When Per woke after his first night aboard, it did not take long before he realized that the ship was behaving differently. He was the first to get out of the bunk and he almost had to support himself because the ship was tossing from side to side. He dressed quickly, went to the toilet, and was eager to get up on the deck to get a better understanding of the situation. On his way to the open deck, he stopped by the bulletin board and read the latest news from the bridge. There he read that they were now in the North Sea, that the breeze from the northwest would continue throughout the day, that the wave height was between three and six feet, and that the temperature was 50 degrees Fahrenheit. All clocks had to be set back one hour, something that they would continue to do almost every day until they arrived in New York. Per oriented himself rapidly and noticed that he was getting used to the new movements and the fresh air. The weather was overcast, and in all directions he saw nothing but the sea. The ship took the waves such that once in a while the sea spray was thrown onto the foredeck. He started to get cold, felt that he was hungry, and moved toward the dining room.

Two others from a different cabin had already taken their seats at the table, and they had already helped themselves from the breakfast buffet. Per soon learned how the food service was arranged. All he had to do was to help himself from the long buffet table. There was no shortage of eggs, bread, and cold cuts. He took a sizable helping and returned to his table, where coffee was served. Little by little the others arrived and the eating was interrupted by small talk. They had all slept well and were looking forward to participating in different activities. Some wanted to play cards and others were looking forward to the evening dance. Per went to his cabin, made up his bed, found a sweater and went back out on the deck. He looked around from the back of the ship, nothing but the sea all around. The huge ship that he had entered in the harbor had somehow become very small in relation to the surroundings. They were alone. Birds that had followed from land for a while had long since given up the pursuit. He looked at the wake behind the ship. It reached as far back as he could see. He took a few laps around the ship before he returned to the cabin and stretched out on his bunk. After a half hour or so, he got restless, got up, and took the stairs up a couple of decks.

He had found a small library onboard and had found a book about New York that contained many photographs. He might as well read a little about the place that they were now sailing toward. He knew something about the place, had heard about all the houses there, the many tall buildings, and all the people that lived there. The book was informative and he took it with him to the cabin. He found it interesting and instructive, but soon he fell asleep. He had slept for about an hour when one of the others came into the cabin. Per was told that different and interesting entertainment was already under way in the lounge and he decided to go there and take it in.

~

The ship's movements changed somewhat after two days on board, as they now had entered the Atlantic Ocean. The relative short waves of the North Sea had been substituted for longer waves, and the ship rocked more in a back and forth direction than it had done before. The earlier movements had been more of a side to side movement.

It had not taken long before he had oriented himself completely and had become familiar with the routines aboard. The routines concerned themselves primarily with the meals that were served between given hours. After he got up in the morning, he got ready for breakfast, thereafter he had to come up with something to do until it was time for lunch, thereafter something to do until dinner, and thereafter something to do until it was time to go to bed. Little by little he learned that there was no shortage of things to do, and little by little he also got into conversation with interesting passengers. He met several young people that were intent on trying their luck just like him, and he also met some elderly Norwegian couples that had been on a holiday trip to Norway after a long stay in America. These told many interesting stories from their experiences and could offer the first-time travelers all types of suggestions and admonitions. It sounded as if the advice from the elderly was quite simple, work hard, stay healthy, keep away from temptations, especially alcohol. If you can manage this, you will find that America is a remarkable country that offers many opportunities and will give you good rewards for your struggles.

The young people had problems with serious discussions that contained admonitions. They were anxious for their future and did not regard it as a problem that one had to work hard to keep up. At home they had heard about the ones that had fallen for temptations and what had happened to them. No, this is not the way they would end up. Their future was ensured because they intended to be successful.

Per did not really know what the girls did during the daytime. It was to take two days before he saw the two girls again that he had seen the first day, the ones he thought came from the same rural district as himself. He saw them after lunch and got into a conversation with them. They went into the lounge and sat down on a sofa. Yes, the girls hailed from the same district. One was one year older than Per and her name was Olga, the other was a year younger and her name was Trine. As most of the other first-time travelers, they also had families and friends to go to in America. None of them had special education and they intended to take a job as housekeepers. They reasoned that if they only got started somewhere, they would learn to manage onward. Their friends had written that this would not pose any problems. They soon became acquainted, and they traveled with high spirits. Both girls were nice and were easy to converse with. They separated with a "See you – maybe at the dance tonight?" They had told Per that they would be met by friends at the dock in New York and that they were to travel to a place on Long Island. After they had told him this, he thought that maybe it would be wise to exchange addresses with them. Who knows what the future might bring.

It did not take long before some of the boys started to play cards. Many played whist but some poker was also played. Per tried his luck with table tennis even though he had never tried it before. He also managed to play billiards quite well. Per put on his sweater and took several trips around the deck. The fresh air was good before going to bed.

Per was awakened when he was just about to be tossed out of his bunk. He concluded quickly that the behavior of the ship was absolutely strange with its strong movements and the loud thuds to the side. The others had also been awakened by the racket and all four got dressed in a hurry and got out into the corridor. They were greeted by a sigh of people who were trying to make their way somewhere. They were hanging onto whatever they could, and Per realized little by little that several were on their way to the toilet. He could see that they did not look well. Per and the others from his cabin had to make a stop at the toilet and when they finally got inside, they found quite a sight. Several men stood, and some were seated, they coughed, vomited, and groaned. It smelled so bad inside that they relieved themselves as fast as possible and got out of there.

Per suggested to his cabin friends that since they had one hour before breakfast would be served, that they take a trip on deck to better see what was going on. They moved along the corridors and up the many steps. They saw several sick passengers that had difficulties getting around. When they arrived at the door leading to the deck, they discovered that it was locked. A notice on the door explained that due to the storm all movement on deck was cancelled. Through the windows they could see that ropes had been attached between the ship railing and deck superstructures for the crew to hang onto when they moved about on deck. They moved higher up in the ship to a location where the view normally was good. Some passengers had found the way there and they were looking through the windows. It was raining very hard and it was so windy that some loose ropes were hitting the mast with loud bangs. What a sight! The sea was white with big waves that came rolling directly toward the ship. The ship bored itself into each wave, and when it came back out again, it shook and provoked all kinds of uncomfortable sounds in the hull. The forepart buried itself completely in each wave, and eventually it emerged again with foaming water flowing in all directions on the deck ahead. The ship was barely free of water on the forward deck when it plowed into the next wave. The ship behaved like a wild bucking horse trying to rid itself of its rider. They could see crew members on the deck that had great difficulty in securing a couple of hawsers that had broken loose. The hawsers knocked with great force at the ship's side and this provoked loud thuds that could be heard a long way inside the ship. This was a frightening situation! An officer who had worked with the deck crew happened to come into the room and was bombarded with questions. He explained that weather like this was common at this time of the year and that it usually lasted only a couple of days. He assured the listeners that the ship had been in much worse weather than this. He recommended that everyone be careful and move about as little as possible. No one dared to ask the question that they above all would like to have answered, namely if they were in any danger.

The young men saw that the clock on the wall was approaching time for breakfast, and they moved in the direction of the dining room. The ventilation on the ship was probably reduced considerably because they could now detect a smell in the air that was a mixture of diesel and food. Once in a while they came across vomit in the corridors that the crew had not had time to clean up. By the entry door to the dining room one of the young men said that he felt dizzy. He said that he wanted to go to the cabin and took off in a hurry. The others entered the dining room where there were plenty of empty seats. Per and the ones he shared the cabin with walked across the floor in the dining room as if they were intoxicated. They felt fine, but to walk in a straight line across the floor was impossible, the ship tossed too much. They managed to find some food and took their seats. The tablecloth had been moistened by the staff in order for the tableware to stay in place. They were told by the staff that if the plates started to move, they should turn up the hinged table moldings. After they had eaten for a while, more people came to the tables, but the dining room was still only half full. The last arrivals explained that the situation in the corridors and toilets was chaotic with many seasick people and with poor air quality below due to poor circulation.

The captain came on the loudspeaker with his morning greeting at the usual time in a calm and monotone voice. He explained that they were in a storm that came directly on the ship and he was afraid the intensity of the storm would increase in the next few hours. He told of a couple of broken legs and arms as a result of falls on the stairways and admonished the passengers to be careful and move about as little as possible. He finished by saying that he would alter the course a little to see if this would possibly make the voyage more comfortable. He promised to come back with new information at lunch time. Well, this was not a desirable situation they were in. They were so absolutely helpless on this endless ocean they were on. They had only one choice. They had to rely on the captain and his crew and do their best to get through this incident without an accident, and not to get weighed down with anxiety.

~

It was to take several days before the storm moderated sufficiently for passengers to be allowed back up on the deck. While the storm raged at its worst, there were not many passengers at the different meals. Most were sick and kept to their bunks, and some had constantly been running to the toilets. Many had taken their helplessness out in anger. They expressed annoyance for having been so dumb when they decided to take this voyage. Others were simply scared that the ship would not make it. Many could not think about food, but some managed to eat some dry crackers and water. It was not easy to get an appetite when one stayed deep down in the ship where the combination of many confined smells alone was sufficient to make one sick. The announcements from the captain sounded so very routine. He explained that they were aboard a safe ship that had gone through many storms and that the crew had a lot of experience. It was important to move about as little as possible, he had said. How could he really know if the ship was able to take this awful sea? Did the captain really have the situation under full control? These were questions that many kept to themselves.

Per kept going day after day. His form was far from one hundred percent and he was fighting with himself just to keep going. He had heard from several before he departed how important it was to keep going even if it was so much easier to give in. If it had been possible to remain relaxed in the bunk with a book, it would have been easier, but who could concentrate between four walls when it creaked and banged all over and when the ship heaved so much that one was almost tossed out of the bunk. In addition one had to listen to the moaning of the sick passengers.

There were less people in the lounges and the air was much better there than in the corridors. It helped to sit there and entertain oneself with an exciting book. Once in a while he would get into conversation with someone, and this would most often be about the weather. When can we expect to get back to sailing as pleasant as when we started, was the question that most wanted an answer to. Pale-faced people started to appear as the storm moderated and among them was the girl that he had met several days ago. It was Trine who showed up in the lounge one afternoon, and she told him how sick they had been in her cabin. One girl had started to vomit and the others had become sick, one at a time. It had been awful and it would be impossible for him to comprehend just how terrible it had been, she said. “Try to imagine,” she said, “four sick girls in a small room, competing for the puke bucket, moaning, whimpering, helpless, crying out for help and being scared stiff when the ship tilted and creaked. Sometimes two girls clung to each other as they staggered down the corridor for the toilet. And that awful smell!” She did not envy the staff who had to clean up the mess that could be seen all over. She felt listless and miserable, and Per suggested that she had to do her very best to get to the next meal. He believed that she would be able to get something down, and reminded her that the staff would gladly recommend something suitable for her.

Thus it was that they got Trine to their table for dinner. It had turned out as Per had indicated, she had found something that she could eat at the prior meal and felt better already when she left the table. Trine said that she would do her best to get her friends up for the next meal, because they had to be hungry, even if they did not realize it. Trine brought along some crackers and a pot of tea to the cabin. Per used the opportunity to get her address on Long Island.

~

Two days before they were to arrive in New York the storm subsided and the ship started to behave as it had done in the first days of the voyage. Little by little normal life returned aboard, and it was a relief for many passengers to foresee the end of the voyage. They dared leave their cabins, participated in meals again, and shared stories of how sick they had been.

Per knew that Uncle Tor would be on the dock. "I wonder if I will recognize him from the pictures that I have seen of him?" A friend of Per that he had corresponded with would also be on the dock, and the arrangement was that Per was to move in with him to begin with. He was sure that Uncle Tor would not have any objection to this, as he lived rather far from the central part of the city. This had been discussed around the dinner table while they were under way, and all were in general agreement that it was important to arrange for a central place to live from the start, because then it would be so much easier and faster to get into the new routines. Per had also been told that he would be able to get along just fine with the Norwegian language all over the Bay Ridge part of the city.

In ample time before the ship was to reach New York City, the passengers had been informed about what would happen when they arrived at the dock. All had furnished their baggage with tags that contained a color code based on their type of cabin and location on the ship. Per was ready with his preparations early because he wanted to observe what was happening when the ship closed in on the dock in New York City. He soon realized that many people had gathered on the pier to greet the ship, and even before the ship touched the dock, he heard passengers calling out to family and friends dockside. The ship was soon cleared by the authorities, and rushing passengers started down the different gangways. Per had not experienced any problems when he presented his papers to the immigration and health authorities, and he was soon on the section of the warehouse floor where the baggage had been assembled. He found his suitcase and followed the people who were walking toward the customs inspectors. That inspection was quick and in a few minutes he saw his Uncle and friend among the many people gathered on the dock.

It turned out that the two who had come to meet him had both driven their cars to the dock. Tor and Erik, Per's friend, had talked while they waited. They had exchanged telephone numbers and had discussed the plans they had for Per. The three of them engaged in small talk, including greetings from family and friends, and conversation related to experiences on the crossing. Tor broke off this line of conversation by saying that he had something important to finish at the office and therefore needed to drive there right away. Erik had decided that he would drive directly to his home. They talked a bit more before they started their cars. Tor waved good-bye with one more "welcome" toward Per and said that he would call later in the evening. When they arrived at the apartment, Per was directed to a small room where he moved his few belongings. He was well cared for by Erik and his wife, Gerd.

Form worker

Lars Tunet worked as a carpenter doing formwork and had worked on the top floor of a new building all day. The sun rays had been intense all day from a cloudless sky. The temperature had been in the high eighties Fahrenheit and the relative humidity had been near ninety percent. The workers on the floor did their best to avoid the direct sun but that was not easy, as the newly built floor where they were offered few shady areas. He and his partner were a team that had been assigned to erect forms for columns and beams on a reinforced concrete construction project. They were soaked with perspiration so that the breeze they felt once in a while was cooling and almost cold.

Lars worked as a partner with Andreas Neset. Both were familiar with the different types of work they could be assigned by the foreman. Andreas had been on this type of work for about five years. He had followed the same construction firm for much of this time, primarily because he got along well with the foreman. He had worked on a huge foundation for a multistory office building in Manhattan, expansion at an electric generating plant that required precise placement of anchoring bolts within large footings for gas turbines, and several high-rise buildings similar to the one they were working on now. Andreas had been a good teacher for Lars, who had only worked for one year as a carpenter on formwork. Together they performed their work skillfully, and they knew each other so well that work related conversation was almost unnecessary. They put up forms for several columns consisting of four panels during a day and the columns were erected at a common distance of twelve to fifteen feet. The ironworkers had extended the reinforcing bars that followed each column up from the foundation before the carpenters started to work on them. The four panels, in lengths of ten to twelve feet, depending on the ceiling height, and widths of two to three feet, were fastened together securely with clamps.

Lars and his partner saw to it that one of them would end up on the shady side of the newly erected forms for a column when they were to be fixed in place. This is where one carpenter would seat himself near the swinging plumb bob, hung from a nail near the top of the panel, with a ruler in hand to read vertical adjustment on both sides of the forms for the column. The other carpenter fastened two braces, one for each column direction, to the top of the column forms. The other end of the braces would be fastened to secure points on the floor. This final securing would take place as soon as he was directed to do so by his partner, who was keeping an eye on the plumb bob. Two-by-four nailing strips were fastened horizontally on the column forms, at a height equal to the location of the bottom of the beam that would eventually be connected to it. The engineer would be checking all measurements with his instruments before the carpenters continued with the installation of forms that would make up the floor for the next level. Before they left the erected forms for a column, they double-checked that it was erected square and in plumb.

The panels were put together by another pair of carpenters, who were able to avoid direct sunlight by putting up their workbenches under a provisional canvas on the floor. These carpenters worked with panels that had been used before, and they were brought to them by helpers or strippers from the floor below. Every carpenter pair had a helper who was responsible for bringing all materials needed by them to a convenient location. As much as possible used panels were repaired by being cleaned for concrete and nails and by replacing damaged boards. As soon as a panel was ready, carpenter helpers brought them to the next location where columns were to be put up.

The workers followed the recommendations of their foreman regarding drinking plenty of water throughout the day and in small quantities at a time. The small paper cups used for drinking the water were scattered all around the water can. It had also been recommended that everyone should take a couple of salt tablets that were placed near the water can, and they would usually swallow three or four during a day.

During the lunch break they would seat themselves with their backs against a pile of lumber while they ate the food they had brought along in their lunch boxes. Lars and his partner usually sat with the other carpenters and they engaged in small talk. It could be about work, cars, something of interest from the newspapers, restaurants, women, and family back in Norway. This was also the time when different types of stories and jokes were told that usually brought much laughter. When the food had been consumed, most lit a smoke. They were sitting or reclining with closed eyes and were almost asleep when the whistle blew to indicate that the break was over.

The assembly of forms for a beam started by placing a panel

horizontally between two columns at the height given by the engineer. Beam supports of solid material, typically four-by-four inch pine wood, were made into the shape of a "T" and placed under the panel and spaced evenly every three to five feet. Height adjustments were made with two wedges placed under each support. These wedges were made from short pieces of two-by-four lumber that had been sawn diagonally such that each wedge was four inches wide and ten to twelve inches long. The panel that became the bottom of the beam was checked with a level and adjustments were made with the wedges as needed. This was verified later by the engineers with their precise instruments. The next step in the process was to lift up the panels that would become the sides of the beam. The carpenters crawled up and stood on the beam bottom while they lifted one beam side at a time that was handed to them by their helper and put it into place. The sides were braced securely from the horizontal part of the "T" shaped support that had been placed under the bottom beam panel.

The installation of the beam side panels, especially for the outside beams of the building, could be unpleasant and dangerous. It would not take much wind before a carpenter could loose his balance, and this became only worse as the building became taller. The carpenters worked without any form for protection, not even a belt or a rope around their waists. If they should be unfortunate and fall down, they would end up on the ground. The ground was no comfort in case of a fall, because it could be a long way down and the ground could be a pile of rocks from the excavation of the foundation. After the forms for the columns and beams were in place, the installation of the flooring forms between them would follow. The ironworkers followed with many reinforcing bars that were tied together with numerous wire ties.

The ironworkers belonged to a strong union, and they had a

better pay scale than the carpenters. They usually worked at ground level when they put together reinforcing rods for beams. The lengths of the rods were five to six feet longer than the ceiling height in order for the additional length to give sufficient overlap for continuation of the reinforcing rods to the next floor. Part of the work was done at ground level for safety reasons and by necessity, as the unfinished floors did not offer sufficient space for this work, and also because it could be performed more easily on the ground. Several ironworkers were busy cutting bars to length and in forming the bars with their bending tools. All reinforcing profiles were put together with bars that had been formed to the proper profiles. This was the case for columns, beams, and floors or ceilings. The individual details were gathered only shortly before they were put together for the final unit, to simplify storing. The finished units were hoisted by crane and placed into the proper location, after which the ironworkers tied the new section to the reinforcing bars that extended from the previously poured sections. Reinforcing bars for floors and ceiling was hoisted by crane as needed and as the carpenters were finishing new forms.

The different services needed for the building would be installed under the concrete ceilings. These would include things like water, gas, heat, telephone, air-conditioning, electric supply, and electrical controls. This form of installation gave good flexibility, in that the individual entities simply were hung under the ceilings with metallic attachments. In this way the services were easy to modify and expand. The visible ceiling would also be hung from the load-bearing concrete ceiling.

When everything was ready for concrete to be poured, columns, beams, and floors were poured at the same time without interruption. One or two pairs of carpenters were chosen to be on duty when the concrete pouring was taking place. Their job was to make rapid repairs to forms that might give under the pressure from the concrete as the forms were being filled. Many hours could accrue that could include Saturdays and Sundays. Work in excess of normal weekday hours and Saturday work was paid with a 50% increase for each hour, and Sunday work was paid with a 100% increase. It happened very seldom that a form gave in from the weight of the concrete and the vibrators that were used to ensure complete filling of the forms. But, it became very hectic for the carpenters if a failure occurred. The priority was for getting the forms repaired fast, and with flowing concrete all over, it was not always an easy job. The stand-by duty during concrete pouring was sought after as it was usually problem free and it gave good earnings on account of the overtime. Lars and Andreas were to be on duty at the next concrete pour which was expected in about one week.

Lars was tired at the end of the day. He was dirty, and he smelled far from good. His eyes were sore after having squinted against the sun all day. The ones who worked on the floor below them had at least shade against the sun. He was dressed in overalls over only underwear. When the day was over, he exchanged the overalls, work shoes, and cap for clean shirt, trousers, and a pair of light shoes. The overalls were usually washed once a week and were kept in a locker with his tools. With his lunch box under his arm he was ready for the trip home in a few minutes after the work whistle had sounded.

The carpenters started to work at seven o'clock and worked eight hours with a half hour for lunch. They were four that drove the half-hour trip to and from work and usually they were back home at about four in the afternoon. The driving was shared so that each man drove every fourth week. If a passenger did not own a car, he would compensate the driver on a weekly basis. The three passengers used the opportunity to take a nap on the way to and from work. Often they separated to their favorite bar, where they had two to three beers before they walked home, each to his own. This had been a tough day, and Lars needed a shower and a nap. His wife, Kari, would be coming home soon from her job.

Their apartment on the second floor could be warm in the summertime even if all the windows and doors were left open. They could get a good draft through the rooms if there was a breeze. The pressing heat today probably signaled thunderstorms later in the day or evening. The layout of the apartment was such that the rooms were in line from the street to the back yard. The apartment had three rooms plus a bathroom with entry to all rooms from the hallway and the bedroom. The room facing the street was the living room, and the room facing the back yard was the kitchen with entry from the end of the hallway. The room in between was the bedroom. Entry to the bath was at the end of the hallway on the opposite side of the entries to the other rooms.

A small room at the front end of the hallway, with a window to the street, was part of the apartment. This room was a natural usage of the floor space over the staircase. The room had sufficient space for a bed, a dresser with three drawers with a mirror over it, a small wardrobe, and a spindle-backed chair. The hallway room was let for five dollars a week. The renter had access to the bathroom but not the kitchen.

Lars tossed his dirty clothes near the washing machine that was installed in the bathroom. He showered, drank a glass of cold water from the icebox, and went to the bed that was located in the middle room. It did not take long before he was sound asleep.

Factory worker

Lars Tunet and Kari Solbakken Tunet hailed from the same part of the country. They came from small farms on the West Coast of Norway and had kept their farm names as their family names. The Tunet farm, where Lars came from, could support a horse, three cows, fifteen to twenty sheep, a couple of pigs, and some chickens. His father had always had to take occasional work to support his family, whenever he could justify being absent from the farm. He had taken occasional work as a tradesman or a fisherman. Lars was the oldest of the four children at Tunet. He had learned several different tasks that a small farm demands, and he had worked with his father as a carpenter. Lars was an able and handy fellow and he was easy to associate with.

Kari also came from a small farm. In earlier times it had supported one or two cows, a horse, and some sheep. These days they only kept a few sheep. The father had secured permanent work at a factory for many years and the Solbakken farm was therefore worked more or less as a hobby. Kari had worked for a while in a textile shop where she had been mostly assigned to sales work.

Kari was two years younger than Lars, and they had taken notice of each other after they were confirmed. Kari was twenty years old when Lars proposed that they become engaged, and this had made her very happy. They were content with each other, and their relationship with their respective parents was good. A big church wedding took place almost two years after their engagement. The new bride and groom settled in a centrally located apartment and they were happy.

They had mutual friends who had crossed "the pond" to try their luck and they had discussed among themselves if this could be something for them. They discussed this with their families, and even though none of them liked the idea of them traveling so far away, they understood that this possibly would be a good way for them to improve their living standard. They could always return to what they would be leaving. It was to take almost two years after the wedding before they packed their belongings and made ready for the trip. Kari exchanged tearful good-byes with her parents and her younger sister. Both families followed the two when they bid farewell at the bus station. The bus would take them to the city where they would board the large ship that would transport them over the Atlantic. The families had been helpful in lending them some money for tickets and a little extra in order for them to get established over there.

They were met by friends when they arrived safely in New York City. They stayed with these friends for a few nights until they had rented an apartment and both had found work. It had not taken much time to get established, thanks to the help from their friends.

Kari worked at a can factory. The factory produced mostly cans for the beer industry, but occasionally they also produced cans for the canning industry. The production of the cans started with small thin steel sheets that had been punched out of long rolls. The ends of the small plates were first tinned and then given a round form and soldered. The small tube that was thereby created could easily be corrugated to give it more strength before the bottom plate was soldered into place. The lids were shipped separately with the cans and were soldered into place by the end user after the cans were filled. The processes were fast, and the different operations, with a transport belt between them, were so noisy that normal conversations near the transport belts was impossible.

For some time the factory had experimented with the possibility of manufacturing cans from rolls of thin aluminum alloy stock. These new cans appeared promising. They could be produced fast, they were cleaner, would not rust, and were lighter and less expensive. The soldering process could be eliminated with these cans because it was possible to fold the lids into place, and do it in such a way that the cans would be perfectly watertight. In addition, such cans could be recycled, as they were easy to melt down and could thereby again be used to manufacture rolls of thin stock material of different dimensions. The factory was hoping that they would also be able to establish an extrusion process whereby one of the ends could be formed with the forming of the body of the can to avoid making one separate lid. The can factory delivered cans and lids separately for their customers. The lid was fitted with a strip of foil that could be pulled off to open the can. The ultimate customer fitted the lids onto the cans that were used for a variety of liquid products. These could for example, be for different types of soda, beer, or soups.

The work in the factory was not really heavy. It could be rather boring. Kari had been assigned the job of sorting out bad products from the belts. She had a belt directly in front of her and had to pay close attention to the cans that passed by her quite fast. Once in a while a can would be lying on the belt instead of standing upright; she would grab the can quickly and put it upright. She could see inside the cans with a mirror arrangement, and if she saw dirt in them or if they were pinched, she would grab them and toss them aside. It was warm in the factory and noisy for her and all the other women who worked there from morning to night. It was mandatory to use the earplugs that they were given. They worked eight-hour days, and every other hour they were given a ten-minute break on a rotating basis. This was sufficient for a quick trip to the toilet and a smoke for many. In emergency situations, the women signal a relief person that would take over while the women took care of their problems. The lunch break was a half hour long, just enough time to consume the food and drink they had brought with them. The work in the factory continued night and day, with a three-shift arrangement. When the whistle blew to indicate the end of her shift, Kari straightened herself and moved away from her chair. A new girl moved into place rapidly and they greeted each other with a quick "Hi."

It felt good for Kari to get out into fresh air and away from the noise. She walked with two friends to the bus station and the conversation was mostly about what kind of plans they had for the evening and the coming days. Kari's bus came after only a few minutes, and she was home in the apartment in a matter of a half hour. On the way up to the apartment she brought along the mail.

In the bathroom she could see that Lars had come home. She did not have to see his dirty clothes. She could smell them a long way off. She went into the kitchen and checked the icebox and discovered that they needed to buy an assortment of groceries. But she did not feel like going to the delicatessen just yet, as dirty and tired as she was, the purchasing of groceries had to wait. She returned to the bathroom, tossed the dirty clothes from Lars into the washing machine, added soap, pushed the start button, and the machine started to take in water. She tossed her dirty clothes in a basket next to the washing machine and entered the bathtub. She pulled the shower curtain and adjusted the faucets for a suitable water temperature. It felt wonderful to wash off the perspiration and dust from the factory. She dried herself, went to the kitchen, picked up the mail and a glass of soda and went into the living room. There she tossed herself down on the sofa to relax a little and to read the mail. Today they had received a notice from the landlord, a letter from home, and two bills. The landlord informed them that the icebox would be replaced with an electric refrigerator this coming Saturday. She looked forward to this exchange because an icebox had really become an old-fashioned appliance by now. They would not have to worry about ordering ice blocks any more and make sure that the iceman had access to the kitchen. They would also be able to sleep later on Saturdays mornings because their iceman had a habit of coming very early. The letter from Norway was pleasant and it informed that all family members were well. She relaxed and soon had problems keeping her eyes open. This evening they had plans for a fun time with good friends. It was Friday.

The lodger

The new lodger of the hall rom was the nineteen-year-old Per Bakken who had arrived in Brooklyn a short while ago. He hailed from the same part of the country as Lars Tunet and Kari Solbakken Tunet, and their impression of him was that he was a decent, reliable, and friendly fellow. He had found work as a carpenter on framing, however as an apprentice carpenter. He had been told that he should expect to be working as an apprentice for a while before he could become a full member of the carpenter's union. Per appreciated this arrangement and had no doubts of becoming a full-fledged carpenter in due time. He had become acquainted with several who had managed the transition in a short time, and he was looking forward to this, because his wages would increase substantially.

Per had also been informed of the importance of getting a certain number of hours worked up to become eligible for health insurance. Normally this would take about six months. Anyone unfortunate to get seriously sick without health insurance coverage was really in a serious predicament. One solution for many who were stricken with an illness that prevented them from earning an income was to return to their original home in Norway. Friends in the immigrant community and family in Norway would contribute to make the return possible. The alternative could be a life on skid row, death, and burial in a potter's field.

Per had handled a hammer before he came to Brooklyn and he had experience from a carpenter shop. He did not have any direct experience with framing of houses, but he learned the routines fast, the work became easier, and he was able to produce more every day. He had found a reliable and capable partner and they collaborated excellently. The tempo at work was at full throttle every day, and he knew all too well what the result would be if he did not give every minute of the day his best effort. He had seen several who had been fired before their first day was over because they did not maintain a steady work pace throughout the day, or they did not perform in accordance with the expectations of the foreman. He was tired and stiff after the hard and new pace in the first days. It had been so bad that he almost had to crawl up to his hall room. He had been bone tired, he ached all over, and it felt so good to stretch out on the bed for a while. He only had to guard against falling asleep for the night.

He had gotten a job on a large housing project on Long Island. The new houses were put up with little spacing between them on the flat land there and the work progressed based on well-proven methods. Carpenters were separated into groups with different specialties and the work progressed as these carpenter groups followed each other closely. As soon as one group was finished, for example, after the framing, the erection of the roof would follow. There were four to five house patterns that repeated. All were on one floor with different numbers of bedrooms and baths, and could be with or without a garage.

There was usually time for some coffee and a few words from the foreman when the carpenters arrived at the job site in the morning. This was also the time when the foreman assigned work for the day with rapid orders, and this was often done in Norwegian. The carpenters had time to exchange a few words with others as they were gathered around the foreman at this time and again during the short lunch break.

The layout of streets and housing lots at the construction site were carried out precisely in accordance with the architectural drawings. The streets were furnished with drainage, fire hydrants, and sidewalks. The housing lots had been supplied with water and sewer services and electric and telephone cables. Sidewalks and access to the garages and main entry for each lot were poured concrete, while the streets were usually finished with asphalt. The foundations for the houses were put up as directed by civil engineers. The formwork and concrete work were specialties that appeared to be dominated by Italians. They had their helpers who often appeared to be young immigrants that spoke Italian.

Large quantities of construction materials were brought to a central location inside a fenced area on the job site, which was locked up and guarded at night. In many cases helpers brought the various construction materials to the many footings, because it was not always possible for trucks to drive close to the foundations. The greenest workers were usually given these assignments. The carpenters fetched, or were brought, necessary materials as needed from stacks that were placed near the foundations. It was easy for the boss to see how much an individual carried, and if it was insufficient according to his judgment, it meant being fired. These helpers also functioned as helpers for the carpenters and it was, as an example, their duty to lift heavy beams and rafters into place. The work that these laborers performed was without doubt the heaviest, and it was also the lowest paid. Youngsters who found it necessary to start in the construction trade tried to get jobs as carpenters as soon as they got a feel for this trade. Among the laborers who carried heavy loads were also older, strong men who had specialized in bringing lumber as needed, and they could obtain piecework contracts for such work. The youngsters who started in this trade had a difficult time and a day with this type of work took the courage from many. Their character and perseverance were severely tested and this often resulted in doubts being raised about the choice that they had made in coming to this country; and this in turn brought forth a longing for home. But, as greenhorns it was not easy to find alternative work so they had to continue to work in order to sustain themselves. If they were fired on one job, they had to try a different job site. The carpentry trade was without doubt the trade that appealed to most Norwegian immigrants. Other first-time work demanded that the laborer be conversant in English, and the starting wage for such work was considerably less than for the construction trade.

By far, most houses were put up on concrete slabs that were poured inside foundations at a height of about six to eight inches above the ground. The water supply was embedded in the slabs with copper tubing. The houses were sometimes heated by a hot air system in which the air was circulated by force within ducts placed between the rafters. Or, the heating system could be hot water, or steam, where the heated water was circulated through radiators to the different rooms. Electric and telephone connections were installed from the nearest distribution pole to a point on the house that gave sufficient clearance from the ground. It could be a point on a wall or a point on the roof where the electric wires were brought to a fuse panel through a conduit. The telephone wires were brought to a convenient point in the house and connections were distributed to other rooms from there.

In the rare case where a house was to have a full basement, or what happened more frequently, that a house was to be put up over a crawl space, the floor beams would have been placed at the ready next to the foundations when the carpenters started in the mornings. Some carpenters were assigned to install the flooring beams between the house foundations, and others were assigned the task of starting the framing. The framing consisted usually of two-by-four pine lumber that was erected to the pattern that the boss or leading carpenters had laid out from the drawings. The pattern was prepared with three two-by-four nailing strips, one on top of the other. The two top ones were nailed together and they were tacked to the lower two-by-four that was permanently fastened to the beams. In the case of a concrete slab, the lower two-by-four would have been fastened directly to the floor and would have been of pressure impregnated lumber. The three two-by-fours constituted the plate and these would be marked jointly where the studs were to be fastened, the locations of doors and windows, and where connecting walls were to be attached. The necessary headers would be installed over doors and windows. The top two-by-fours would make up the top of a wall and the upper of these would be notched for connecting walls where applicable.

When the assembly of the framework started, the carpenter couple would free the two top two-by-fours for a wall section and temporarily pull them further in on the floor or beams. Studs of proper length were fastened where indicated between this double two-by-four and the permanently remaining two-by-four. When all studs were fastened to the top part of the plate, the entire side was put upright. A carpenter pair would often have to get help from a carpenter pair of a neighboring house to set a large wall section upright and to get the temporary braces fastened. Only some of the studs were fastened to the bottom two-by-four at this time.

Carpenters, who had some experience, were put to the task of nailing the two-by-four studs to the corresponding marks on the floor plate. This required one nail on each side of the stud, approximately one inch from the outside edges, and it was toenailed into place in rapid succession. A newly erected wall was soon shored up securely and plumbed as additional adjacent walls came into place. Two men were able to put up all the walls for a regular house before the end of a day. In addition, all the headers would have been nailed into place above windows and doors. Often the roofing beams would have been put up on top of the walls ready for the next day's task.

The beginners started by filling their nailing pocket from the nail cask. They would set a nail by hitting it with the hammer held in one hand against the head of the nail that they held between the index finger and thumb of the other hand. After the first blow, the hand that had held the nail went to the nail pocket to get another nail that would be fastened as soon as the first nail had been seated completely. It was to take only one blow to seat a nail completely. They worked with bent backs and heads hour after hour on floors or roofs. The novices clenched their teeth and carried on. The most clever ones asked the experienced carpenters for advice, how best to hold and swing the hammer and so on. They soon got blisters on their hands and once in a while the hammer hit a finger or the wrist instead of the nail. It was just impossible to avoid, and thereafter it was not easy to get a good grip on the nail. How were they to hide that they had gotten a thumb banged up after a miss with the hammer? How were they to hide that they were so tired, thirsty, and hot that they were about to collapse? How were they to straighten their backs without the boss seeing it? It was necessary to appear as if one had no problems with the work assignments or the pace. It was necessary to appear as a fellow who could tackle the job without complaints and without showing weakness of any kind.

This was a tough school. The ones who managed the first two to three weeks became quite skilled after a couple of months. The ones who could use their heads in addition to their muscles soon stood out. They became leaders, and the ones who really dared to test themselves often became subcontractors with their own firm before too long. All carpenters who worked outdoors were of course dependent on good weather. There was no work on days with rain, snow, high temperatures, or extreme cold. However, the workers always had to show up at the job site, and they could risk being sent home if the weather or job conditions were not satisfactory. A day without work meant a day without pay. On days with inclement weather sometimes some carpenters could be assigned to work for a day or two on something that could be done under cover. A day off could be a blessing for the newcomers because this would give them a chance to take care of their wounds and give their bodies some extra rest. They also used such days to get better acquainted in the neighborhood and to find out where the best, or next, jobs was to be found.

Fortunately Per had sense enough to eat before he went to his room in the evenings even if his body was stiff. If he had gone to his room first, he would most certainly would have stretched out on his bed just to rest a little with the result that he would have fallen asleep for the night. Often he needed only to think of lying quietly and he would soon be asleep, because he was so tired. He slept soundly for the most part, and once in a while he had problems hearing the alarm clock when it started every morning at five o'clock with its cowbell sound. That allowed just enough time to get up fast, get dressed, take a quick trip to the bathroom, and go to a nearby restaurant for breakfast. At the restaurant he could also purchase a sandwich or two that he put into his lunch box and brought to the job site with a thermos full of coffee. He did not need many tools for the job he was assigned to at this time and he brought what little he had back and forth each day. In this way he always knew where the tools were to be found. This was also smart, because he would then be ready immediately if another and better job should be offered after he got home from work.

An older Norwegian carpenter, who knew Per's family, had brought him to a hardware store and helped him with the purchase of the necessary tools and work clothes soon after he came to this country. This man had also lent him some money for these purchases, and Per had been able to repay the amount after just a few weeks. Per felt that he knew the area after a short time and he had managed to save up some money. He had investigated rather quickly how to open an account in a bank, and this he had done. When he saw one day in the local Norwegian-language newspaper that there was a hall rom for rent nearby, he decided to move there to become independent. He was grateful to his friend where he had lived the first few weeks, but now it was time for him to manage his own affairs.

Per had been in touch with Uncle Tor from before he left Norway and had continued to do so after he arrived in Brooklyn. Tor had wanted Per to move in with him and he offered several possibilities to help Per get started in some kind of work. But Per felt that Tor lived too far from the center of the Norwegian milieu and he wanted very much to try and manage on his own. He thanked Tor for all the assistance he was willing to offer and asked instead that he be permitted to get back to this question after he had become better acquainted. Wherever he decided to settle in the Scandinavian section of Brooklyn, he was sure that there would be someone he knew from Norway living nearby. He would be able to meet and talk to Norwegians every day in this area. Tor understood him well because he had been in a similar situation himself several years ago. He asked Per to stay in touch and wished for him to come for visits often. Tor was a pleasant fellow and he and Per were often in contact with each other. They met approximately once a month and their get-together were always friendly.

Per liked to browse in different stores. He soon became acquainted with places where he could find clothing, shoes, entertainment items, kitchen appliances, tools, and food. Among the kitchen appliances he noticed a couple of things that he thought his mother would appreciate. He had investigated and found the easiest way to send items to Norway. Now, of course, the easiest way of all was if someone he knew, who was returning to Norway with their belongings, would be willing to bring along a little extra. What had caught his eye was a coffee maker, a so-called percolator. That had to be a better way to make coffee than to carry on with the boiling of coffee that they had always done at home. As his mother always was baking one thing or another, and he thought that the mixing machine that he had seen would be terrific for her. She would even be able to knead the bread dough in this machine. He knew that he had to purchase one suitable for the Norwegian line voltage and he knew where to buy these things. He wrapped and boxed the items and had them sent by a transport agency. In the package he also wrote a few words about how these items were to be used. He estimated that he would be receiving a letter from his mother in four to five weeks and was anxious to learn how these gifts would be received.

Per Bakken was satisfied. He had learned a few English words over time, but his experience was that he managed well wherever he ventured with his Norwegian language. He wrote diligently to his mother, brother, and sister and heard from them in return that they were doing fine and that they missed him. He had purchased some nice garments and the small sum in his bank account was increasing. First of all he was saving money for a return ticket on the transatlantic liner. Such a sum was to be considered as a type of insurance, and it gave him a feeling of security. In addition he had started to save money for a used car. One of the men from work that he had become acquainted with had taken him to an area with little traffic a couple of times in order for Per to try his hand at driving. He would have to drive a few more times before he dared apply for a driver's license. He had obtained a pamphlet for the requirements for drivers' license that he read in spare moments.

Per had a rather long way to the job site and therefore came home to his hall rom nearly always some time after the landlord and landlady had come home. He rode with another man who worked at the same job site as he and paid him on the way home after they had received their pay for the week. This solution was good for both parties. The newcomers who were without a car and not familiar with the area were helped to the job site, and the one who owned the car got his expenses covered for gasoline, insurance, maintenance, and possibly a little extra.

On his way to his room this evening he noticed that the bathroom was not occupied. He took off his dirty clothes in his room, grabbed the bath towel and went to the bathroom. He understood from the dirty clothes in the hamper and the wet shower that the landlady and landlord had come home before him. It felt good to stand under the warm water in the shower and to get washed clean of dirt and perspiration. The warm water that he let flow onto his sore back felt so wonderful. After he had dried himself, combed his blond hair, and brushed his teeth, he noticed that he was hungry. He fancied a large steak this evening in one of the restaurants on the avenue, topped off with a couple of glasses of beer. He applied some lotion to his sore hands and tanned face from tubes that were placed on his side of the bathroom cabinet. Before he opened the door to the bathroom, he wrapped himself in the towel. He opened the bathroom door as quietly as possible, looked to the left and right to ensure that he was alone in the hallway, and walked quietly toward his room. Dusk was setting in, but he did not find it necessary to turn on the hallway light.

After four or five steps, he became totally stunned. He was as if frozen in place. On his way to the bathroom he had not noticed that the door to the living room was ajar, and now the opening was facing him and he could see into the living room with the window toward the rear. He saw the landlady lying on the sofa with her left arm under her head and her right foot pulled up toward her left knee. She lay there and slept, nude, with all her feminine magnificence directly in front of him. The landlady was in her mid-twenties and she was quite pretty. She had always been pleasant and friendly toward him in the few conversations they had had since he answered the advertisement from the local paper in person only two weeks ago. Now, here she was just a few small steps in front of him and his eyes could only enjoy her well-shaped body. He had seen glimpses of naked girls while growing up at home and at the bathing place in the summertime. But, this was something completely different. He saw how her stomach and breasts moved up and down in time with her breathing. The light from the window cut through her light hair on both her head and body. He moved quietly a couple of steps closer to the door to see better and noticed that his manhood reacted under the towel. After a short time, he pulled himself together and walked quietly to his room.

What a sight! Now his manhood reacted severely. Per had

difficulty sorting out what had happened in the last few seconds, or was it minutes? Had she forgotten to close the door, or what? She knew that he would be coming home when she lay down, and she knew that he would be using the bathroom. She had to know that she could be seen from the hallway. But maybe she was just tired this warm and sticky evening. She had possibly thought about getting as much draft as possible through the apartment, had therefore opened the door, and had perhaps fallen asleep.

Little by little he clarified a couple of things for himself. Firstly he had to settle down, and secondly he realized that this sight would suddenly complicate his life. He had worked so hard since he arrived in Brooklyn that he had not thought about girls at all. However, this would now change. How would the relationship with the landlady and landlord develop from here on? He had to react as if nothing had happened, even if this might not be easy. As the landlady was asleep, she was not aware of what had just happened. He dressed, tossed the dirty clothes in a bag that he brought along on his way out of his room. He walked quietly, thought about taking the extra couple of steps toward the living room door, but decided instead to go directly down the steps and out. His goals were to go to the laundry first and then to a restaurant. What a sight this had been!

Kari had not heard when Per came out of the bathroom but awoke with sleepy eyes when Per was standing by the door staring at her. Her mind was going a mile a minute, "Should I scream or make out as if I am asleep?" She elected the latter and hoped that Per could not see that her eyelids were partly open. She studied Per, who gazed at her with a look that expressed a combination of surprise and admiration. And, she could see movement and the increasing bulge under his bath towel. When Per finally withdrew, Kari remained totally confused for a while. She noticed that Per had awakened certain feelings in her. She waited until she heard Per walk down the steps and out the front door before she got up, closed the door to the hallway, and looked at the nearby clock. She had to awaken her husband in approximately one half hour in order for them to get ready for the evening. In her state of mind she decided to creep under the sheet with her husband. It did not take many movements and touches by her before she noticed reaction from him.

Dockside meeting

Tor had to endure many difficult days after Susan's death in the tragic automobile accident. He had stayed in close touch with her family and friends, but with time these contacts had become less frequent. He had never had anything against her parents, far from it. They got along well and they always had a good time whenever they got together. There was only one drawback with these contacts in that every time he thought about her parents, the history of Susan surfaced again. Susan's name came up every time they talked over the telephone; it was just unavoidable. This is why he gradually had deliberately avoided frequent contacts. Her death was, of course, a tremendous loss for her parents, and they continued to talk about her just about every day. Tor knew that he was lucky in the sense that he had people in his office to interact with and he always had lots of work that helped to divert his thoughts from Susan. His was always busy. Solutions had to be found for the planning of every day and future projects, or it was preparation for meetings in the evenings that demanded his attention.

Anders, his collaborator and partner for so many years, and his wife had been very helpful after the accident, something that Tor appreciated very much. It had also been a pleasure to have his nephew Per to talk to, and they he had met several times. He was pleased that things had turned out so well for the young man, and he felt sure that he would manage well in the future. He had been thinking more and more in the direction that he eventually would make an offer for Per to join the firm. In the meantime, he would not force Per in any way; he would show an interest in what Per was doing and consider whatever he did as a valuable experience for him. Tor would try to influence Per based on his own experience, primarily regarding education. If the plans that Tor had for Per should develop favorably, it was possible that Per one day could hold an important position in the firm. Because, he figured that one day both he and Anders would have had it with all this toiling and would have to find someone competent who could take over the operation of the firm as they reduced their involvement. Every time he came upon such thoughts, it was so easy to bring Susan into the picture. It was especially at the time when he was to withdraw from active participation in the firm that they had planned to fully enjoy their companionship.

He understood all to well that his friends were often busy trying to find him a mate, and there was no shortage of ladies for him to meet. Even if he appreciated his friends' willingness to help, he considered this a matter that he would have to solve himself. This was not really a problem, and his opinion was that his friends were making it a problem. However, where was he to find a suitable lady friend? He knew with certainty that no matter who he was to meet in the future, they would be measured against Susan. This would place every newcomer against a difficult and demanding test. With Susan it had been so easy, they had met in a delicatessen shop. He had been to the same delicatessen shop several times since, but what happened when he met Susan happens only once in a lifetime. When he fell into such thoughts, he broke off his thinking with the thought that this matter might solve itself somehow, and he forced himself to get his thoughts back to his work.

Today was an unusual day because he was going to the Manhattan dock in New York City to meet and greet his sister, Signe, and her daughter, Helga, his niece, who were arriving on the transatlantic liner from Norway. He was really looking forward to this meeting.

New immigrants

The passengers had received detailed instructions from the staff aboard the liner about how they were to prepare for the arrival in New York. It had been recommended that they should not wait until the last minute before making their luggage ready and have it placed in the hallway outside their cabins. They were reminded often of the importance of identifying their baggage with the tags of different color code combinations that they had been issued. The reason for this was that the management on board knew from experience that as soon as land could be seen, the passengers wanted to stay on deck as much as possible. To be able to see land after ten or more days at sea was in itself a big occasion, and when they came closer to shore, it was possible that some of the famous landmarks would be familiar to some passengers. When the first landmarks came into view, it was also time for the ones who had not managed well during the crossing to get on their feet. They had to collect themselves and be ready to do what was demanded of each passenger when they came ashore. During this time it was customary to see fairly weak and pale passengers move toward the toilets and showers with stiff legs and dull looks.

Signe and Helga were in good shape and their excitement increased. They had been told that the first landmarks would come into view early in the morning, if the fog and morning haze did not spoil the visibility. They were expected to pass the famous Statue of Liberty at about noontime, and the time for docking was scheduled for 13:00. It turned out that the fog was there when they approached land and the only thing they noticed was that the ship was moving slower. The movement of the ship ceased almost completely. They heard the sound of the foghorn from their and other ships and possibly they also heard foghorns from land-based stations. Helga could not resist the temptation and often ran to the upper decks, looked around, and ran back to her mother and related what she had seen. Signe sat in the lounge and looked out into the fog. The passengers were told over the loudspeakers that the fog was expected to lift little by little. Helga was the first one to see the Statue of Liberty and she pointed excitedly to it for her mother. With this sighting, most people in the lounge ventured out on deck to see better. It turned out that the fog had been so dense that the ship had moved between Staten Island and Brooklyn without the passengers having seen land. This is when the excitement among the passengers started in earnest because they caught a glimpse of Lower Manhattan and the many skyscrapers there. These appeared gradually as the fog lifted, while the ship approached land and the dock at slow speed. The buildings that came into view looked like mystical fairy-tale structures that were swept in a veil of thin fabric that gradually moved upward on the buildings and disappeared against the sky.

The activity on the ship increased considerably when the

tugboats came about. The pilot had come on board early in the morning and was the one who had the responsibility for getting the ship into the harbor; now the tugboats had the responsibility of moving the ship to the dock. It looked as if everything was done in slow motion, but they obviously knew what they were doing and soon the large buildings along the dock came into view. They were on the west side of Manhattan Island, on the Hudson River, and they passed several ships that were berthed against their designated docks. The tugboats were responsible for finding the right dock for their ship and for securing the mooring. The personnel on board had long since started to move all of the specially marked luggage of different shapes, from cardboard boxes to large steamer trunks, toward the closest door of the cargo hold. Larger pieces, including luggage that had been kept during the crossing, would be hoisted from the cargo hold directly to the dock. The passengers were encouraged to stay in their cabins or in the lounges until further notice, as the traffic in the hallways was hectic. They sat in small groups, with a good grip on their valuable papers, and talked anxiously and nervously about what would happen in the next hours. Those who were on deck or those who were located by a window on the port side could see the large warehouse building that drew near. All of a sudden they felt a small jolt to the ship and knew that it had touched the dock. Now it was time for the authorities to come on board to inspect the ship documents. The passengers were ready to disembark, but they had to await orders from the authorities. The passengers were informed to have their passports and medical declarations ready for the authorities, and where to go for the inspection. After they had passed through this inspection, the order would be given that would start the flow of passengers toward the gangways. These were indicated according to class, and the passengers were given instructions for how to move there in an orderly manner.

The first thing that they had to do after leaving the ship was to locate their baggage.

The ship personnel had arranged for space in different lounges where the health and immigration authorities could examine the passengers and their documents. The passengers had been notified which documents they had to have ready for the authorities, and they let a small number of travelers at a time proceed toward the inspectors. It was not certain that all would pass the first inspection without problems, because especially the health authorities were demanding in their work. Signe and Helga Bakken passed through the inspections without difficulties. They made sure that they had all their hand baggage, glanced back at the ship, and joined the stream of passengers on their way down the gangways.

They had been told that a stevedore would be found near the baggage who would assist with the baggage. The stevedore would bring the baggage on his dolly to the customs inspectors and farther, according to the owners wishes, for a tip. One of the things that the passengers had been informed about before they left the ship was how much of a tip was customary. But, the stevedores were not shy in telling the passengers how much they expected as a minimum for each piece of luggage. Several passengers who were not comfortable with handing over the baggage to the stevedores, or simply could not afford to or refused to pay for such a service, struggled with their baggage on their own. When the customs inspectors, as the last official stop, were satisfied, everything was cleared and the passengers could move toward the large group of people who stood and waited behind the barrier to receive the travelers. The immigrants had arrived in America.

~

One person who was waiting on the dock was Tor. A long time ago he had decided that when this day came, he would use plenty of time to enjoy the occasion, and he had arrived at the dock early. He had followed the increasing activity on the dock, and had seen how the place was prepared to accept all the baggage. Tor had not been at the New York docks since he had met Per when he arrived and he found it interesting to watch what was going on. He had arrived at the same dock himself many years ago. It was announced that the ship was in the Hudson River and that it was getting closer to the dock, assisted by tugboats. Tor secured himself a spot with a good view.

It was an exciting and interesting sight when the ship slid in, bow first. When it was almost at the dock, things started to get busy for the personnel on board the ship, and several heaving lines with a monkey's fist at the end landed with a thud on the dock. These lines were connected to mooring lines that longshoremen pulled ashore and fastened to designated bollards on the dock. The ship was actually pulled the last few yards against the dock with the mooring lines that were connected to winches on board. The ship was once again docked at the Norwegian America Line Pier 42 at the foot of Morton Street in Manhattan. Tor could see that there was high activity on board and he looked eagerly at the people on the different decks for someone he might know, but he did not see anyone he knew. Some relatives or friends must have found each other because he heard shouts that were exchanged between people on the dock and someone on board. In all the commotion it was doubtful if they could exchange anything intelligible between them. The most important thing was that they had seen each other.

Tor felt that he was drawn into the excitement that erupted between the people on the ship and on the dock. A family near him had brought along three children, and he estimated them to be between seven and twelve years of age. They all talked excitedly about who would recognize their grandparents first. It had been a few years since Tor had seen Signe, and he was anxious to learn how much she had changed and wondered if he would have difficulty recognizing her. He knew that he would not have a chance of recognizing Helga, because she had been just a baby when he saw her last. Maybe she resembles her mother, he thought.

Tor noticed when the inspectors walked on board to clear the ship and knew that it would not take too long before the first passengers would been seen on the gangways. He went to the barrier that separated the customs inspectors from the visitors and tried to talk to one of the stevedores on the inside. They were just standing around with their dollies for the time being, and were hoping for some busy hours ahead with good earnings. Finally he made eye contact with a stevedore that he beckoned to come over to the barrier. Tor asked if he could go to the luggage that was accumulated under the letter B, for Bakken, third class, and stand at the ready to help a woman and her daughter onward from there. The stevedore commented that he could not afford to limit himself to just one party, but he promised to keep an eye on that area of the floor. Tor realized quickly that if he provided a good tip, the man would surely help. He pulled a bill from his wallet with a rather large figure and gave it to the man and said that he would receive one more just like it when he brought the ladies to him. The stevedore smiled satisfied – his daily wage was almost secured before he had lifted one suitcase. Yes, he would deliver the ladies, he assured Tor and they agreed on a place where he was to deliver the passengers with their baggage. Tor realized that he had taken a chance with this tip, but on the other hand he knew that it was highly probable that the stevedore would make more money by helping him alone than if he was to compete with the other stevedores for work. Tor was confident that this would work out.

Two official-looking gentlemen, who stood on the gallery of the warehouse with a good view of the large hall below, had a lot of experience with this type of surveillance. It happened that they spotted someone who behaved suspiciously, and they were able to tip off their colleagues below to perform a thorough examination of such persons. The inspectors above were ready to monitor the passengers from the Norwegian transatlantic ship that started to move to the gangways and streamed onto the floor of the warehouse. The passengers oriented themselves quickly and dispersed to the different sorted baggage places where they picked up their baggage and headed for the customs inspectors. The activity below reminded the gallery inspectors of the annual sorting of animals after a grazing season when the animals are herded into different pens as determined by their markings. The people that came off the ship were separated similarly, by colored luggage tags and name. Often one could hear people, outside the customs barrier, call out to someone known to them in the multitude on the inside: “How was the trip? Did you get seasick? Who is meeting you? Where are you going to live?” The ones who had found acquaintances assured them that it would be wonderful to get together again and waved with, “We will see you before too long,” while they watched for their family or friends. The passengers on the other hand shouted to each other, “Thank you for being such great company, be well, good luck, hope to see you again soon.”

Several passengers were escorted by stevedores who had stacked the passengers’ baggage on his dolly. After the last inspection of the baggage was completed, the passengers could put away their papers, put the customs barrier behind them, and concentrate on what was waiting for them on the other side. They followed their stevedores and kept a close eye on their baggage the whole time. Most would be met by family or friends outside the barrier who would arrange for transportation onward for the passengers. The crowd eventually moved to the outside of the dock area, where the passengers were separated and transported to their final destinations.

Tor followed as best he could and saw how the passengers started to find their baggage and noted that it did not take long before the first dollies, which were loaded with baggage, came through the stations of the customs inspectors. He thought to himself, "What in the world could an immigrant have in his or her baggage that could be of interest to a customs inspector." No matter where he looked through the opening of the barrier it was impossible to see anyone that looked familiar. He just had to wait and see.

When Signe and Helga came to the area where the baggage was gathered in alphabetical groups based on the last names, there were already many people around them and they heard both English and Norwegian spoken in several dialects. The passengers oriented themselves as fast as possible. Most expected to be met by someone, but some were pleased to see references for assistance written in both English and Norwegian. The Travelers Aid Society was located on the dock and assisted many who were to travel farther by train, to Chicago and other places in the Midwest.

A stevedore came over and asked if he could assist Signe and Helga. They were just about to say yes when another stevedore rushed over and said something to the first one so that he moved away. The second stevedore explained himself and Signe gathered that he intended to bring them and their baggage to a gentleman who was waiting outside the barrier. Okay, they thought, we have to get away from here, and it could not be anyone but Tor who had made this arrangement. The stevedore loaded their baggage on his dolly and asked them to follow him. They went straight for the customs inspector, who asked a few and simple questions that they answered as best they could, and were waved on with, "Welcome to America." The stevedore took the lead, and after only a few steps outside the barrier they saw a smiling and very recognizable Tor. He had no difficulty recognizing his sister. Helga had become a grown and beautiful girl with her mother's likeness. Handshakes and hugs followed that were interrupted by the stevedore who indicated something to Tor. Oh, yes, he was to get money, and Tor asked him if he could bring the baggage to his car that was parked outside the building. This was arranged, and they walked arm in arm out of the dock area with the stevedore on their heels. They located the car and the stevedore helped to load the baggage. The stevedore received a very god tip for having done the job well and he was one big grin because his day had been very good indeed.

The dock area was a busy place with people rushing in every direction. Trucks were backing up to the dock to take on cargo from the ship, other trucks delivered freight that the ship was to carry on its return trip, and a large number of private cars and taxis drove in both directions on the street outside the terminal. The immigrants followed their dear ones closely. They were afraid of getting lost in the crowd. They were glad when they could take a seat in the cars on instructions from their family or friends, and when they could start to get away from the area. Once in a while someone waved and shouted greetings between the cars. The drivers used their horns as farewell greetings and to draw attention when they finally left the area slowly and slid into the street traffic.

Signe seated herself in front with Tor, and they talked about memories from the time when Tor was in Norway. Helga, who sat in the back seat, was busy looking from one side to the other. She looked at the traffic, the shops, the tall buildings, and the people who scurried in all directions. Tor explained that they were now on their way to the section of the city that was called Bay Ridge, the place where one would find the largest concentration of Norwegians in this country. Before long they would be crossing the Brooklyn Bridge and Tor could tell a little of its history. Among other things, he explained that the bridge was 486 meters long, and when the bridge was opened in 1883, it was the longest of its kind in the world. It was not difficult for Tor to understand that neither Signe nor Helga was very interested in listening to his statistics. As an architect he could not resist, however, he refrained from coming with additional such comments. They had heard what Tor had said but were much more interested in taking in all the new sights that appeared along the streets. When they had crossed the bridge, Tor said that they had approximately fifteen to twenty minutes left until they would arrive at their destination. He had not told them what would happen there and they had not asked. The only thing they both had mentioned was that they were anxious and eager to meet Per.

Tor was driving them to a planned surprise. He and Per had worked together on getting an apartment rented and fixed up for Signe and Helga. The plan was that Per was to be in the apartment and he was to open the door when they rang the doorbell. Tor was wondering if Per had arrived at the apartment while he was driving, and once in a while he looked nervously at his watch. He would simply just take a longer route to use up more time in order to arrive on time. There was no harm in doing this, because the passengers he had today were so interested in everything they saw in the streets and they did not have to know that he was taking a detour.

Per had come home from work at the normal time. He had washed up, changed his clothes, and had had enough time to take his dirty clothes to the laundry. Thereafter he had walked to the new apartment, and on the way he had bought a bouquet of flowers and a fresh coffee cake. He found a vase for the flowers, added water, and put it on the kitchen table. He had bought different food items the day before and placed them in drawers and cabinets in the kitchen. The refrigerator contained milk, butter, jam, and some soft drinks. Coffee and the coffeepot were ready. He put the cake on the kitchen counter, where he already had placed a dish with some apples and oranges. He walked about the apartment nervously to make sure that everything was in order, and once in a while he glanced toward the street. Of course, he knew Uncle Tor's car by sight, and he saw that there were plenty of parking places right outside the apartment.

Tor parked directly outside the apartment and took the few steps to the entry door with Signe and Helga on his heels. He rang the doorbell and the door opened quickly by a smiling Per, who stood there with extended arms. Signe was taken aback for a few seconds and hesitated slightly before she entered the apartment. She embraced Per while she expressed through a flood of tears of joy, "My dearest Per, my Per." Suddenly she remembered Helga, and yielded so that she also could get to hug her brother. After a short while, as Per was looking at Helga he burst out, "How tall you are, you look all grown up, and how beautiful you have become. Yes, she is one we will have to look out for," as he addressed the others with a smile.

Per and Tor went to the car and brought in the baggage while Signe and Helga took a tour of the apartment, as the men had suggested. They were more than satisfied with what they saw, here was everything they needed. They saw two bedrooms, a bath, a kitchen, and a living room with a view to the street. Both saw that with a little creative work they would get themselves a cozy place to live. With the baggage in place, they all sat down in the living room, and Signe and Helga started to answer questions posed to them by Tor and Per. They had so many questions about family, friends, and acquaintances in Norway, they wanted to know about their voyage, and they wanted to know if they felt tired after the voyage. They talked and had a good time and everybody managed to get a word in now and then. After a while Tor looked at his watch and told them that it was time to start for the restaurant where he had reserved a table for dinner. They walked directly to the main street and continued toward the restaurant. They met several persons familiar to Per along the way that he introduced to his family. They also passed the building where Per's apartment was, and several shops were indicated where Signe and Helga could purchase the most important items they would be needing in the coming days.

The restaurant was fairly full of customers, and often they heard Norwegian being spoken. They were directed to a suitable table, and when they received the menus, it took some time for Tor and Per to explain the different items for the newcomers. They agreed on a meat dish, and when it was served they got a surprise. Signe and Helga looked at their plates with a large steak surrounded by potatoes and vegetables. The food on board the ship had been creditable every day, but it could not measure up to this meal in any way. They had plenty of time and therefore ate slowly and used the occasion to talk about many different things. Eventually Signe had to say that she just could not eat anymore, even if she had some leftovers on the plate. She felt awful for not being able to eat more, but she was assured by Tor and Per that to leave some food on the plate was not a problem. She was told that this was acceptable in this country. She was also told that she could get a sack to bring the leftovers home if she wanted to. They agreed that this was not appropriate this time, but Signe appreciated knowing about this possibility for some other time.

Tor paid for the excellent meal, and they walked back out of the restaurant onto the sidewalk in the direction of the apartment. Each woman walked arm in arm with her brother. When they were back in the apartment, the coffeepot was started, and the conversation between them continued. Per found the cake that he had bought, and even if they had consumed a lot for dinner, they managed to find room for some cake also. They all expressed their pleasure and gratefulness for having come together again, and they had so much to talk about. Signe told of how everyone in their families in Norway were doing and she did not forget to tell about how Ole was doing in school. Per was the first to bring up that he unfortunately had to think about the following day. He explained that he had to get up early and that it was therefore time for him to get to bed. As this was Thursday, they would all get plenty of time to talk over the weekend, he said. Tor explained that he had decided to take off the following day in order for him to be with Signe and Helga the next day and over the weekend. The sleeping arrangement was solved with Tor sleeping in Helga's bed and she was sleeping with her mother in the large bed of their new apartment.

When the three were in their beds of the new apartment, they were grateful for this day and were looking forward to many good days together in the future. Helga gave her mother a hug, turned on her side, and was soon sound asleep. Signe after reflecting on having met her son and brother again, was satisfied and fell asleep with a smile.

Per was quick in getting back to his hall rom. He found work clothes for the next day and slept well satisfied knowing that his mother and sister would be living nearby from now on.

~

All three woke up the next morning after a good night's sleep in the new apartment. Tor was the first one up and he had left the apartment quietly and gone to the bakery to buy, among other things, fresh rolls for breakfast. He made preparations in the kitchen and set the breakfast table. When the smell of freshly brewed coffee drifted throughout the apartment, Signe opened her eyes wide. In a short while the three of them sat around the small table in the kitchen having a conversation that in many ways was a continuation of last night's talk. Signe and Helga had so many things they wanted to tell Tor, and he had different things that he had to inform them about. This involved several practical matters: helping Signe establish a bank account, they had to get registered with the authorities for what was called Social Security, and they had to establish contact with a doctor and a dentist as soon as possible. It was natural for them to contact a Norwegian-speaking doctor that Tor could recommend. This doctor was also connected with the Norwegian Hospital that was located centrally in their part of the city. Furthermore it was important to get Helga enrolled in a school. She had always wanted to study but first of all she had to be accepted in a school that offered English education for students of immigrant families. She had learned some English at her school at home, but it would most likely be a good idea if she were taught more as soon as possible.

In the afternoon when Helga left with her mother and Tor to get her enrolled in school, she dreaded the thought intensely. It was only a short walk to the school and they were well received when they got there. Tor explained the situation and they were assured that Helga was not the only student there with a similar background. They were told that many of the students were children of immigrants, and that even if they had a little difficulty at the start on account of the language and the foreign teaching materials, the school administration wanted to assure them that the students got into the new routines fast. The necessary personal data for Helga was recorded and the different subjects that Helga was to take were presented to them. It was explained that her class had mathematics at present and they were all invited to go to that class. The school principal led the way down the hall and knocked on a door. When it opened, Helga saw approximately 25 students inside of her age. The principal introduced the teacher to Helga, her mother, and uncle. The teacher asked if the students who were Norwegian or of Norwegian heritage would put up a hand. The newcomers to the class were surprised to see six hands in the air, four girls and two boys. The principal then asked if anyone spoke Norwegian and five answered in the affirmative. Finally the class was asked to say in unison, "Welcome, Helga."

They were invited to find a place to sit, and the teacher continued with the math education. It was interesting to follow what was said and what was written on the blackboard. Helga was attentive, she followed everything that was going on and at times she looked around the room. Tor was so anxious to get an answer to a question from Helga that he could not contain himself any longer and asked in a whisper if she understood what the teacher was talking about. "Yes," answered Helga, "This is something we covered last year." Tor smiled and thought, "This is going to turn out well."

When they were back at the apartment, Signe wanted to start with preparations for dinner. Her plan was that they were to eat as soon as Per came home from work. First she had to look into what kind of food items the menfolk had purchased for dinner, and then she had to learn how to utilize the stove that used natural gas as fuel. She asked her brother for help, and he instructed and demonstrated for her. But Tor did not want to hear about her plans for making dinner today. He assured her that dinner plans were already taken care of. As soon as Per arrived, they would drive to a certain restaurant for a pleasant meal. "In the days that I will be spending with you, we are going to enjoy ourselves," Tor said. The day came to an end all too suddenly, but they had achieved much.

~

It turned out that Tor slept in the apartment that night also. The next morning he was again the first one to get up. He found his way around the kitchen and made preparations for breakfast. The coffeepot was started and he was all set to fry eggs, bacon, and make toast as soon as the others showed up. When Signe awoke, she heard someone speaking Norwegian with an unfamiliar voice in the kitchen. What in the world, did Tor have a visitor this early in the morning? Who could this be? Shortly thereafter she heard Norwegian music, and when she came into the kitchen, it dawned on her that Tor had turned on the radio. Tor explained that he usually listened to the Norwegian radio program that was broadcast every Saturday morning. The station sent news and a mixture of Norwegian music and advertising for firms in the community. This was a surprise. Signe had no idea that she would be able to find a Norwegian program on the radio in Brooklyn. She was told that in Brooklyn one could buy Norwegian newspapers that were published in America, and Tor gave her a copy of the latest edition of a local paper that he had just purchased. It was in *Nordisk Tidende* that Per and Tor had seen the advertisement for the apartment they were now in.

Tor wanted to use this opportunity to tell her a little about Norwegian newspapers in the United States. He had seen a copy of a list that was put together by Olaf Morgan Norlie and published in December 1946 in Northfield, Minnesota. "It is almost unbelievable," he started, "that the first Norwegian newspaper in this country was published in New York City as far back as 1847. The publication of several Norwegian newspapers followed rapidly in the years thereafter in the different states where Norwegians settled. Norlie's[1] list shows that this country had as many as 561 Norwegian newspapers at the end of 1943."

"Since we are talking about Norwegians in America, I want to mention a little about immigration from Norway," Tor said. "This will make it easier to understand why so many Norwegian papers were published. As you know, one considers the first Norwegian immigrants to be the ones who crossed the Atlantic in the small sloop *Restaurationen* in 1825. The voyage for the 46 passengers and a crew of seven was planned by Cleng Person. They arrived in New York City on October 9 after a voyage of fourteen weeks and settled near Rochester, New York. The flood of immigrants from Norway was at its peak in 1883, when more than 28,000 left the country. At least 800,000 Norwegians immigrated over a period of one hundred years. In the 1880's it was only Ireland who had a larger percentage of immigrants than Norway. For comparison: Ireland had 16 immigrants per thousand inhabitants, Norway 11, Sweden 6, and Germany 4." When Tor had completed his comments on immigration, he looked at

---

[1] Western Viking published the list in its centennial edition on May 17, 1989. At that time only two newspapers remained, *Western Viking* of Seattle, Washington, and *Nordisk Tidende* of Brooklyn, New York.

Signe with an apologetic glance. Signe thanked him for the information and said she was very impressed with the statistics and for Tor's knowledge about this subject.

Per had bought along fresh rolls when he joined them and they had a long and pleasant breakfast. Thereafter they took a walk up and down on both sides of the main street in the Norwegian colony. "Maybe we will meet someone known to us," Tor said. One thing that surprised Signe and Helga was how often they heard Norwegian spoken by people standing in small groups on the sidewalks. They heard different dialects and all age groups were represented. They entered some stores and were surprised to hear Norwegian spoken there also, even behind the counters. This was in some ways like coming to a large shopping area somewhere in Norway.

When they walked by a vacant lot that was ready for sale beside the main street, they noticed a group of men that stood around a kneeling person who was picking something off the ground. They were young men and it looked like they had a good time as they were joking repeatedly. The kneeling person stood up, shook whatever he had between his hands, and as he tossed it up in the air, he called out, "Heads." Tor understood immediately what was going on. "They are playing a game that I know, tossing coins at a stick," he said to the others, "Let us go a little closer and have a look." The man who had tossed the coins into the air was now busy picking up all that had the "head" side up, those were his share. The next person was busy picking up the coins with the "tail" side showing. He mixed the coins well between his cupped hands, and tossed them into the air and called out his favorite side of the coin. After all the coins had been divided in this manner, in accordance with the individual standings, they were ready for the next round. Tor could not resist. "May I join you?" he asked and received a quick answer, "Yes, by all means." This was said by one of the men who was keeping a lookout toward the main street in case the police should show up. What they were doing could be considered as gambling and would therefore be unlawful. He explained that this was a game that they had not played before in this country. A few Norwegians had been talking of nothing in particular while standing on the sidewalk when suddenly they got the idea of playing the game, as they had done it in the old country. “That bare spot on the empty lot here looked so inviting,” he admitted smilingly. Tor examined his pockets, and came forth with four five-cent pieces and walked to the designated spot to toss the coins. “This takes me back many years,” he said. He aimed and tossed. One coin landed quite a distance from the stick that was stuck into the ground, and Tor aimed and tossed the next coin. He tossed all the coins, but none were placed close. The next person tossed his coin much closer than Tor’s coin. However, Tor had revived memories from the past and was satisfied. He thanked them, and he and his three companions continued their walk.

Tor told them that when he was young at home, it was a sure sign of spring when *stikkespillet*[11] started after the winter. The youngest had played with bottle caps, and he remembered coming home with his pockets full of caps on a good day. The pockets would also be full of sand and mud from the graveled roads they played on, something that his mother did not really appreciate, he said with a smile. Tor explained that the older fellows used to play with coins. Five *øre*[12] pieces were used by the youngest, and the big boys who were employed and made money played with *krone* coins. It was impressive for the younger ones to see all the *krone* coins that could be tossed at the stick. Tor explained that there were usually rules set up by the participants for how many coins they could use, but sometimes there were no limits. That meant that an individual could toss all the coins or bottle caps he possessed, which could make for a large pot. Per said that he had also participated in this game, but it sounded like Tor had played much more because he had such detailed knowledge about the game.

The conversation up to this point had only been about what kind of games the boys had enjoyed, and Signe wanted to tell about the kind she, and surely also Helga, had been playing. Their first sign of spring was when they marked a pattern on the gravel road and started to play hopscotch. They competed with several different combinations, as for example one foot in each square, one foot in some squares and both feet in others, to some squares with a jump forward and to others with a jump backward. The object was not to lose one's balance or step on a line. They could be busy with this game for hours, Signe said, and the final winner would be chosen before they gave up for the day. Another game that was popular among the girls was to bounce a large ball against a wall. They had a variety of patterns that they had to master, as bouncing the ball three times from the head, followed by three times from a shoulder, thereafter three times from the chest, and so on. The one who dropped the ball was out of the competition for that round.

Per asked Tor if they played the same type of ball game in America as they had done in their native district in Norway. Tor knew right away how the game Per made reference to was played; he had participated in the game many times himself. Tor said that the youth in this country played a similar ball game in the streets called stickball. But the main ball game in this country is called baseball, he said. Tor explained a little about how that game was played, with up to three attempts to hit the ball that was hurled at the batter by a pitcher. He explained about the four bases, and how one got there, and how points were earned. "It is quite an exciting game," said Tor, "and one day when we get an opportunity, I will take you to one of our two stadiums; one is located not far from here. We have two of the best professional teams in the country close by," he explained. They spent the entire day and evening together and had a great time. Tor explained that he intended to spend the next day, Sunday, also with them.

~

Tor was again the first one to get up in the morning and he prepared breakfast as he had done on the previous days. While they were eating, he suggested that they should go to the Sunday service in the Norwegian church. This ought to be interesting for them, he figured, and in addition they would meet many Norwegians there. The service impressed Signe and Helga, and as Tor had indicated, they met and talked to many Norwegians during the church coffee. In the afternoon, he had to excuse himself and be on his way home because he had several matters that he had to prepare for Monday morning. He promised to keep in touch and come again soon for a visit. Per who had also accompanied them to church, staying with his mother and sister until bedtime. He very much wanted his mother to prepare his favorite dinner this Sunday, veal fricassee, and he had seen to it that all the ingredients were purchased.

The men were not concerned that Signe and Helga would be alone come Monday morning. They had already seen enough of the neighborhood and could easily find their way to the shops on the main street, and the way back, on their own. Signe had plans of tidying up and reorganizing a little in the apartment at the first opportunity.

The bakery

It did not take long in the new environment of this part of America before Signe Bakken had established contact with several people her age from different parts of Norway. One day she had a conversation with the Norwegian owner of the popular bakery on the main street that resulted in a job offer from him. She had accepted the offer immediately and enjoyed the job. Often she thought how strange it was that the language spoken in the shop was as much Norwegian as it was English. She had no difficulties with the communication; if there was something she did not understand from a customer, she only had to ask one of the other salespersons for help. Little by little she learned the routines and understood more of the language. A conversation across the counter or a few words on a street corner were sufficient for her to make many acquaintances in a short time. On Sundays, there were always many people gathered on the main street, especially when the Salvation Army came in the afternoons with its orchestra and choir.

They had so many Scandinavians in the choir that several of the songs were sung in Norwegian or Swedish.

The conversations of late had often concerned the large celebration that was planned for May 17, in honor of Norway's Constitution Day. Signe and a couple of her women friends from work had decided to take a trip to the main dance for the fun of it. Helga had not spent many days at school before she felt comfortable and had made several girlfriends. These girls also had plans for celebrating May 17, but they could not participate in the celebration with the grown-ups. Their celebration would primarily be to participate in the May 17 parade, when their school was one of many that would take part. Helga was to march, and the students would be told where and when to assemble. They had purchased flags and bows for the occasion.

On the Saturday of the May 17 dance, Signe and her women friends took the bus to the hall before the celebration was to start. They bought tickets and were directed to a large hall that was nicely decorated in line with old traditions. Even though they arrived early, there were many people already there, and they had to stand on their toes and turn about several times to locate an empty table. Finally one of the ladies located a table and they hurried to occupy it. They took a seat, ordered something to drink, listened to the music, talked, and enjoyed themselves. A large orchestra played a mixture of old and new dance music from a raised stage. It happened often that one of them, or all, were invited to dance, and they danced merrily about and became so warm that they began to sweat. A cool drink felt good while they discussed what they had been talking about with the men while they danced, and how they felt about the dancing skills of the different men. Some of the dancing partners had talked endlessly while others had not said a word, except for "thank you" when the dance was finished. Some danced stiff-legged, some were excellent dancers, and others, were types that fancied themselves as experts and were really trying to show off. The women started to wonder how long they would be able to carry on in this warm place with this hurried pace. They looked at their watches and it turned out that a couple of hours remained before the evening was over.

All of a sudden a man appeared before Signe. He bowed nicely and asked if she would dance with him. He was half a head taller than she, with light hair, blue eyes, and appeared rather shy. They moved out onto the floor and danced quite acceptably. It turned out that he was Norwegian and that there was very little difference in their dialects. Even though there was quite a bit of noise in the dance hall, they were able to exchange their names and what part of Norway they came from. Other than that, the conversation was on the subjects of, "How long have you been here? Do you like it here? Do you live nearby? What line of work do you do?" and so on. When the dance was over, he escorted her back to her table and thanked her courteously. Her woman friends had not returned from the dance floor, and he asked if it would be all right if he sat down in order for them to talk some more until the others showed up. It turned out that he was of her age and he was easy to have a conversation with. When the woman friends returned, she introduced him to them, and as he was about to leave, he turned to Signe and asked if she would permit him to drive her home when the party was over. She said that she had come with her woman friends and that they had plans of returning together. He offered to drive them all home, and said that he would return to the table in about a half hour.

When it happens, it happens fast, as the saying goes, and there was no mistaking it, a spark had been ignited. How in the world was she to handle this? Her friends wanted to know everything about this man and she told them that she knew little beyond that his name was Jakob and that he was Norwegian. They discussed his offer and agreed that if he wanted to drive them all home, there was nothing wrong with that – they could not get home easier. They decided that they would permit him to drive them to a certain street corner from which they would get home on their own.

Jakob returned to their table as he had said he would, sat down after he had been offered a chair, and they talked for about a half hour. Jakob learned that Signe and her friends worked at the popular bakery in the middle of the main street and he learned a little about each of them. It got so late that they decided to leave the dance hall. They got out on the sidewalk and Jakob showed the way to his car. It was not a very long drive to the street corner they had agreed upon, where all three stepped out of the car and thanked Jakob for the ride. Jakob and Signe agreed to meet again, in two days, before they parted. He was to come to the bakery store just before closing time. With that he started his car, waved good-bye and drove off.

The three friends waited and all talked incessantly and at the same time about Signe, who seemingly had found a really nice chap, a man who appeared interested in her. Signe did not know that much more about him. His name was Jakob Torgersen, he had talked about the place in Norway that he came from, and he was working in a travel agency not far from where they were at the present time. The friends said that they would try to help her to find someone who knew something about this man, and Signe intended to contact her brother and enlist his help. As encouraged as Signe had become with this attention, she was certain that she had to maintain a clear head and not fall in love like a young schoolgirl. She could not hide that it was a long time since a man had shown her so much attention.

The following day was Sunday and that was when the Grand

May 17 parade was to take place. The parade route was a long one, and the streets that had been selected were decorated with American and Norwegian flags. Flags of both countries were displayed from many windows and on many balconies along the route. It was a wonderful day with sunshine and a suitable temperature. People came from far away to this part of town to celebrate Norway's Constitution Day. Signe had never experienced nor heard of a May 17 parade with such a huge turnout. She had read about May 17 parades for different places in Norway, and especially how large the parade was in Oslo from year to year. But this parade was larger; it took several hours before all of it passed the bystanders. It was an assembly of many different organizations, Norwegian-American groups, orchestras, schools, and schools orchestras, and the parade even had an element directly from Norway. The people who were lined up along the parade route, three to four deep, were for the most part of Norwegian origin, but even those who had no connection to Norway were lined up and cheered for the country that they had only read or heard about.

The parade ended in a park where many people had gathered to listen to the main speaker for the day. The people responsible for the parade and the arrangements were introduced, and finally the event was turned over to the speaker. This time it was the governor for the state of New York who was the keynote speaker, and he had many flattering words to say about Norway and the many people with Norwegian roots in New York State and the country. The governor took his time after the speech and talked to many people that had surrounded him.

This was an excellent day to meet people from near and far and to make new relationships. It was a big day for the shops. The delicatessens and bakeries were very busy, because there was no limit to how much food was needed to satisfy all these festive people that were celebrating the day. The large number of bars in the area were popular gathering places, and this day was actually one of the busiest days for these establishments. Restaurants that advertised Norwegian food and Norwegian service were busy serving individual customers and family groups.

New drawings

Andreas Neset had worked with several partners in his time as a carpenter. As so many others, he had started on housing construction and had gone through the hard apprenticeship that had given him so much pain and so many sore muscles. He could easily sympathize with the beginners who were put to the task of nailing from morning to night. On his own initiative he had taken some evening classes when he started out as a beginner on framing to learn how to read construction drawings. With that education and the experience he gained with time, it did not take long before he was selected to do the layout of the plates in accordance with the drawings for the different houses that were being built.

After a while he was offered a job as a carpenter on concrete form - work at the suggestion of one of his earlier partners. At first he had been skeptical, but his partner had persuaded him and now after several years as a form worker, he admitted readily to anyone that he was glad that he had changed his line of work. He had learned the assignments fast. His first partner had moved to a different city after about one year, and he ended up with a somewhat younger partner in Lars Tunet. He was well satisfied with Lars as he was able and easy to associate with. Their friendship at work had expanded to a friendship that also included their wives. They had all been together for evenings and over weekends and had always had enjoyable times.

Andreas had been employed much longer than Lars and he had managed to purchase a car. Two others plus Lars drove back and forth to work with him every day and they paid Andreas the customary amount after they received their cash payments on Fridays. They had been on the same job for many months and Andreas knew that it was coming to an end. They had only two floors left, which meant that in only a few weeks they would have to look for a new job.

One day the big boss told Andreas that a new project would be starting up as soon as this job was completed, and that he had been designated as the foreman. He would be pleased if Andreas and Lars would follow him to work there, he said. The boss had become well acquainted with these two and he would very much like to keep them for the next job. It was not difficult to find willing newcomers, but a pair experienced as Andreas and Lars was not so easy to find. He had just recently received a set of drawings for the new project and had heard as late as yesterday that the excavating had started. He had started to study the drawings because he liked to familiarize himself well ahead of his actual start on the job. He knew also that it was necessary and important to find time to get acquainted with the architects. A close relationship with them from the start was required to get a project completed on time and within budget. The drawings he had been issued were for a large building that was to be built in the University area. It was an eight-story building, and after a quick assessment, he estimated that the job would provide work for about one year. The location of the job site was advantageous because the trip back and forth could be done by different means: bus, subway, or private car.

He looked at the bottom right-hand side of the drawings and noticed that the design was by Dale Architects and Builders, Inc., with Tor Flaten as the principal architect. He did not know the firm immediately and made himself a note to establish contact with them as soon as possible. The name of the architect looks very Norwegian, he thought.

Domestics

Tordis Hansen and Sofie Larsen came to Brooklyn full of expectations and ready for new experiences. They had heard many positive comments about the conditions there from friends and people they knew that had taken the trip. When the opportunity for travel arose, they decided that this venture was something that they also were willing to try. They left their homes in Norway without any professional experience, and with elementary schooling as the only formal education. From a very young age they had to help out with many tasks in and around their homes, and this was their only work experience when they left. They both had plenty of courage and abundant amounts of spirit and figured that they would manage as well as others they had heard of with similar backgrounds.

Tordis and Sofie were well received in Brooklyn and were soon introduced to the type of work that was the easiest to get started on. Based on recommendations from other immigrant girls who lived nearby, they pinned their hopes on getting jobs as domestics. The girls started out by assisting experienced women on their jobs. After a short while they were able to secure their own jobs, where they worked part-time for some hours, depending on the size of the house or apartment.

The girls would work for one or more households during a week. If a position was unsatisfactory for one reason or another, it was easy to find another. The salaries for the domestic jobs were paid in cash after the job was completed each day, and the income was not documented officially by either party. Often the girls established a good relationship with the people they worked for and would receive gifts like perfume, used jewelry, and clothing from their employers. This was much appreciated, especially in the beginning, because the recently arrived girls had come with limited amounts of such things.

Some girls were lucky to obtain employment as housekeepers on a full-time basis. This was a big advantage because lodging and food would be included.

Others, tried their luck as au pairs, a profession that was well suited for the ones who liked children. This type of work gave an excellent opportunity to learn the language, because the girls became quite isolated from other Norwegians. Even if their compensation were limited to room and board, some received a little pocket money also.

Girls who had the ability to prepare food were appreciated. As an example for what could happen to an inspired youth, reference was made to a woman in the colony who had started out as so many young girls and had ended up as the chef for a large household in Manhattan.

As the large concentration of Norwegians in the colony was longing for Norwegian food, some women tried their luck in the restaurant business. The menu included the traditional Norwegian dishes with well-known desserts. Carpenters really appreciated a meal of meatballs, green peas, and potatoes covered in brown gravy after a hard day in the construction business. This was also a good place to meet friends and acquaintances, and job prospects could be discussed during the meal.

As the girls became accustomed to the milieu and began to master the language, they started to seek positions in offices and shops. Many positions dealt with immigrants, or Norwegian import and export activity. A capable person with ability for office work and who had command of both languages was in demand.

Older women who no longer had children living at home, or other obligations at home, often tried to find employment. Income from these jobs was often used to procure different domestic items that they intended to bring back to their homes in Norway. Many items were popular, including items for a bathroom, curtains, kitchen appliances, refrigerators, shirts, blouses, and dresses.

For many of the young immigrants this was their first experience being away from home, but it did not take long before they were confident with their new situation in Brooklyn. They had found their own apartments, which they often shared with someone else from the start, they selected their own work environment, and they found the way to work by bus or subway. This was for most a new experience that they handled in an excellent manner, and they gained added freedom when they achieved financial independence. They became confident, resolved matters on their own, and used their income where and when they wished. However, they were not only concerned with their own well-being, they never forgot their loved ones that they had left behind.

Three Norwegian girls lived in a basement apartment four houses beyond Tordis and Sofie. They were often in conversation with these girls and had been informed that they were quite active in the

Norwegian churches of the colony. One girl sang in a choir and had been the featured soloist on several occasions. As they were working on plans for an evening with much entertainment in connection with the annual church bazaar, Tordis and Sofie were asked to help. Norwegian dishes were on the program and they needed help with these. Several work teams were engaged for this church project, and it was estimated that the church would be visited by several hundred people over the three days the various activities were to be carried out. Meatball and *lutefisk*[13] were to be served with caramel custard and chocolate pudding for dessert. *Kransekake*[14], buttered *lefse* and *potetkaker*[15] with *eggost*[16] were to be served with the coffee.

One evening when Tordis and Sofie were in the girls' apartment to work on the planning, something happened that was new to all five of them. When one of the girls went to the toilet, she turned on the light outside the door and stepped inside quickly. She was barefoot and suddenly noticed that she had stepped on something that was moving. She glanced quickly down on her foot and saw that she had stepped on a two-inch-long insect. She saw several similar insects that scurried on the linoleum-covered floor toward their hiding places. She had partially smashed one of these that was still moving under her foot, and the girl screamed in fright and fear. When the others came, the insects were out of sight and the girl who had seen them explained to the others and pointed in a shaky voice to where they had disappeared. One of the girls found a rag and wiped off the partially crushed insect from under the foot of the unlucky girl. They summoned the Norwegian landlord and complained to him. He apologized, and explained that it was quite common that a basement apartment would have water bugs or cockroaches. He cautioned the girls that the areas around the toilet and the drip pan under the icebox were especially vulnerable. He promised to put out poison and assured the girls that the creatures were harmless. The girls were emphatic, such nasty and disgusting creatures were something that they would not tolerate. They regarded this matter as most serious, and said that if the landlord did not solve the problem, they would be forced to move elsewhere. What if one should find such an insect in one's bed? The girls did not like the thought of having the insects possibly crawling up into their beds. These thoughts would not leave the girls even if the landlord assured them that the insects kept close to water and moisture.

Never before had Tordis and Sofie had so many possibilities to associate with so many people their own age of both genders, as they did in Brooklyn. They did not regret having left their homes. Life in Brooklyn was good. They were satisfied, but at the same time they were determined to return to their homes in Norway one day.

Eventually Tordis met Karl Fredriksen and Sofie met Andreas Neset in the Norwegian colony in Brooklyn. They were married in the Norwegian Seamen's Church there.

Inquiries

In the afternoon two days later, when Signe Bakken seated herself by the small table in the room next to the shop to take a deserved break, she started to sort out all of the information that she had collected about Jakob Torgersen. No negative comments had come in from any source. Could this be right? Jakob Torgersen had apparently been married in Norway several years ago, and his wife had died quite young, maybe in connection with childbirth, someone had said. He had been a valued worker in an office in his native district, and had, as so many others, traveled to America after his wife died, the story continued. After a while in Brooklyn he had been going steady with a girl for a long time. One day the girl had suddenly said good-bye to Jakob and had taken off with a man to another state. Jakob had taken this hard, and he had been seen seldom in the colony. Once in a while someone had seen him go into some restaurants nearby. He did not have a habit of hanging out at bars. No one knew what kind of work he did, but it was quite certain that he was not a carpenter, because no one had seen him on such work sites. Signe knew that he worked in a travel agency because he had told her about this when they first met.

Well, if this was the whole story, it was not frightening to Signe. On the other hand, it was funny that the girl should have broken off with Jakob so abruptly. Could the problem be Jakob? Signe left these thoughts by reasoning that it probably was the fault of the girl who had taken off with an old sweetheart.

Signe's brother had asked her to be careful. Be skeptical, do not hurry, he had said. This was both good and understandable advice that Signe took seriously because she knew it was sensible and correct.

Signe was ready when Jakob came into the store a few minutes before closing time. He came toward the counter, greeted the nearby employees, thanked her for their last time together and wanted to purchase a small bread and two Danish pastries. Signe was assured by this that he was living alone, because if not, he would have bought more. He paid, and Signe confirmed that she was ready to go with him. With the paper sack in his hand, he guided her toward his car that was parked right outside the store. Jakob knew that she had been in Brooklyn for only a short time, and he suggested therefore that he was going to drive her on a short trip in order for her to get better oriented with the area of the city she lived in.

They drove to different areas, and she was informed on many things and places that she had not seen or heard about before. They drove, among other places through a large park, and they drove along the shoreline and saw ferryboats traveling to and from Staten Island. They talked a little about themselves and about their homes in Norway, and she learned a little bit more about him during the trip. After an hour's time he was of the opinion that they had driven enough for one evening and suggested that they should have dinner in the restaurant next to where he had stopped. Signe had no objections, and they were directed to a nice table with a view of the harbor. Jakob, who was capable in the English language, found his way around the menu easily and suggested several dishes for her.

The dinner was delicious and the time from appetizer to dessert passed all too fast. She learned that Jakob had two older sisters and a younger brother living in Norway. He told her that he had been going steady with a girl for a long time after he came to this country. He had known her from Norway and it had kind of been an understanding between them that they would marry one day. However, for different reasons, this important decision had never been made, and one day she suddenly disappeared with another man. Jakob was disappointed and still had difficulties talking about it. But now he was happy for being able to sit and talk to Signe so easily about this. She was a good listener and contributed with sympatric comments. She told of her marriage and how she had become a widow several years ago. She talked about her three children, and she talked about the small farm that she had leased to her neighbor before she left Norway. She did not in any way feel that her story had troubled him.

When he opened the car door for her outside her apartment, they agreed that this had been an afternoon and evening that they both valued. They realized that they had many things to ponder in the next days after what they had experienced in this first meeting. He squeezed her hand when they separated, and they agreed to meet again in the same place and at the same time on Friday.

Signe had told her children that she would be coming home a little late this evening, but nothing further. Well, they were far from children anymore, teenagers and more, but for her it was difficult to think of them as anything but children. Per and Helga had agreed that they were going to a movie, and they had not yet come home when

Signe unlocked the front door and entered the apartment. "I wonder if they have any idea of what I am doing," Signe thought. She knew that she had to offer an explanation, and she was determined that they would be told about the situation very soon. These kinds of thoughts would have been impossible for her to talk about while they had lived in Norway, but now she was not inhibited at all. She was actually looking forward to getting their reactions.

The reactions from the children were positive when she told them about Jakob, much better than Signe would have thought. They were full of questions and they were mature enough to understand that Signe would have a need for a companion. They had always been very open toward each other, and even though this was something completely new, it was talked about in an understanding and open manner. The children wished all the best for their mother, they advised her to advance slowly in the relationship because they did not want her to be disappointed or hurt. Signe agreed with what they said and she promised to be careful and keep them informed. She gave each one of them a good hug before Per left for his rented room and she and Helga withdrew for the evening.

Signe had difficulty falling asleep that night. There were so many things that had to be sorted out. Did she dare, did she want this relationship to develop further? What was to become of it? Was she in love? Could she really trust everything that Jakob had told her? What could his purpose be with this relationship? What did she expect? She was doing fine, why not just settle down and enjoy herself without complicating matters with a boyfriend?

Get-together

It took a short time before Lars Tunet realized what he felt behind his back, on his neck, and behind his ear. When the sleep left him, he understood the signals from Kari's warm body. He wondered for a split second what the reason could be for these advances from her but did not let that prevent him from enjoying her softness. It did not take many minutes before his posture changed from passive to active participant. In a short while they were able to satisfy each other.

The agreement for the evening was that they were to meet their friends in a restaurant, and they were prepared for the short walk with time to spare. Both were dressed lightly because of the pressing heat. They noticed that the sidewalk was wet when they came outside, so the rainy weather that had been predicted earlier had already produced a shower or two. Their spirits were high when they walked arm in arm toward the avenue and the restaurant. It would be evident to any passerby that this was a couple that was were very much in love.

Andreas Neset and his wife, Sofie, had already arrived at the restaurant and had only waited a short while when Lars and Kari came. They were assigned a table for six people, sat down, and ordered a drink each as they waited for Karl and Tordis Fredriksen. They showed up after a few minutes, and soon all were busy studying the menu that tempted with an assortment of dishes. When the waiter took the orders, it was for grilled chicken for some, others preferred deep-fried shrimp, and others again decided to go for the specialty of the house, prime rib steak.

All six were in an excellent mood. The conversations between them were easy and uninhibited. The ladies talked about their jobs and the men about theirs. All had been paid for the week, all were in excellent health, they were young and enthusiastic, and the food tasted excellent. The meal was completed with dessert for the men, and coffee and a cigarette by most.

After a while they were ready to drive to the first dance location that they had agreed upon during the meal. When they came out on the sidewalk, they saw that the rain had started in earnest. Andreas was the one who had volunteered to be the driver for the evening, and while they waited under a roof overhang, he ran down the sidewalk to get his car. They ran for the car when it came to the sidewalk in front of them, piled in fast, two in front and three in the back, and they drove off with all in great form.

They were lucky to get a place to park when they arrived at their first destination, because a car pulled out from the curb on the same side of the street as the dance bar and not far from the entry door. The rain was coming down hard. They ran for the entry door, and the last ones out of the car slammed the door behind them. There was quite a commotion at the crowded bar, and several were dancing to the music of a three-man band. They found a small table in the dimly lit room and were soon able to give their drink orders. A new tune started and all danced. As they got used to the noise and the dim lighting, they were able to look around, and once in a while they saw people who were familiar to them. They took a break from the dancing and Andreas went to the toilet.

On his way there, Andreas was spoken to, and to his amazement it was a good friend from his native district in Norway that he had not seen for a long time. They exchanged a few words before Andreas had to excuse himself. On his way back from the toilet he asked his friend to follow him to the table in order for him to be introduced to his wife and friends. Andreas explained that he and Gunnar had, among other things, been together at a camp one summer while growing up in Norway. The others did not know this stranger, even though they knew well the area where his home was located. Before they separated, Andreas and Gunnar agreed to meet one evening as soon as possible to talk of the old days and exchange information on new experiences.

The stop at this dance place was successful, but they had decided from the start that they should visit a few more places before calling it a night. They had been at this place an hour or so and the men had consumed three drinks each. They were ready for the next place. It was still raining when they got out on the sidewalk, and Andreas ran ahead to open the car doors. The others also ran and got seated as soon as possible. Andreas had a major problem by not being able to see because the windows were steamed up. He asked the ones closest to the windows to open them a little, and he adjusted the fan to full speed to get the windshield cleared. The passengers were merry and demanded loudly that Andreas should get going. He was too slow, they shouted, and they wanted him to take off at once and fast. He started out carefully, staring through the windshield where only a small spot had cleared. The windshield wipers were moving steadily but with little or no effect. The view was also reduced by the oncoming headlights that reflected so irritatingly on the dark and wet surface of the street.

He could see that he had a full stop at the first cross street, the mist on the windshield had reduced such that his vision was somewhat better. He stopped, looked to both sides as best he could, did not see any oncoming cars, and drove carefully ahead to cross the street. The passengers were loud and nagged him that they were in a hurry to get to the next place. They complained that he was too conservative a driver and demanded that he drive faster. After only five to six feet, he noticed a car coming toward him from his left side and it looked like it was coming at him without showing signs of slowing down. Andreas reacted by stepping on the gas pedal to get across faster as he kept his eyes on the other car that was approaching rapidly. The street was slippery, his tires did not get good traction on the wet surface, and then he noticed that the other car was coming at him sideways. But luck was with him. His tires got a grip and his car accelerated forward suddenly and at the right moment, such that the car that came sideways toward him was able to pass just behind his car. Andreas drove his car across the street and parked at the curb on the other side. He did not react to questions from several of the passengers about why he had stopped, and he ran out of the car. This happened so fast that the others in the car who had not followed what had just taken place, and did therefore not understand what had happened, sent only puzzling looks after Andreas who had hurried out into the rain. Andreas sought temporary shelter from the rain against a house and saw that the other car had braked, and that it had pulled to the side and parked at the curb of the crossing street.

With his heart in his throat and, pulse rising, Andreas ran across the street and over to the other car to check on the situation there. He found an elderly couple who had fortunately had their seat belts buckled and they looked unharmed. Andreas talked to the driver through the window that was halfway open on account of the rain. They agreed that both had been lucky, none were hurt, and the cars had not received a scratch. They agreed quickly that they were both guilty; Andreas had not had a clear view before he crossed, and the other driver, who did not have an obligation to stop, indicated that he probably had been negligent by driving too fast under the circumstances. He said that when he saw the crossing car, he had braked hard and suddenly, and his car went into a skid. It had looked bad for a while, he and his shaking wife explained. Both drivers agreed that they had consumed too much alcohol and that they did not need or wish for interference from the police. Andreas was probably at fault, but they separated with a handshake commenting only that they had been lucky, and both apologized.

Andreas ran back to his car and was soaking wet when he sat down behind the steering wheel. He expressed a sigh of relief, shaking from the experience and his wet clothes. The others had become quiet and waited anxiously for word from Andreas. After a while he recovered sufficiently to explain what had happened, by describing how close they had been to a collision, how lucky they had been. He referred to the conversation with the other driver and noted how soaked he was. Andreas said that he could not continue to another dance location in his present condition. If he was to continue further this evening, he had to go home first and get out of his wet clothes.

The others in the car started to realize how close they had come to a serious accident. They understood that Andreas had to change his clothes, and they suggested that he should drive to a particular bar that was located such that they all could walk to their respective homes from there later. Sofie was in agreement and wanted to go to the bar with the others. "Remember to bring an umbrella," she told her husband when they were dropped outside the bar. Andreas was to drive home, change, and walk back to the bar. This bar had music from a jukebox and there were no problems getting to dance even though the dance floor was rather small. It did not take Andreas long before he returned in a set of dry clothes. The incident earlier in the evening was not mentioned by anyone. They had an enjoyable time in this bar and a fine conclusion to the evening.

They were far from alone in this place. It was packed with happy people. The jukebox had a good selection of popular Norwegian and English dance music. Many spoke English, and many talked and sang in different Norwegian dialects. When they separated on the sidewalk outside the bar, the weather had changed. Now it was clear, refreshing, and with a new moon. Andreas and Sofie did not need the umbrella when they walked home.

Job offer

On the way to his assigned table in the restaurant, Per Bakken caught sight of an acquaintance who sat alone by a table. He went to the table and was invited to sit. Both were eager to have company during the meal and to get updated on happenings and experiences. The conversation concerned itself with work, what the prospects were for increasing their earnings, transportation arrangements to the job, what kind of person the boss was, and their relationship with the carpenters' union. After they had finished an excellent steak, they agreed to go to the bar that was connected to the restaurant to get a drink and to possibly meet with friends.

Per had brought his union membership book. It was time to pay the dues. This could be arranged easily with the help of a retired carpenter who earned a few dollars by doing the active carpenters a favor. He collected the union membership books from members, the necessary amount for dues, plus a couple of extra dollars for each book for his service. The pensioned carpenter took the books to the union hall at the first opportunity. There the payment for each member was registered and each book stamped. The books were returned to the owners at one of the many bars in the neighborhood. The owner of the book could not be without the book too long because there was always a chance that the job site would be inspected by union representatives. It was necessary for a union member to have a book that showed that the dues had been paid. It was essential that the union membership book was up-to-date at all times.

The conversations were jovial around at and around the bar, and Per met several that he knew and others that he had seen before. Many of the conversations were in good fun – the many jokes that were told were rewarded with much laughter and each joke told challenged another. Something that was a sure bet for laughter was when a story was told about how a beginner had struggled through the first days on the job. Most at the bar had gone through the same hard work, and no one took such a conversation personally. The heat was talked about, how tan they were, the blisters on their hands, and how exhausted they were at the end of a day at work. It was unavoidable that carpenters would compare how much a pair of them had completed in one day, and from such talk there would always be some bragging. The newcomers listened with some admiration to the ones that had gained some experience, and at the same time with apprehension for what was in store for them. When the conversation took on a serious note, it was often with reference to the status of the individual's job and the possibilities for future jobs. It was important to prepare for the next job in plenty of time before the current job was completed.

An elderly man who had not participated directly in the carpenters' discussions engaged himself in conversation with Per. He said that his name was Karsten Hansen and that he had surmised where

Per originated from based on his dialect in the conversations he had overheard. He explained that he also came from the same general area in Norway. They moved away from the others and sat down at a table.

Hansen asked Per to tell a little about himself, and Per told him how long he had been in Brooklyn, what kind of work he had found, and how he was managing. Karsten Hansen said that he was running his own business and that he had some workers installing wall-to-wall carpets. He talked in great detail about this type of work and Per was a good listener. Karsten highlighted some advantages of this type of work in comparison with a job as a carpenter. A carpenter depended on good weather to work and this was not the case for a man who installed carpets. Karsten had been busy for quite a while, and he was taking on more work, he said. A job with him offered overtime quite often. When, as an example, carpets were being installed in hotels, the work was often done over a weekend. From time to time his installers would have to travel to different areas of the county, at times even in different states, he explained. The job was best suited for a bachelor who was willing to work long days, and at times over weekends, with little time for sleep. Karsten asked Per if he was interested, and he was offered an hourly wage that was considerably higher than what he was getting as an apprentice carpenter. Karsten needed his answer by Saturday. Per was surprised and grateful for the offer and told this to Karsten. He also said that he had not purchased a car as of now and was therefore dependent on getting a ride to and from a job site. It was also important for him to tell that he had no idea how wall-to-wall carpets were installed. Karsten said that he was aware of that, but at the same time he was confident that Per would learn fast. In addition, he said that Per would be working within the city and that it would be possible for him to ride with others who worked in the same firm. He should therefore be able to manage without a car for several months.

With that said, Karsten Hansen thanked him and left the bar.

Per Bakken was seated alone by the small table and was about to roar loudly. What luck, what an encounter! Of course he had not had time to consider the offer in detail, but he knew that this had to be celebrated in one way or another. He determined that it was best not to tell of this conversation to others. He drank the rest of the half-full glass of beer and returned to his carpenter friends who were standing along the bar. The mood of this group was still high and most of the bachelors were in favor of going to a dance hall. Per had heard about the hall they talked about, but he had never been there. This evening he had something to celebrate and was willing to join the group. The easiest and quickest way to get there was to take the streetcar and several of them took off for its nearest stop. They continued with their rather loud conversations while under way.

The hall was a combination of restaurant and bar, with a dance floor. Many people had already gathered in the place and almost all the seats around the bar were occupied. Dancing was ongoing, and the smoke-filled air and high heat and humidity made for an uncomfortable place. The new arrivals seated themselves around a couple of small tables near the dance floor and were ready to order something. Some decided on both food and drink, others wanted only drinks. They got used to the noise and the reduced lighting after a while. Among the many tables they could see some that were occupied by couples, some by only women, and other tables, as their own, only by men. Most of the dancers were couples, but there were also some women who danced together. Per was in conversation with his friends and was looking at the dancers while they were eating hamburgers, cheeseburgers, or hot dogs, with big appetites. He glanced around the room and at the dancing women. At the sight of the dancing, twisting, and smiling women, the experience with the sight in the apartment returned, and he found himself imagining some of these dancers in the same position that he had seen his landlady on the sofa in the apartment. Per did not consider himself a good dancer, but he was not afraid to test himself. He had studied the women for some time before he got enough courage to engage one in a dance. It turned out just fine, and he continued to engage several throughout the evening. Finally there was one that stood out. She was not only good looking, but she was quick in her replies in a witty way and in a beautiful dialect. After having engaged her again she seemed interested. They danced one dance and waited for the next. In the middle of that dance he asked if he could escort her home. Thus it was that he left his friends, she her girlfriends, and they got out of the hall to a fresh and cooling breeze a short while before the dance was officially over for the evening.

They walked side by side and the scent from her was pleasing. Once in a while they bumped into each other, and both apologized at the same time. He would have liked to embrace her because she caused a strange warmth in him and he felt so comfortable by her side. They walked and walked, but eventually she said that they were by her door. He was not aware that they had already walked many blocks. He was totally bewildered, had such desire to embrace her, feel her closeness, experience her tenderness. Did these feelings have anything to do with the sight he had seen in his apartment? Finally he managed, "What is your name, and can we meet again?" She answered his questions and departed with a smile and a handshake. But, they were to meet again, on Wednesday, "girls' day off." As he continued his walk to his apartment with lightened steps, he became aware that it had rained a little and he saw lightning in the distance. All that he knew about her tonight for sure was that her name was Inga Hansen and that her dialect was that of a person from the southern part of Norway. The conversation between them had flowed so easily this Friday evening, and he was already looking forward to Wednesday evening.

It had been busy on the job for a long time. Per knew that additional people had been employed the last few weeks. The boss had asked someone every Friday if they could work the following day. Before they left the job earlier in the day, the boss had asked Per if he could work overtime the following day. He had replied with a, "Yes and thanks." The extra income would come in handy. The boss had told Per when and at which street corner to be at in the morning and who his partner would be. Now he had been out late and with his unique experiences during the afternoon and evening it was difficult for him to get to sleep. But, he had to sleep the few hours that were left of the night, because this Saturday he had to get up early, at the regular working day time. He had a long and strenuous day ahead of him. Maybe Saturday would be a work-free day on account of the rain and thunder he heard when he put his head on the pillow.

Correspondence

Even though Signe Bakken had come into a hectic and exciting period in her life, she had never forgotten her younger son Ole, who had remained in Norway. She remembered all too well how they all had been sitting and discussing different plans for the future while at Bakken farm, among others, the possibility of traveling to America. Signe had been steadfast and the entire time said that she would never leave Helga behind. This she had advanced early on in the conversation, and had stated that she would not listen to any arguments along that line. Helga had indicated that she did not know anyone "over there," that she had her friends in Norway, and that she liked what she was doing. Signe had comforted her by saying that she could use the same argument, but she knew for certain that they had to make the most out of the chance they had before them, and that it was not certain that the conditions would be as favorable for them in, for example, five to six years, she had said.

She was mostly worried about Ole. He had not hesitated when he made his decision of wanting to get more education. He liked to study and he was able and eager for more learning. They had contacted Uncle Tobias, who had become a schoolteacher and had settled in the city. He knew all of Signe's children well, and when Ole had said that he wanted to get more education, Tobias was determined that they had to see to it that this would be provided him. Tobias also said that he and his wife had talked about this and come to the conclusion that it would not be a problem if Ole moved in with them. This would give him a short distance to school and they were only eager to help him. Their own son, who was three years older than Ole, had no problems sharing the house with Ole; far from it, he was looking forward to it. Signe had thought aloud that this was in no way a solution that was the beginning of a lifelong separation from the family. She and Helga were after all just traveling to America for a trip to check out the conditions there, primarily to satisfy their curiosities. In order for Ole to continue with his studies, he had to leave home in any case because additional studies after high school could only be had in the city. They were very fortunate in having Uncle Tobias, for he himself had studied and could therefore give good support and advice in all respects. It was also obvious that if Signe and Helga should take a liking for and manage well in America that there was nothing to prevent Ole from also taking the trip like the others had.

Thus it was that Ole was left behind. But it was dreadful for Signe when they were to depart from him. She cried and cried. Ole comforted her as best he could, and both promised to write often. The departure was not easy for Helga either, and there was no lack of tears also from her. They had been good at writing regularly to each other. Ole had been told that all of them were managing well, how they worked hard, and that they were healthy. They told of good friends that they were together with and of many new ones that they had established. They told about the work, the work places, and how they traveled back and forth. They also told of apparel that they had acquired and about trips to parks in the city and to bathing beaches.

Ole told them about school, how satisfied he was, and that his grades were good. He also said that living with Uncle Tobias and Aunt Irene was a pleasure. They had been most helpful and friendly toward him and he had found many new contacts his age. They had also arranged for contacts that had given him small jobs that earned him some pocket money. Signe had put a five-dollar note in the letters to Ole from her first wages to help out with pocket money. She had also been to department stores and bought a couple of shirts and pants that were now on their way to him in the mail.

She had not told Ole about Jakob. That had to wait a little longer, she thought, even if she had informed Helga and Per. She knew that she could not wait too long before she told Ole of this situation, because she was sure that news like this would be conveyed by others in letters to their families and friends. She knew that when news like this came to Norway, someone there would see to it that Ole would be informed quite soon. Signe knew that the first information to Ole about Jakob had to come from her. Immigrants who had been in America for a while often used to make reference to Norway, and the place that they had left, as "the old country." She herself had difficulty calling Norway "the old country," at least "I cannot do it yet," she said to herself.

Increasing interest

Jakob came and fetched Signe as prearranged on Friday evening. The entire staff of the store knew about her gentleman friend by now, and she had to tolerate many questions and comments during the day and afternoon, including a certain amount of friendly teasing. When Jakob showed up, Signe introduced him quickly to the staff that was not occupied with customers and then they disappeared, waving from the doorway with a, ”See you,” from Signe.

Jakob suggested that they should take a ride like they had done the last time. He wanted to show her one of the parks nearby. Thereafter they could find a place to eat and possibly also a place where they could dance, if she were interested. She responded by saying let us take one thing at a time, and they drove toward the park. They walked around the lake, looked at the flowers, looked at people who were rowing small boats on the lake and at the birds that were fighting for the breadcrumbs tossed to them by an elderly woman.

They sat on a park bench and Jakob said that he could recommend a place to eat nearby where they also had a small band with a possibility for dancing. She thought this sounded good and they drove there. Jakob helped her understand the menu and he explained the different dishes as he had done when they were together in a restaurant for the first time. She took his advice and had a very good meal this time also. They danced a couple of times, settled down with a drink, and talked about various subjects, from the weather in their home areas of Norway to politics.

Jakob told her a little about his work in the travel agency and mentioned, among other things, that from time to time hotels offered employees very inexpensive weekend rates. This was a form for advertising by the hotels. They wanted travel agencies and agents to know what they could offer and the kind of standards they maintained. He said that he had taken advantage of such offers several times and once in a while he had even been able to spend an entire weekend at outstanding hotels for free. He asked if she would be interested in accompanying him if such an opportunity should arise again. Her answer was that it sounded interesting, and she promised to think it over.

Jakob said that he had several places in mind for them to visit, like the Bronx Zoo, the Brooklyn's Botanical Garden, the Brooklyn Museum, the Empire State Building, and Radio City Music Hall. But first of all he suggested that they take a trip to a bathing beach. He recommended a trip to Coney Island as the first trip and explained how easy it was to take the subway. He asked her if she had ever been swimming in an ocean and she admitted that she had not, but she was looking forward to trying it. Jakob, who knew that she had informed Helga and Per about him, suggested that they could accompany them on such a trip. "This will give us a better opportunity to get to know each other," Jakob said, "and we can make this into a picnic." Signe thought this was an excellent idea and said that she would inform her children of these plans.

When they parted company that evening, he kissed her lightly and quickly on her cheek while he was holding her hand. They thanked each other for the evening and agreed on the next date.

The following day she was with her friends after work. They wanted answers to all kinds of questions. Their impressions were that she had found a decent fellow, and from the little they had talked with him the first evening and the little they had seen of him since, they hoped that she would continue to be satisfied and they wished her well. None of the others had been as fortunate as she. They had to remain active, they said, with considerable laughter. Signe said that she had kept her children informed during this period and that they had been understanding and had really offered only encouragement.

The last evening they had been together, Jakob had given her something new to think about after she had gone to bed. She knew that she did not want to break off the relationship with Jakob, but could she really accompany him to a hotel? She was determined not to be too hasty in her relationship with Jakob. It would possibly be too hasty if she traveled with him to spend a night in a hotel? She fell asleep after she had reasoned that it possibly would be acceptable providing they had separate rooms. Signe had informed Jakob of her decision when they talked to each other a couple of days later.

The decision about traveling with Jakob to a hotel in the neighboring state came four weeks after Jakob had mentioned the possibility. The trip was organized such that they were to drive to the hotel on a Friday evening and were to stay over until Sunday afternoon. Jakob had shown her brochures on the hotel. It was a medium-size hotel with indoor and outdoor swimming pools and was situated in beautiful surroundings. Jakob had respected her wish and had reserved two rooms.

Decision

It was Friday evening, and Per had finished his duties for the day. He had even tidied up a little in his room. He was sitting on the only chair in the room and was looking out the window at the coming twilight. Several things had happened in the last few days that he needed to clear up, and he had some important decisions to make for the future.

He had worked overtime last Saturday. It had turned out well even if he had been tired after the short sleep the night before. It had been a warm day at work with threatening rain all day. He and his partner had been putting up the framing for a house. They had not seen much of the boss during the day and had taken a couple of extra breaks once in a while. Of course they could not overdo this, because the boss knew well what to expect from his carpenters.

He had looked forward to being with Inga again on Wednesday and they had met as agreed in the combined restaurant and dancing place. After they had eaten, they danced for an hour or so and talked to several others their ages that were enjoying themselves as they were. They conversed about many different topics, places, episodes, and experiences from Norway, or new experiences and their work places here. As they walked home, Per told Inga that he had something rather difficult on his mind that was troubling him, something that he had to take a stand on and that he unfortunately could not talk to her about at this time. When Inga was told that this in no way had anything to do with her, she accepted that he was so secretive. He promised that he would give her a full explanation when they met next time. They parted by her door with an agreement for meeting again the following Saturday evening.

On Thursday he had received a big and pleasant surprise on the job. When the boss and the union representative had looked him up, he had become perplexed. They had taken Per aside and told him that they liked the way he did his work and that he therefore, from next week, would be considered as a fully qualified carpenter and would thereafter receive union pay according to the prevailing scale. The entire conversation had taken only a couple of minutes. They separated after congratulations and handshakes, and went back to their respective duties. Per was very pleased and told the news to his partner immediately, who congratulated Per. He had gone through the same routine some years ago and knew well what this meant for anyone's self-esteem, and the increased income was appreciated.

But in the joy of the great news that he had anticipated for several weeks, Per had this other problem that had to be solved. Tomorrow he was to meet with Hansen – how was he to respond to his job offer? Per reasoned that he would earn as much, or possibly more, as a carpet installer, than as a full-fledged carpenter. This was on account of additional working hours over a year plus the fact that Hansen had indicated the possibility for considerable overtime pay.

The job could not possibly be more demanding than his carpenter job, could it? The fact that the work was indoors had big advantages, especially during the cold season. He reasoned that he could always return to a job as carpenter if it should turn out that he did not like carpet installations. His carpenters' union book would show that he was a fully qualified carpenter, and he could maintain that situation by paying the dues on time. However, it was also a shame if he moved to carpet installations because he had been lucky to get a nice and competent partner. His boss had never been unreasonable toward him; all in all he was quite content being a carpenter. This was difficult. After much thought back and forth he came to his decision, he would accept Hansen's offer. His reasoning was that he had to seize this opportunity, and he could easily resume the carpenter trade if this new trade should not turn out to his liking. But, after he had said yes to Hansen, he had to notify his boss, his partner, and his everyday traveling companions. He was not looking forward to this. Before he talked to Hansen, he would attempt to reach Uncle Tor with a telephone call to get his reaction to his decision.

The trip back and forth to the job, and the daily activities in the neighborhood before he withdrew to his little room, had become routine. Eventually Per got to bed and made sure that the alarm clock was set correctly, because tomorrow he was to work overtime again. Even if the decision had been difficult for him, he did not have any problem falling asleep, because he was quite tired after a long day with heavy work and many positive happenings. He managed to say a silent good night to his mother and sister who were living in their Brooklyn apartment, and to brother Ole who was living with Uncle Tobias and Aunt Irene in Norway, before he was sound asleep.

Per knew well and had proven to himself many times how important it was to arrive well rested on the job each morning. It was so much easier to tackle a day of hard work after having slept well, and he was sure that he would also be working easier and safer. But, it was not always easy to get sufficient hours of sound sleep. In late summer with high temperatures and humidity, his room was like a sauna on a still night. After such a night he would get up soaked with perspiration when the alarm clock went off. The sheet, which he had rolled into a ball in his restless sleep, was moist and disgusting and had to be washed every day. Per decided to buy a small oscillating fan. Maybe a little air circulation would help cool down his small room.

Coffee break

Per was practically awake when the alarm clock went off the next morning. It did not take him many minutes before he was dressed in his light summer work clothes after he had finished up in the bathroom. He took off, down the stairs, out the main door that he locked securely behind him, and set a course for the restaurant that for the time being was his favorite. There he would order his traditional breakfast and lunch to be taken along. Several spoke Norwegian at the counter and tables. Many were in the same errand as he. This restaurant gave good service and it did not take many minutes before he had the smoking hot food in front of him. Usually he ate the breakfast in a hurry but today he had a little more time to really enjoy the food. The luncheon food and the thermos bottle with coffee were secured in the lunch box. His next stop was the agreed on street corners and there he met one of the other fellows who were to be passengers. The car came shortly after, with Per's partner already in the car, and they proceeded toward the work site. This day was no different from others in that it did not take long before a couple of passengers fell asleep.

The boss assigned Per and his partner to start the framing on a new house today. Others would finish what remained on the house they had been working on the previous day. It was a damp morning, and they soon agreed that it was only a matter of time before it would start to rain, it was as if it was hanging in the air, just waiting to fall. The started out and worked nonstop for a couple of hours until one of them suddenly felt a couple of raindrops. He thought at first that it was a drop of sweat, but now he could see on the poured concrete slab that it had started to rain. Per's partner called attention to a large rain shower that was on its way toward them, and they agreed to gather their tools quickly and seek shelter. Oh yes, this was surely going to turn out to be a rainy day because now it also started to thunder. They took it easy where they were sitting under cover and found their lunch boxes even if it was a little early to take the lunch break. When they had been sitting and eating for a while, talked and looked at the threatening clouds and on the rain that did not let up, the order came from the boss: "Let's call it a day men, you have earned a half day's wage." Per and his partner grabbed their toolboxes and lunch boxes and ran for the car. The other two who shared the car also came running with their toolboxes, and in a few minutes they were on their way toward the city and their apartments. To be a carpenter on house framing, one is dependant on good weather to get in a full work day. Per had not told the others of his plans, he thought to himself that from this day on he did not have to concern himself with weather any longer at the place of work.

This suited Per well that it was to be a short work day, because he had several things to take care. He found a telephone booth after he had returned to the city and called Uncle Tor in his office. By chance he was present this time, and Per told him in some detail what had happened to him, of his new status as fully qualified carpenter and of the offer from Hansen. He also added his decision and finally said that he would appreciate hearing what Tor thought about this. Tor thought he had advanced rapidly and had no problems with Per's reasoning. Far from it, he would absolutely recommend a change because he felt that it would be valuable for Per to get experience in other trades. At last he reminded Per, as he had done several times before, about getting started in an English evening class a couple of times a week. Per thanked Tor for the talk and the interest he had shown and promised to get signed up for an English class one way or another. He knew someone who had done it, and they had told him that it was both an easy and inexpensive matter to get started with. But it required initiative. After a long day at work it did not sound tempting to sit down at a school desk. He understood well why Tor suggested school attendance so strongly. Tor had started somewhat like Per with hard work, and had found time to take a few hours of schooling in the evening, and therefore his feeling was that Per should also be able to do it. Some elementary courses from the beginning had led Tor to exams in several subjects and to the excellent education that he had acquired. Tor meant that if he could do it, almost anyone ought to be able to do it. OK, Per thought, as soon as I get into the routines on this new job, I will sign up for a course.

The matter was really straightforward after his conversation with Tor. He wanted to go to his room, take care of some laundry and rest for a while. Later in the afternoon he planned to go to a certain restaurant to have dinner and thereafter he would meet with Hansen at the prearranged time and location.

When Per came up to the hallway landing for his room, he saw that the door to the kitchen was partially open and he heard someone making noises inside. Shortly Lars came into view and he greeted Per with: “Hello, I see that you were sent home early today also.” Lars said that he was fixing coffee and invited Per for a cup. Per thanked him and asked to be excused in order for him to take a shower and changed into clean clothes and said that he would stop in as soon as he was finished. Lars said that would suit him just fine and that he was to stop in whenever he could. Per felt sweaty and clammy in the half-wet work clothes and it did not take long before he had washed up and changed. Thereafter he felt like a new person.

Lars had put some simple food on the kitchen table and Per helped himself after he had been offered. The conversation changed quickly from a how are you and how are you doing, to work and the work site. Lars explained that he and his partner were working on the next to the last floor on a building that was to be twelve stories high, and that he for the first time this year had felt that fall was on its way. It had been raining and quite windy on their job for a while, and been cold and uncomfortable. When the shop steward blew the whistle to signal the end of the day, the workers were all happy to get into their cars and drive home. He had been like Per, almost soaked to the skin, and now felt good for being able to sit and enjoy a cup of coffee and look at the rain. Lars told a little of what kind of duties he and his partner had been assigned, and Per listened with interest and had many questions.

When Per got a chance to explain a little of what he was doing on Long Island, Lars also showed interest. Per had big news today as he was about to change type of work, and he explained what he had decided. Lars indicated that he had made a sensible decision. He happened to know a couple of fellows who worked with carpets and from what he heard from them, they were well satisfied. The only negative he had heard was that once in a while they had to take some heavy lifts and that they could experience considerable amounts of dust when floors were being swept clean before the new carpets were put down. Lars also knew of problems that many of these fellows acquired with time, especially with the knees on account of the bending and pressing with the knees against the special tool that was required to get the carpets stretched out. It was rather common for these fellows to develop water on the knee. Per said that he knew little of this trade, but as he was enjoying coffee with a piece of a Danish pastry, looking at the rain and listening to the wind, he was actually looking forward to Monday and the new job that he was about to experience, which would not be affected by weather at all.

After a while, Per had to break off this enjoyable conversation, he had laundry to deliver before closing time, and he had a couple of men that he had to locate before Monday. Before they parted, Per promised to keep Lars posted and inform him later how he was doing on the job. When Per went out the entry door with his laundry under his arm, he met Kari who was coming home from her job. Her work was not dependant upon the weather and she had worked a full day. They greeted each other a little awkward and Per explained that he had just had coffee and a good conversation with Lars. He was thinking: “If you only knew that I saw you naked on the sofa.” She was thinking: ”Little do you know that I saw you starring at me from the hallway.” They exchanged positions in the doorway with a “see you.” Kari shook off the rain from her umbrella and got inside and Per started out with long strides and at a fast pace for the laundry.

Weekend trip

Again it was Friday evening, and Signe Bakken and Jakob Torgersen were on their way to the hotel that was located a four-hour drive from the city. Jakob had finished rather late in the office, and now they found themselves in terrible traffic. It looked like everybody was leaving the city at the same time. They had to be patient, and as it looked now they would not reach their destination before around eleven o'clock. When they had been sitting in traffic for more or less one hour, and with the traffic moving so poorly, they decided that they might as well stop and get something to eat. Maybe the traffic would improve after they had eaten. They were looking for a suitable place and finally ended up in a nice restaurant with a view of a lake. It had started to get dark, and it looked like it might rain. They ate a good meal and talked the entire time. Signe had long wondered how she was going to clear up the rumor of Jakob having been married in Norway several years ago. It probably was not all that important for her to know, but it was just that she was thinking about it from time to time and concluded that this opportunity was as good as any. She told him what she had heard, and Jakob reacted with easy laughter and a: "No, I have never been married." He could see that Signe felt relieved after this was cleared up. Signe showed a satisfying smile when she explained that it was not exactly that it would bother her if he had been married before. It was simply that she felt she knew quite a bit about him and it was just that she would be relieved to get this rumor cleared up once and for all.

They studied a brochure from the hotel while they ate. It explained that there was a path from the hotel to a fairly high mountain nearby and that the hike would take about one hour at a reasonable pace. The brochure also stated that the hotel would furnish their guests with a box lunch if they were interested. They agreed to start out on this trip in the morning and that it therefore behooved them to get a good night sleep. As soon as they arrived, they would check in, sign up on the list for the mountain trip and locate their rooms. They agreed to meet at seven o'clock for breakfast.

When they got back to their car after dinner, it had started to rain, but the traffic moved better. Jakob did not drive fast. His speed was a little over the speed limit and he drove defensively. Signe noticed that she was getting sleepy, but she did not dare to lean back in the seat because she was afraid that she might fall asleep, and that would not be fair to Jakob. But they had several things to talk about that used up some time. After a while Signe started to sing some of the old Norwegian songs that all Norwegians know from grade school. Jakob joined in also and it turned out that he had a quite useful singing voice. Once in a while they had to help each to other remember words of a song, and the result was that they enjoyed themselves and stayed awake.

When they arrived at the hotel, they each registered in accordance with the reservations that Jakob had made. The reservations were in order, Jakob's stay was to be charged to the hotel, and he explained that Signe's room and all expenses that they might incur by her was to be charged to his account. They did not need assistance to carry their things to the wing of the hotel that they had been assigned, as they each had only a small suitcase and a bag. The rooms were on the first floor and next to each other. They were both quite worn out and parted company with a small kiss at the door as prearranged.

Signe turned on the lights in the main room and the bathroom and was quite impressed with what she saw. She opened the curtains a little, and in the darkness, aided by floodlights, she established that the view was toward the garden and the swimming pool. It did not take many minutes to hang the garments from the small suitcase on the clothing rack and to get her toilet articles placed in the bathroom. She fixed herself quickly for the night and was soon in bed. Just to be sure she ordered a wake up call at six thirty. Even if she was in new surroundings, she had no difficulty falling asleep as tired as she was.

Confirmation

Per met Karsten Hansen at the appointed time and place. He explained with as little introduction as possible that he had considered the offer for a long time and that he had made his decision. Per wanted Hansen to understand that it had not been easy to decide because he had just managed to meet the requirements and was now a fully qualified carpenter, something that called for higher pay and more demanding assignments. He also said that he had a good working relationship with his boss and his partner. But in spite of all these advantages as a carpenter, he had nevertheless decided to accept Hansen's offer. He based this on being able to work independent of weather conditions, which he saw as a major advantage, plus that he was willing to try something new. Hansen thanked Per and offered him dinner at a nearby restaurant.

During dinner Per had to confess that he was a little unsure of the proper and most practical way of giving notice at the job he now had, and how to notify his partner. Hansen assured him that this was something that he was not to agonize too much over. All that he needed to do was to inform his boss and partner over the weekend. Hansen explained that things like this happened all the time among carpenters and he assured Per that this was easy to solve. Hansen therefore felt that Per would be able to start working for him beginning next Monday. Per had his doubts if it really could be arranged this easily and promised to contact his boss and partner as soon as possible. If problems should arise, he would contact Hansen again. When they parted company, they had agreed on where and when Per was to be picked up on Monday morning. Per had been told not to worry about tools for the first days because he would be able to borrow all that he would be needing. The last thing that Hansen said when they parted company was that Per was from that time on to call him by his first name.

Per had so many things to take care of before Monday. First and foremost he had to contact his boss, thereafter his partner, his mother and sister, and his Uncle Tor. He and Inga had agreed to go to a movie this evening. This is when he would tell her of all that had happened; he would especially explain to her why he had been so secretive when they were together last. Per had several times been thinking that it was about time that he introduced Inga to his mother and sister. But this had to wait a little longer, he felt, because at the present he was so busy with many things. Inga became happy when Per explained what had happened and why he had been in such deep thought the last time they were together. With everything cleared up between them, they had an enjoyable evening with a good movie.

When he met his partner on the main street the day after, he took the news well and congratulated Per on his decision. Per was quick to inject that it was only his plan to try out as a carpet installer over the winter. If he did not like it, he would return to the carpenter trade and would therefore maintain his membership in the carpenters' union. The boss also took the news well when he was told of his decision. Per explained how difficult the decision had been for him because he liked the job he was on so well. He explained that he had talked to his partner, who had simply said that he would arrange for a new partner and he had wished Per well. The boss was understanding, and he also wished Per good luck when they parted with a handshake. Per was pleased that the meetings with these two had gone so well because he had really dreaded these meetings. Now it was done and it had actually turned out as easy as Hansen had indicated.

Hotel guests

Signe came into the restaurant for breakfast at seven o'clock and looked around for Jakob. When she did not see him, she seated herself on a bench by the entrance. She looked around and noticed that the hotel had selected rather merry color combinations. Well-kept plants were placed strategically in the hallway and the walls were decorated with paintings. The area was neat and pleasant. A smiling Jakob came into view after only a few minutes, took her hand, and guided her into the dining room. They were directed to a table by the window with a nice view, and on their way there, they glanced at the magnificent breakfast buffet that they were to help themselves from. Both admitted that they were hungry, and as soon as they had been served orange juice and coffee, they went to the buffet table to fill up their plates. Getting food and good coffee was wonderful and they ate well. When Jakob asked the server about food for the mountain trip, they were asked to help themselves from the buffet and the hotel provided a suitable paper container. Jakob had brought along a small backpack where they placed the food, some fruit, and something to drink.

It turned out that several guests from the hotel had decided to take the trip. There were so many gathered outside the hotel entrance that the hotel had decided to send along a man who was familiar with the area to explain the sights along the way. The rain from the night before had continued toward the east and now the sky was blue and the temperature a lovely 70 degrees Fahrenheit. Signe and Jakob were dressed lightly and had on good walking shoes. Both were in good shape and had no problems following the pace of the guide. The path began to wind after a while, and the climb got steeper, while the view became only prettier with every turn on the way up. The guide stopped the small group often to show them different places in the terrain around them and in the distance. After almost two hours the goal was reached. The many stops on the way had taken time, but it had been most interesting to hear the excellent descriptions from the guide.

All in all there were nine persons who had taken the tour. They seated themselves on the ground when the reached the end point and brought out their box lunches. The food tasted good and the view was just magnificent. They could see almost unobstructed in an arc of some 270 degrees. The saw green fields, forests, a river far away, and the next mountain range behind the river. The view behind them was blocked by the mountain they were sitting on. It turned out that it was possible to go even higher but the path onward was more difficult to walk. But this was cozy, and the guide surprised them by producing three bottles of wine that he shared among them. The guide could tell some of the history from this area, how it was that many Indians had been living in this vicinity years ago, and how they had been forced further inland by the white man when he developed a taste for crop-land. He said that it was possible to find traces of the native

Indians, especially by the river where they had ground their corn. Many hollowed out places in the rocks could be seen.

After an hour of relaxation, it was time to continue. Some opted for going to the very top and others for returning to the hotel. The latter group included Signe and Jakob. They walked side by side, stopped once in a while to take in the view and really enjoyed the trip and each other. They were both in such excellent shape that the trip was not demanding for them at all. They walked and talked about what to do when they got back to the hotel. Signe was thinking about taking a shower, she said, but Jakob reminded her that whatever she did, she had to try the Jacuzzi and the swimming pool. This was something she had completely forgotten.

Jakob and Signe went to their rooms when they arrived at the hotel and met only a short time later by the swirling bath in their bathing suits and with a towel over their arms. The water was so wonderfully warm and soft, and the jets of water that massaged the entire body created a relaxed feeling. After a while when this bath became a little too hot, all they had to do was walk a few steps and jump into the swimming pool. The pool was large and one could really get exercise by swimming back and forth. They alternated between the swimming pool and Jacuzzi two or three times and then took a seat in one of the lounge chairs on the lawn to sun themselves a little. Jakob located a waiter and ordered a drink for each of them. They had a wonderful time, were completely relaxed, and were in agreement that this was an excellent place to spend a weekend. They had brought along a book each, but there was little time for reading. They enjoyed each other's company and talked about all kinds of things.

They noticed that it got colder when the sun was about to set behind the roof of the hotel; it was getting to be late in the afternoon. They had to go to their rooms to get ready for the evening, when a better dinner was planned. This was a part of the advertisement package that Jakob had received from the hotel. They elected to take a last trip to the swimming pool and after a few times up and down the length of the pool, they got out, collected their towels, and walked toward the rooms. Signe's room had an entry from the swimming pool side, and when they got there, Jakob followed her inside and she did not object. When the door was locked and the heavy curtains pulled, Jakob embraced Signe and gave her a long kiss and she reciprocated. After a short while he started to fumble with the buttons on her bra and let it fall to the floor. He looked down at her breasts, held one in each hand and noticed that they were cold and moist. He played with the stiff nipples while he continued to kiss her gently. Signe noticed that she started to get excited. She was anxious for what she knew would happen, but at the same time she was willing to continue. As if on a signal they removed the rest of their bathing suits and in the next minute they were in bed. Jakob continued to touch her while he held her in his arms and continued to kiss her. She assisted by letting her legs slip apart and was ready for what would and had to happen. When she looked up, she noticed that Jakob was also ready, and what she saw almost scared her. It had been such a long, long time since the last time. Suddenly she felt Jakob and in the next moment it was just enjoyable. They soon found the rhythm and before long their feelings were satisfied.

Eventually it became necessary to get up and get ready for dinner. They were already running a little late and needed to hurry. Jakob opened the lock to the common door between the rooms on Signe's side, wrapped the towel around himself, opened the door to the hallway, looked both ways, ran to his door and opened it to his room as fast as possible. When safely inside his room, he opened the common door on his side. He heard that Signe was already in the shower and he made for his own shower. With the shower completed, they met in the common doorway for a fast hug, and each of them proceeded to get dressed as fast as possible. They were all smiles as they walked hand in hand to the dining room.

The dinner was delicious, and they took their time to enjoy it and each other's company. They had so many things that needed to be discussed and they sent many loving gestures to each other between the comments. Signe wanted to talk about something practical after a while. She was wondering if they could cancel one room to save some money. Jakob reasoned that it was already late in the day and it would therefore most likely be difficult to arrange, as they were after all leaving for home the following day. He suggested they should forget this matter. But Signe felt that it would not hurt to ask, that is, she added, if Jakob did not have anything against sharing a bed with her. Of course he did not, and when they had finished the meal, they went to the reception desk to investigate. This turned out to be very possible; the hotel had a rate for late checkout that they would use. When the difference was calculated, it showed that they had saved considerable money on the suggestion that Signe had introduced and for which Jakob now was grateful. This solution meant that they would have to move her things into his room as his room was at the expense of the hotel. This took only a few minutes, and on their way out of the hotel to take a walk, they dropped off the key and told the woman at the reception desk that the room was now cleared and available.

Twilight was coming on when they stepped outside. They elected to walk on a dimly lit path that wound itself around the hotel. They saw the spotlight on the building, the lit pools, and once in a while they heard laughter from people that were in the hotel garden. A half-moon played hide-and-seek with the clouds. With the fine aroma from plants and trees and the newly cut grass from the many lawns and the ideal temperature, this was an absolutely romantic evening for the couple, who were walking arm in arm along the path. They enjoyed each other and talked easily of trivial matters, while they each knew all too well that a serious conversation that would deal with their future had to come. But nothing was said in that direction – they both postponed such references and continued with conversations that had to do with the present.

They sat down on a park bench, and now they could hear soft music from the hotel. They decided to go dancing. The last time they had danced to a large band was actually at the big May 17 celebration, when they had met for the first time. They therefore decided to go to the ballroom. It was a four-piece orchestra that played. The music was acceptable and gave them several good dances before they withdrew for the evening. The day had been wonderful and they were looking forward to the next.

Anxiety

It was Sunday afternoon when Signe Bakken and Jakob Torgersen were on their way back to the city to get ready for another workweek. They had agreed to start the return trip early to get their apartments cleaned up a little in the afternoon. Signe had also promised Helga that she would not be late, and she had invited Per for dinner.

Signe and Jakob had spent a good night and the relationship between them was very good, and it had only grown better with time. None had mentioned future plans. They simply continued to postpone such a serious discussion as long as possible. Or were they both a little anxious for how the other part would handle a discussion like that? Signe could not help that she was having unpleasant thoughts. She was so terribly afraid that Jakob's reaction would simply be that now he had conquered her and would leave her to conquer another woman. If this were to happen, she knew that it would devastate her. Why did she have to look at this from such a negative point of view? Jakob also sat with his thoughts. They concerned themselves with questions like, if Signe was really interested in a future with him, could he offer her a good future, and how would her children react to this?

When Signe began with, “Say, Jakob,” after what appeared to be a long silence from both of them, they both knew that this signaled the start of the serious conversation. Signe simply continued with the question, “How are we going to handle our relationship from now on?” Jakob started carefully with several hesitant half-finished sentences, and pauses and then finally said, “I was wondering, had kind of hoped that we could continue our relationship. Well, what do you think?” They were in total agreement that what they had found in each other this weekend was not something to make light of, both admitted that they had become very fond of each other, and that this after all was the most important thing. Both were interested in continuing the relationship, but how were they to tackle the details about it? Both were in deep thought and broke the silence once in a while with short comments. When they started to see the skyscrapers of the city, Jakob arrived at a suggestion that they both agreed upon. Jakob simply said that he understood the situation to be such that they both were interested in a future together. He suggested that they were to have a date next Friday at the usual time and place, and that they at that time were to arrive at a decisive solution for their future. In the meantime both were to give this much thought and Signe was to take the matter up with her children.

Jakob drove her to her door, and before she left the car, they hugged and kissed each other. Jakob carried the little she had of luggage to her front door and said, “We will see each other again soon.” He went back to his car and drove off. Signe stood in the open doorway and waved to him, and when she closed the door behind her, she felt totally alone and confused.

Jakob was interested in getting home to his apartment as soon as possible, but his thinking was clear enough to remember that he had to purchase some food for breakfast. He therefore stopped by the little store, near where he lived, and grabbed a few things in a hurry and almost forgot to greet the clerks that he had become well acquainted with. He had to get home to think. Somehow this had happened so fast – was it too fast? Signe was great to be with and they had enjoyed a wonderful weekend. He could not see how he could be without her in the future, but was he at this point in time ready to take the serious step of marriage?

Per was visiting his mother and sister, who had invited him for dinner. His mother had said several times said that she would like to have Per move in with them but Per was determined to manage on his own, in any event for a while longer. They were surprised when Per told them that he was going to change his occupation and they speculated for a while on how this new job would develop. Per explained as well as he could what this new job would entail, with the limited knowledge he had of this trade. He explained briefly how he had arrived at the conclusion of switching from carpenter to carpet installer and that he had sought advice from Uncle Tor.

They had a good dinner together. His mother had made meatballs, one of his favorite meals. They had eaten and talked until it became time for all to go to bed. Per had almost mentioned Inga a couple of times during the conversation. He was especially close to doing so when Helga wanted to know how he liked the last movie he saw. They did not know if he had seen the movie alone or had been with someone at that time. He almost revealed her name when he was explaining a couple of scenes in the film about which he and Inga had disagreed. Inga had felt that especially one scene was too unrealistic and Per had felt that it was just a bit exaggerated. Signe had her own secret from her trip to the country with Jakob, and she also elected not to mention anything directly regarding the relationship between Jakob and herself and how it was developing. She said that the trip had been interesting and she mentioned with a few words what they had seen and let it go at that.

Friends meet

The afternoon was rather gloomy. The weather could not make up its mind if it was to be rain or simply continue with the nasty cold wind that blew through the streets. This Sunday was not suitable for conversations on street corners as would have been the case if the weather had been better. People kept to their apartments or met with friends and acquaintances in popular places.

Andreas and Gunnar were sitting in one of the popular bars of the area with a glass of beer each. They had met as they were coming home from work one afternoon and had agreed to meet the following Sunday in this place. They had discussed and updated each other for quite some time on the conditions at their places in Norway and their families there. They had many mutual acquaintances so that this part of the conversation took considerable time.

It turned out that they had several glasses of beer before their conversation turned to their jobs. The story of how and why they had come to Brooklyn was more or less the same for both of them. Not having a special skill or trade that they could use immediately when they arrived in this country, they had as most newcomers taken advice from people they knew who had gone through similar routines to secure jobs. Andreas explained how it was that he ended up as a carpenter doing formwork. He told how much experience he had gained with this trade and that he had an excellent partner and was comfortable with what he was doing.

Gunnar explained that the first contacts he had established were through installing hardwood flooring and this occupation had been highly recommended to him. For one thing they had compared this trade with that of house framing and had several times indicated how strenuous that type of work was, and how there would be no income in bad weather. They had told him that safety precautions on such jobs were minimal and of accidents that had happened. Carpenters had to balance on the new beams as they were put up and they sometimes would fall down. The beams could become quite slippery after rain and they were often slippery from snow and ice in the wintertime. Falling down one story was usually not too bad, providing the person did not get hung up on a beam or land badly on the floor below. Of course it would result in the person getting some scratches and black-and-blue marks, and having gained an experience. Gunnar's friends had, among other stories, been told of a young Norwegian who not long ago had been put to work on the roof of a house that was under construction. This happened early one morning and the partially completed roof was probably covered with dew. The man had fallen down and had apparently been killed on impact. Even if this put a scare in the beginners for some days, they continued to work without safety precautions. They simply did not have a choice if they wanted to continue on the job. Such work accidents were practically forgotten after a while and seldom discussed. Gunnar's friends had also told of a carpenter who had been so unfortunate as to step on a rusty nail. The workers had to be on the alert constantly for where they stepped, because many boards could be laying on the ground with nails sticking out of them. The people responsible for keeping the workplace orderly were not always so conscientious. It therefore happened that young men, who had not taken any precautions, were unfortunate and ended up with bad cases of tetanus and loss of pay for several days.

Gunnar had also heard of a different form of carpenter trade that sounded interesting. This work was independent of weather conditions as it was indoor work and did not require heavy lifting. The work was called trimming. These carpenters were responsible for hanging doors and putting up molding, including baseboards, and trim around doors and windows. Carpenters who selected this type of work, and who were given the opportunity to get these jobs, were often those who had some experience with more precise types of work as, for example, cabinet - making. Special tools that cost a good deal of money were needed for this type of work and it was therefore not easy for beginners to get started before they had managed to save some money.

Gunnar's friends, who installed hardwood floors, had been very convincing. They had emphasized advantages like always being able to work under a roof, and that it was probably the easiest occupation to establish piecework rates on. Usually this would be worked out so that the individual would be paid a certain amount for each installed square foot of floor. During the conversation it was brought up several times that a person who had the knack for this type of work could make good money. Gunnar did not really have much of a choice, and when he had accepted their arguments and reasons, and when his friends offered to help him get started, the choice was made. Gunnar told Andreas how terrible the floor installation work had been for his back. The first few weeks he almost had to crawl at the end of the day.

Gunnar explained how difficult it had been for him to work up the skill of putting down the narrow flooring boards. They were usually oak and they were to be fastened securely to the underlayment with special nails. These were blunt at the end to prevent splitting of the wood, and the nailing was not easy to manage at first. From the beginning he had been fortunate to be assigned to work with two men who had considerable experience. The first days he was helping to bring the flooring material into location, and to put out the lengths of flooring so that the seams would not occur in the same spot row after row. Gradually he was given the task of putting down small floors at first, for example in closets, and he was told to ask the experts for advice often.

Little by little he dared to cut lengths of boards and he learned quickly how important it was to use available board pieces sensibly. The boss would not be pleased if he discovered many and long pieces among the remnants that were to be discarded. It was with short lengths that Gunnar first tried the nailing. One of the fellows who had long experience showed him where to place the flat cut nail, put it on an angle, give it a solid hit, follow up with the next hit against a new nail, that was used as a nail punch and placed flat against the head of the first nail. This resulted in the first nail being driven in until it was flush with the groove in the flooring board. It looked like it was easy, but it turned out to be far from it. Of course one had to hit the nail. If one hit the flooring board instead, it had to be discarded, which meant removing the entire length of board and starting all over. When the experts drove the nail in with one hit, Gunnar needed several blows that he let fall with care in order not to hit the flooring boards with the hammer. Not all blows hit the nail, especially in the beginning the hammer head landed on the fingers that held the nail. It became more difficult to manage the nailing after such mishaps, as it was not easy to hold the nail steady with a swollen and sore thumb. The fact that beginners were given the task of putting down small floors was understandable for a couple of reasons. First in so doing they were isolated from the experts who were working on the main floor areas. Secondly, the short lengths were easy to exchange if needed. Gunnar was managing fairly well after a few weeks, and he was permitted to test himself on the larger floor areas little by little.

The work assignments that these carpenters were given could be for private homes, public buildings, indoor sporting arenas, and often in bowling alleys. It was popular to restore old bowling alleys with new floors and automatic equipment. Many carpenters were used for the larger projects, and usually these came from different firms. It was important to get finished as fast as possible in order for the owner to get the business started up again. The owner had his fixed expenses and had no income as long as the work was taking place. Carpenters were often able to negotiate for piecework for a certain amount for each installed square foot. This was highly sought-after work by the experienced carpenters, but almost impossible for apprentices to be permitted to participate in because the experts did not tolerate anyone slowing down the work and thereby the earnings. A way for the apprentices to participate on these large jobs was to work as an assistant or helper to the experienced carpenters and accept a regular carpenter wage from these.

All new floors in hardwood, usually oak, had to be sanded down and varnished before they could be used. The sanding was done with a six-inch-wide roll of sandpaper that was driven around a drum of a fairly large and heavy machine. The machine was noisy, and even though the machine had a bag mounted on it for the collection of the dust, the room still became dusty, and the workers had to use ear plugs and face masks. Finished sanded floors were swept and vacuumed before they could be lacquered. Multiple coats were applied with long mops over a period of several days to permit drying between coats. As the smell from the lacquer was intense, and not entirely without risk, it was necessary to provide good ventilation.

"But, now listen to this," Gunnar continued. A friend of his had told him that many newcomers had obtained work on fishing boats farther north on the coast. Gunnar had learned that in the city of New Bedford a celebration called the Scallop Festival was held once a year and he had traveled there to see what was going on. It appeared as if the entire city participated, it smelled scallops all over, and he had simply eaten too much of this delicacy. He had also met several Norwegians his own age who worked on fishing boats. They told him a little about this occupation and, of course, about the income that was based on lots. On certain trips they had earned exceptionally well, but they had also had trips where the earnings had been poor. A young Norwegian fisherman had invited Gunnar aboard a fishing boat that was tied up by the dock, and he explained that it seemed like most Norwegians who worked in this type of fishing came from the west coast of Norway. It was therefore natural to assume that these young men had a certain experience with fishing before they left their homes. The boat itself was not impressive at all – it was small, and the room allocated for each person was tiny. He was told that it became very busy on the deck when the catch was hauled aboard in a large net. The net contained other catches in addition to scallops. The task was to sort out the scallop shells and toss most of the remaining catches overboard. If they did not have too many days left on the fishing field, they usually kept a few lobsters and cod that they brought home for private consumption. The fishermen who cut the scallops out of the shells with well-directed cuts at a rapid pace were standing by the railing with their special knives. The scallops were tossed into a container and the shells were tossed overboard. The exception was that some nice types of these colorful shells were taken home, where they usually ended up as ashtrays. The work was manageable in good weather, but became both difficult and dangerous with wind and high seas. Gunnar was told that the fishermen who mastered the art could remove unbelievable numbers of scallops from their shells in an hour and that a competition was held annually to choose a champion.

Gunnar had also met the owners of three fishing boats who had offered him a job. Two owners were in need of a new cook but that was an occupation that Gunnar knew with certainty that he had not mastered. The occupation of a fisherman did not impress him at all. The small boats would surely toss something awful in a rough sea; that is to say, he saw seasickness as a certainty. Gunnar's only experience with the sea was his voyage across the Atlantic, and even that large ship had tossed considerably, sufficient for several passengers to get seasick. He admitted that the sizable income that some fishermen had earned was sufficiently tempting for him to not put this job prospect entirely out of his head. He did not know if he would ever do anything with this opportunity. But, he felt it was good to have something else to fall back on if the work he was doing now was to suffer a slowdown.

Andreas glanced at a clock that hung on the wall behind the bar and apologized for having to break off the conversation because he was to have been home half an hour ago. Both agreed that this meeting had been good, that the time had passed much too fast, and both appreciated being updated on each other's activities. They admitted that there was a high probability that they would be granting themselves a short nap after they had eaten something because they had consumed too much beer. When they parted on the street corner, they promised to get together again before too long.

Inquiry expands

Several days had passed since Signe Bakken and Jakob Torgersen had returned from their trip into the country. In this time she had been troubled and uneasy. Her friends at the store had noticed a change and had asked her several times if something was the matter, if there was anything they could help her with. She assured them that everything was fine in all respects and that she did not need any help. She could not tell them that she was so troubled, possibly regretted what had happened, and that she was afraid that she had been taken advantage of. She had to confess that many a time she had been thinking about getting a life companion again, but now that her wish seemed about to be fulfilled, she had become uncertain.

Signe and Jakob had talked a lot and knew each other's background in some detail by now. Suddenly she had come upon the thought, suppose Jakob was not the person he had passed himself off to be. These were terrible thoughts; she had no reason whatsoever for not believing what Jakob had told her about himself. But it was simply that she needed to assure herself that she was not being duped into something that she would regret later, when it might be difficult or impossible to escape.

She had thought long and hard about a solution for getting rid of these thoughts. This required her to write a letter to her son Ole and explain the relationship between Jakob and her. In the letter she would ask Ole to travel to Jakob's home area and inquire discreetly in different places about people there who could tell about Jakob. It was not a long trip for Ole, and he would not have any problems in doing such an investigation for her in a way that it would not attract attention. The more she thought about this, the more certain she became – feedback from his home area was what she needed to solve her state of confusion. "But, what in the world," Signe said to herself, "I cannot use my own son to spy for me and especially not regarding a relationship that has to do with a suitor." She had pondered this problem, had speculated back and forth on it too many times. The result was that she became more and more worried and uncertain for how to go about it. She had started a letter to Ole and had come to the point where she would be asking for his help. To spy was possibly too strong an expression, even if it was the truth, and she elected to write "ask you for a king-size favor." She just could not let go of the negative thoughts. She had to get confirmation from the old country about what she had heard from Jakob and others. If she received confirmation, she was prepared to stake out a future with him.

It was at this time that luck came to her aid. She picked up the telephone that rang in the evening while she was doing the dishes, and it was Jakob on the other end. After having made some small talk for a while, "Thank you for last time, cannot wait until we meet again," Jakob said that he had an idea. The fact was that he had been thinking about something for a while. He had written his family about it and had now received an answer. The plan was that Ole should take a trip to visit Jakob's family as soon as he was free from school. The family had promised to take good care of him and would see to it that he would have a look around in the area. Signe became nearly speechless; we have so much in common and now it appears that we are also thinking alike, she thought. Signe did not hesitate in agreeing with the suggestion and she promised to write Ole right a way. Jakob had given Signe names and addresses that she was to convey to Ole. Signe became really relieved, and did not remember much of their conversation thereafter. She noted one thing. She noted that she would be picked up at the same time and place Friday afternoon.

Imagine, for several days she had walked about being worried, even had several sleepless nights, and then the matter was solved so easily with just a phone call. This had to be a good omen for her future, she thought. She seated herself and started to rewrite the last page of her letter to Ole and explained the task she had for him. The pen flew over the paper with all the news that she had to tell her youngest son.

Carpet installer

Per Bakken showed up Monday morning at the agreed time and on the given street corner as he had been instructed by Karsten Hansen. He stood there and saw one car after the other pass him by. After a while he started to wonder if he possibly had misunderstood Hansen and was standing on the wrong street corner, and if the car he was waiting for was standing at this other corner waiting for him. Suddenly a car drove up to him, a window was opened, and he was asked if his name was Per Bakken. He answered yes, and was told to "jump in," and as soon as the car door was closed behind him the car started up again. In the car there were three young men in addition to the driver. Per had never seen any of them before, and when the introductions started, it turned out that they were all Norwegians. The driver explained that they were on their way to Manhattan, where they had worked for several days already, and that the boss, that is Hansen, considered this to be a good location for Per to get started. Per mentioned that he did not have any experience with carpet installations and was told not to worry, they had all been in the same situation not long ago. They promised to take good care of him and assured him that he would be dropped off at the same street corner in fine shape later in the afternoon. This was of comfort to Per, even though he thought he detected a sly smile from one of the men in the back seat. Of course these men did not know anything about Per and his physical condition, and Per considered himself every bit as fit as they appeared to be. It will work out, he thought. I am after all much better prepared than when I picked up the hammer for the first time on Long Island.

It turned out that the job site they were going to was a hotel. They simply drove into the bottom parking garage, parked the car, and took the elevator to the fifth floor. All who arrived in the same car plus a group from another car were to work on this same floor. Carpets, carpet pieces, and tools were scattered on the floor just as the installers had left things the evening before. Per was told that it was important to finish one floor at a time in order for the hotel to be able to make the rooms available for guests as soon as possible. Hansen had put on extra crews to finish the job quickly. The carpet installers worked in pairs like the carpenters, and Per was assigned a couple that he was to work with until he learned the routines. He was told this was an unusually large job in which all the hotel rooms and hallways were to get new carpets. The carpets were delivered to each floor directly from the factory in accordance with the purchase order from Hansen, and therefore the installers did not have to struggle to get the carpets delivered to the individual floors. The installers told Per how much the hotel lost each day they were without guests, and why it therefore was possible for them to pay extra in order for the work to be completed fast. He was told that the carpets they were removing could have been in use for as much as seven to eight years. He was told that the replacement was not necessarily on account of wear, many times it could just be that new owners wanted their own color combinations installed. He was told how the most successful carpet installation firms collaborated when they were awarded large jobs like this one, and how in this case Hansen had borrowed installers from firms in the neighboring state. Per was told that he should expect this to happen with Hansen's people also from time to time.

The first workers in each room on every floor were assigned the job of pulling out the old carpets and sweeping the floors clean. This was a nasty job. The dust was terrible, and even if the windows were open, and they used fans and masks, one could hear how the workers coughed and cleared their throats constantly. It was necessary to use brooms in addition to powerful vacuum cleaners. The carpet underlayment had to be swept up and carried out in bags as it often was made of a rubber compound that had dissolved with time. Many bags of dust and trash were removed from each floor. The old carpets were cut up in suitable sizes that were easier to handle and brought to the first floor. There they were taken care of by people who organized the carpets in bundles before they were picked up by a company truck and brought to the garbage dump. After a day on the job, with the sweat running, these men were very dirty. The only part of their faces that was somewhat clean was the area around the mouth and nose after they removed their masks.

Per felt terribly awkward as he was looking at the carpets being installed. But little by little he was able to give a helping hand here and there, he pulled carpet pieces into the hallways, he picked up the nailing strips and saw how they were fastened. He was given the task of fastening the strips, and he had to be shown how and where to place them. It did not take long before he understood that assignment. He learned quickly to be careful when handling the nailing strips because it was so easy to get scratched on the sharp nails in them. As this job involved installation of carpets in rooms that had had carpets before, many of the old nailing strips were reusable and therefore it did not take long to make a room ready for the new carpet. He saw that the new carpet would follow the layout pattern of the old carpet; as the new carpets were of the same width as the old, the joints would fall in the same places. It was therefore not necessary to do much planning for a layout. The rooms were almost alike, so it did not take long to roll out the carpets and get them stretched out and fastened to the nailing strips that had been installed along the edges.

Per felt fine when the day was over. In fact, he was not as tired as he had been after a day doing carpenter work. He was let off at the same street corner as he had been picked up in the morning, and he walked with satisfaction toward his room.

Task completed

Almost three weeks had passed since Ole had received the letter from his mother wherein she wrote about Jakob and asked for his help. What a big surprise that had been! He had read the letter a couple of times before he really comprehended the news. He had to admit that this was almost unbelievable. He had never thought that his mother would be interested in a man again, because he had never detected that she had given any indications in that direction. Maybe she had changed her mind in America? He gave this some thought and the first thing that came to his mind was that he was not willing to share his mother with a strange man. After having given this some more thought, he had to admit that it was not for him to decide on a matter like this for his mother. This was something she wanted and he should be among the first to help her any way he could. He was permitted to be skeptical and would only hope that she had made a wise and sensible decision. Ole understood that this would be difficult for him, but maybe it would help when he heard from his sister and brother, who had met this Jakob fellow.

Signe had asked Ole in her letter to let Tobias and Irene read the letter also. He took the four-page-long letter in his hand and hurried to find his Uncle and aunt. Ole studied his Uncle while he was reading and noted that his expression changed from a guarded smile to full laughter. He gave the pages to Irene as he finished reading them and she also smiled when she had finished reading the first page. "Yes, this is big news," said Uncle Tobias. He appreciated that Ole had some difficulty accepting that his mother had fallen in love. This was clearly the way the letter was to be understood regarding the relationship between Signe and this Jakob. Tobias's laughter was happy because he considered this as excellent news. Tobias admitted that since Signe was still so young, that he had many times wondered if she would be interested in a man again. "Well, well, she had to go to America to find a man. Not bad. And it is amazing that her suitor was raised not far from where we are reading this letter," he said. Irene saw the matter in the same way as her husband and they both thought it would be a very good idea for Ole to met Jakob's family. They discussed this big news for a long time that evening, and Ole eventually became comfortable with his task as being necessary and important for his mother.

~

Ole was about to write a letter to his mother to relate everything that had happened in the last few days since he received her letter. Uncle Tobias and Aunt Irene had both promised that they would also write a few words. So much had happened that Ole had some difficulty getting started. This had not exactly been fun at the beginning, but as he thought back, he had to admit that it had turned out well. He did not particularly like to write letters but in this case he knew that several people were waiting to hear from him. He knew that he had to be cautious and choose his words carefully in order that the readers would not misinterpret his intent. So, there was only one thing to do – he had to get started with his response letter.

"Thank you for your letter, my dear mother," he wrote. "I have to say on my own behalf and that of Uncle Tobias and Aunt Irene that what you told us in your last letter was a big surprise for us all. Dear mother, I have to be honest and say that the first thing that I felt after I read the letter was disappointment. I felt a certain fear of somehow losing you and I was not prepared to share you with a strange man. After I had thought it through for a while, it became somewhat better. That is when I reasoned that your relationship with Jakob is really none of my business, not directly anyway, and I just have to accept it as a fact. I am old enough to understand that you could be thinking of having, what is it called? A life companion. Well, well. Mother, you are mine. You belong to Per, Helga, and me. Speaking for myself, I must say that I have difficulties sharing you with anyone else. But having said this, I will also say that this man that you like so well had better watch out if he is not kind and nice to you. If he is not, he can expect big problems from me. Per will surely also support me," he wrote.

Ole told of the reaction in his uncle and aunt's house after they had read her letter. They had been surprised in a positive way and Uncle Tobias had even reacted with a hearty laugh. He laughed because he was pleasantly surprised, he had said. Ole had to admit that the way they took the news had helped him. When you asked me to take a trip to this man's family, I have to say that it did not sound very exciting. I understood easily how important it was for you, and Uncle Tobias and Aunt Irene felt that I had to do it for you. Uncle Tobias said that he would be happy to accompany me there, but that is when I said no, I would manage alone.

Thereafter Ole explained that he had to wait for a week before he could travel because he could not take time off from school. He had planned to travel there on a Friday morning and return on Sunday evening. He said that Uncle Tobias had investigated bus departures, been in contact with Jakob's family, and arranged for someone to met him at the bus stop. So, this is how it was arranged, and Uncle Tobias followed me to the bus, Ole explained.

The bus trip had taken four hours. He did not care to say too much about the trip itself, only that it was long. The bus had stopped several times while under way. Some people got off at the bus stops and some got on. He had never been to that part of the country before and had paid close attention the whole time. Among other things he had seen several interesting farms. He was simply nervous about the meeting and wondered how this trip would turn out. He would be among only strange people who probably were interested in meeting him, his mother's representative. He knew fully well that the introduction in his letter was not of great interest to his mother. She simply wanted to know how he was received, how he liked Jakob's family, where he was lodged, what they ate, and so on. Dear mother, he thought while he was writing, you will have to be a little patient and tolerant when I include some other details before I answer your questions.

He had started from the city in the morning and had arrived early in the afternoon at his destination. When he got off the bus, a woman had approached him and said his name. She had received a description from Uncle Tobias, and no one else his age got off the bus at this stop, so that made the matter easy. The woman who met him was Jakob's oldest sister and her name was Hulda, Hulda Larsen. She was quick to explain that they lived only a short walk away and that Ole was to stay at her house the two nights the visit was to last. Hulda took the lead and Ole had no problems keeping up with her as he had only a small bag to carry. While they walked and talked, Hulda said that she had invited her sister and brother to come over in a couple of hours. In the meantime, she would acquaint Ole with her home and show him where she had planned for him to sleep.

As Hulda had said, it did not take long before they arrived at the house. They left the main road and entered a small path with the house at the far end. Hulda explained that she and her husband had raised five children who were grown-up and had left the home. Three were married and had children, the two who were unmarried did not live too far away and had promised to come and greet him later in the day. Hulda's husband, Jens Larsen, was not too good on his feet any longer and had therefore not come to the bus stop. Their house was quite large. It was painted white and had many windows. Behind the house he saw a barn, and he was told that they did not have any animals any longer, just a small garden with some vegetables. Everything looked neat and well kept.

Ole was introduced to her husband when they got inside the house and he was a friendly looking man. He had been listening to the radio, but when they came in, he had turned it off and invited Ole to take a seat. He asked Ole how the trip had been, if he was tired, and if he was thirsty or hungry. Hulda intervened and said that before they got too comfortable she wanted to show Ole where he was to sleep. He was given a room of his own, a room that one of the boys of the house had used once upon a time. The washstand had a wash basin, a pitcher full of water, and a towel hanging on the side. If he needed more water he could get it from the kitchen, where they had installed water only a year ago. He would find the toilet behind the house and he was told that it was connected to what had once been the barn. The room that he had been assigned was roomy, and he put his small bag on the bed and was soon ready to go back to Jens. He accepted a glass of currant juice and a couple of potato cakes buttered with farm butter and sugar when he returned. He ate these while he talked to Jens and Hulda about different things. Among other things they wanted to know where his school was, if he liked the city, and if missed his mother, brother and sister. Before long Hulda had to excuse herself. She had to get back to the kitchen and get started with dinner preparations because she was to serve many that evening. The men offered to help but she thanked them and said, "No, that will not be necessary. I have everything under control. You relax and get acquainted."

Hulda had not exaggerated when she had said she would be having many for dinner. Ole had to reel them off. The two unmarried children of Hulda came, her sister with her husband and three children came, and her brother with his wife and two children came. He estimated that this group of fourteen was of ages from sixteen to seventy-five. It was a merry group that made it possible for Ole to relax. Those who were of approximately the same age as Ole promised to take him sight-seeing the next day. Several asked if he knew anything about Jakob, which he did not, and others asked him to tell a little about his own family. He was shown pictures of Jakob from when he was a small boy until just before he left for America. Ole had to admit that he looked like a handsome fellow, and one would be inclined to believe that he was acceptable from the way they talked about him. He had been clever in school and had managed well on the job he had in the district. Acceptable as a suitor to his mother? That was something completely different.

They did not live far from the ocean and Hulda had secured a good-looking fresh cod. Ole did not know if someone in the family had fished it or if it had been bought at a fish market. But in any event it was an excellent meal that they had taken their time to consume with spirited conversation the entire time. They did not just talk about Jakob and Signe. Things that affected the family were touched upon, and among other things, the schooling of the youngest members of the family was discussed. It was in that connection that Ole explained to them that he always had a desire to learn more and he told them that he was very appreciative for being able to do so. His education so far was general in nature and he could envision taking some business related subjects later, he said. Several wanted to know if it was difficult to be so far away from his family. He explained that his first goal was to get an education. Thereafter it was possible that his mother would return to their home at Bakken. Or there was always a possibility that he might take a trip to the others in America. In the meantime he was fortunate to be with Uncle Tobias and Aunt Irene, and he was pleased that he was doing so well in school.

The next day he was picked up by a brother and sister who were about his age. They invited him for a bike ride and Ole borrowed Hulda's bike. The area that they wanted to show him was not all that large and he estimated that two hundred people lived there. The area had a couple of shops and a nice harbor for small boats, and he was told that one of their cousins had a boat docked there. Maybe it was he who had fished the cod for last night's dinner? There was a small sandy beach by the fjord where they went swimming in the summertime. They showed him where they went skiing in the wintertime, the place where the boys usually built a ski jump, and the area they used for playing soccer. It was nice and tidy all over, which is to say that the people who lived there took pride in maintaining the area. Ole asked what occupied the people there and was told that most worked in the nearest small city and that most commuted by bus. Ole was told that the plan for the evening was that he was to have dinner at Hulda's sister's home. The youngest would be serving dinner that was to be prepared by them, he was told. When the separated, they showed Ole the house that he was to go to at about five o'clock, together with Hulda and her husband.

When he returned to Hulda's house, it was time for lunch. He found a stranger talking to Hulda's husband in the living room. It turned out that this was their son who owned the boat and who now had invited all three of them for a short boat ride. But Hulda wanted to serve something to eat first. It was suggested that since the weather was so nice, they ought to bring some food and drink along for the trip. Each one of them carried some of the lunch food as they walked to the boat. The boat trip was interesting, they saw how the shoreline was formed at the inner end of the fjord and where the village was. A short distance from the built-up area there was an area with large birch trees. He did not see spruce and pine trees. The fishing was quite good he was told, so good in fact that some of the people obtained extra income by fishing. They explained that when shoals of the mackerel fish came into the fjord in a few days, the boating on the fjord would get very busy. The day passed so quickly with all the new experiences, and before they knew it, they had to break off the trip to get ready for dinner.

More people came to this meal than had come the night before because it was Saturday and more had the opportunity. The food was delicious and the conversations covered politics, local jokes, news from the general area, news from around the world, latest rumors about who had a new boyfriend, and some even had news from relatives and friends in America. Somebody took pictures of Ole together with several others, and they promised to send copies to Jakob. When the clock was nearing midnight, the older ones felt it was time to get to bed. Ole was to get up at about eight o'clock the next morning to take the bus back and he was also ready to retire for the evening. Much handshaking followed with expressions of, "It was nice to meet you. Hope to see you again," and "Good luck with your schooling." It had been a wonderful evening, Ole felt almost as though he had been at home.

Ole was up early the next day. He had breakfast with Hulda and her husband, thanked them for their hospitality, and started off for the bus stop. It had turned out to be a nice trip, and he wrote all of this to his mother. He wanted her to understand that he had met so many that it was not possible for him to remember their names, nor which family they belonged to or how old they were. But to summarize the experience he had with these people was very easy, they were pleasant and appeared to be reliable and genuine.

Uncle Tobias and Aunt Irene had been listening intensely when Ole told different details of his trip. They relaxed with a delighted sigh when he was finished and said that he had done a magnificent job for his mother. It now was up to her to decide how the relationship between her and Jakob was to develop. Uncle Tobias figured that Ole had been received by the matriarch of the Torgersen family. This was understandable from the way the meeting had been arranged and he was pleased that Ole had managed to complete the assignment so well for all concerned.

They felt sure that the letter from Ole to his mother would be forwarded in the same mailbag as letters from Jakob's family. They were certain that reports from there would be written by one or more persons just as Ole had written his report. Ole hoped that the letters from Jakob's family would give a good impression of him. The mailbag with these letters would be going out with the next passenger ship, which was scheduled to depart next Tuesday.

Wonderful news

The wait for the letter from Ole became long for Signe and Jakob. They had continued with their frequent meetings and were fully aware that the letter from Ole about his meeting with Jakob's family was decisive for their continued relationship. This worked partially as a damper in their relationship while they waited, and it was impossible to hide that both were anxiously awaiting the content of Ole's letter.

Signe had also had big problems as she considered how she had bothered Ole with this matter. Should really a statement from her son in such a private matter as this become the deciding factor? Should she not be able to make a decision for her future without bothering her son with it, something that had to be quite difficult for him? This was not fair of her, she had said to herself and Jakob, but it was done, and now she could only wait. They had figured that it would take four to five weeks from when Signe wrote her letter until she received an answer.

The wait became only longer with each passing day and when

five weeks had passed, Signe started to ponder and worry, what could be the matter? Maybe Ole had not been able to take on the assignment? Maybe her letter had not reached Ole? Or, maybe the meeting had to be postponed because somebody was sick? If she only knew something, if she only had not bothered Ole with this whole matter. She let Jakob know of her concerns during this time, and he consoled her as best he could and asked her to be patient.

The letter came in the middle of the sixth week. Signe grabbed it out of the mailbox as soon as she reached her apartment and dashed up the short outer stairway and tore the envelope open while in motion. She read the letter that she held in one hand while she with the other groped in her handbag for the keys to the front door. Her eyes raced down the page, suddenly she reached something that slowed her scanning pace, there she read among other things that Jakob's family members were nice people and that they were straightforward and appeared solid. In addition Ole mentioned that he had been nervous about the meeting, but everything had turned out well. He had met many members of Jakob's family and the time he had spent with them had been good. Signe noticed that her hand was shaking so much that she had difficulty reading. She had seen the conclusion, she had seen and read the words that she had been hoping to find in the answer from Ole. Finally she was able to open the entry door to the apartment. I have to read the letter thoroughly from the beginning, she thought. No, wait a minute, I have to call Jakob right away; he can come here and we can read the letter together. That was a much better solution. She reached Jakob on the telephone and when he heard her voice, he had no doubts about the content of the letter. Of course, he would be right there, he said.

After Signe had talked to Jakob, she went into the kitchen and put on the coffeepot. She arranged for suitable cups and planned to serve some crackers with the coffee. When the coffee was done, the doorbell rang, and a beaming happy Signed opened the door for Jakob. She told him right away that the meeting between Ole and his family had turned out well, something that was not really necessary to say, because her behavior already told the story. She invited Jakob for coffee that was ready and waiting to be served. Jakob looked at her with a sly smile, and as soon as he got a chance, he said that he also had good news to tell her. She wondered what that could be and he pulled two letters from his pocket. "These concern themselves with the same subject," he said. "They are from my family, and now we have a lot of reading to do. Let us get started."

All three letters gave only positive impressions. They complemented each other such that after they had been read and several sentences read more than once, they were left with big smiles. Signe gave Jakob a hug and exclaimed, "Oh, Jakob, I am so happy."

Helga came into the apartment at this time and saw right a way that something positive had happened. Signe talked fast and was almost difficult to understand when she told of the good news that the letters contained, and she asked Helga to sit down and read the three letters for herself. Signe would like very much for Per to be there also and Jakob solved that problem by offering to drive and fetch him. Helga read and Signe could not wait to get a few words with her before Jakob returned with Per. When Helga finally had finished reading the letters, it was she who took the first word with a direct and simple question to her mother, "What do you think now, mother dear?" Well, that was the big question that she and Jakob had to solve together, Signe felt. Helga for her part felt that the matter was quite straightforward, "Get married as soon as possible," she said. This was the first time that the word "married" had been used and it took a little while before it registered totally. When Per came, he was updated quickly, and was also invited to read the letters. Helga could not wait until Per had read the letters completely before she repeated what she had said to her mother earlier when they were alone. All nodded and laughed, yes, there were no doubts, there would have to be a wedding.

Work casualty

Andreas Neset and Lars Tunet had moved up another floor with their toolboxes. This was the next to the last floor of the high rise building they were working on. They had put up a large work bench to modify the panels from the concrete forms of the previous floor that had been brought to them by laborers. The panels that were usable one more time were adjusted for the dimensions of the current floor.

There was considerable activity on the floor below. Here the strippers were busy as they carefully removed the concrete forms that would consist of boards and/or plywood under the ceiling and board panels for the beams and columns. Before these parts could be loosened from the concrete surfaces, all supports and braces had to be removed. It was important to get the pieces down as intact as possible in order for them to be usable again. The strippers had good experience and used long iron bars that they put between the forms and the new concrete and they loosened a form carefully from one side.

Several strippers would have to work together on larger surfaces. One or more ropes had to be used to pull down sections of a form in order for the strippers to get some distance between themselves and the form when it fell down. Form sections from outer surfaces that were removed, had to be secured with ropes also to keep them from falling all the way to the ground. The concrete panels usually fell down onto the floor in a cloud of dust. It was therefore required that all who worked in the area had to wear face masks.

After sections had been freed from the forms by the strippers, they were left on the floor for the laborers to take over. They separated individual sections from each other, cleaned them for concrete and nails, and brought them to the next level. Pieces that could not be used were brought to the ground, collected, and burned. Movement of usable pieces to the next level could be done with a crane via the elevator shaft or by carrying them up the stairs between the floors. The pieces would often be long and heavy, and often it was difficult to get enough space to get them carried up to the next level. Individual sections were brought to a spot on the upper floor as directed by the carpenters there. In this work there was great potential for accidents; sections of form fell down from a ceiling without having been touched. Laborers and strippers usually worked side by side because it was important to get the sections removed as soon as possible after they were brought down. Sometimes sections had to be secured temporarily while the cleanup work was taking place. If the overhead sections were not removed as they were brought down, it became difficult to free up pieces from the bottom of the pile. There was danger for the workers who could easily become unbalanced and step on nails or twist a foot or an ankle. Strippers and laborers were a group of workers who had to use hard hats and face masks constantly, as the work was dangerous and the air was full of cement dust. Their working area was not available as a passage for other workers before the strippers had completed their work and all the concrete forms had been removed by the laborers.

The first thing that was done on the new floor was to erect barriers against the outside and the elevator shaft. The floor of the new level, which had been quite empty at the outset, was soon filled up with different things that are used on these types of projects. Reinforcing bars were hoisted onto the floor and the ironworkers started to extend the reinforcing bars in the columns as soon as possible. As soon as they were completed, carpenters started to set up the forms around the bars for the column extensions. With some forms for columns in place, the forms for beams could be placed between them. Soon the form for the floor was in place and the ironworkers could put in the reinforcing bars there also. Thus the work progressed hour after hour, day after day, until the floor was ready to be poured.

Andreas and Lars had several days of comfortable work ahead of them. They were responsible for the preparation of the sides for the new columns, and other carpenters put up the forms as soon as they were completed. Some of the panels from columns below had to be cut for length and some had areas that had to be replaced. A handsaw did not keep sharp long when they had to cut boards that were partially covered with cement. The permanent saw filer on the job had a difficult time keeping the many carpenter handsaws in order. The workers were dressed appropriately, because the wind could be nasty as high up as they were. Andreas and Lars worked together well, and they discussed different subjects of mutual interest as they worked. The car that Lars had bought recently was, among other things, discussed in great detail. Lars felt that he had paid a favorable price for the four-year-old car. He had driven the car on one long trip so far and he was satisfied because everything had functioned perfectly.

Andreas, who had only been in the car on the trips to and from work, could only comment that from what he had seen, it appeared that Lars had found a good buy.

When lunchtime was approaching, Andreas had to go to the toilet. He had to go over to the other side of the floor where the portable toilet was located. Lars saw when Andreas came out of the toilet and started to walk toward their workbench. He struggled to get the buttons of the overall buttoned and did not hear or see that the load of long reinforcing bars, hanging from the crane, was swinging toward him. The worker responsible for placing the load on the floor had difficulty guiding the load in the wind, which meant it was coming at Andreas like a giant whip. When Andreas became aware of the danger he was in, he was right next to the elevator shaft. The simple railing that had been put up there could not stop the swinging load of the heavy reinforcing bars that were pressing Andreas against the railing. The railing gave way and Andreas disappeared down the shaft together with parts of the railing. The reinforcing bars continued to swing until they were finally stopped on the opposite side of the shaft. Andreas was killed instantly.

Lars, who had seen what had taken only a matter of seconds to happen, remained standing as if paralyzed. Suddenly he came to and cried out in alarm. The shop steward was notified and he blew the whistle to signal the end of the work day. It was unusual for the work to stop like this in the middle of the day and the reason was explained eventually to the workers. All were told to take the rest of the day off, but they had to wait for their departures until clearance had been received from the police. Eventually an ambulance, a fire engine, and the police arrived. No one could do anything for Andreas. The police wanted to question all who had seen what had happened. Among others the crane director, the crane operator, Lars, and the person responsible for controlling the crane load gave their statements. The crane operator had not seen anything at all. He had followed the direction from the crane advisor on the floor. Only a couple of additional workers had seen anything, it had happened so fast. It was pointed out immediately by some workers that it must have been irresponsible to operate the crane in the strong wind.

The police collected the necessary information about the accident, details of the deceased, his address, and eventual family members. In addition to the names of all witnesses, they recorded the names of the foreman and the shop steward along with their addresses. The ambulance took Andreas to the mortuary of the closest hospital. There the death certificate would be issued, which would give the cause of death among other details. An autopsy to establish cause of death was routine in cases like this. Such a certificate would be absolutely essential in case a demand for compensation was raised. In case of a lawsuit, the contractor might claim that the reason Andreas fell down was that he suffered an indisposition or a heart attack and therefore the firm would not be liable.

The shop steward and the foreman took off to notify Andreas's wife and brought along the few items that Andreas had on the job. Lars had given them such necessary information as the widow's name, address, and her employer. Lars knew that Sofie was at work and that the shop steward and the foreman therefore had to call on her there. They would surely drive her home, he thought. But how in the world can they eventually leave her alone? Lars had told the foreman that he would be visiting the widow later in the afternoon. He, who had worked as a partner with Andreas for a long time, had to and wanted to visit Sofie. First he wanted to go home and wash up, and he wanted to wait for Kari to get her to come along. But, suppose Sofie was sitting home alone? After he had evaluated the situation in more detail, he decided that he could not wait for Kari. He would just clean up, change clothes, and go to Sofie alone. At home he would leave a note for Kari to come there on her own as fast as possible. In the note he had to briefly tell Kari what had happened in order for her to be a little prepared.

Lars was shaking over his entire body when he was seated in his car. He was thinking about what had happened and what he had to do. He remained seated for several minutes before he started the engine and proceeded on the trip home. He had to concentrate on the driving, but could not get the picture out of his mind of the load of steel bars that swept Andreas against the railing and to his death The entire tragedy was so unbelievable, it had happened so fast. In the same minute that he had seen his partner button his overall, he was to be lying dead at the bottom of the elevator shaft among parts of the broken railing.

Sad message

Only two or three minutes after Lars swung onto the road from the work site he got stuck in traffic. The traffic on the opposite side of the divided road moved without difficulty. The drivers ahead and behind Lars stuck their head out the windows of their cars and honked their horns. Lars, who was strained with difficult thoughts, started to get impatient when his car had not moved for some five minutes without knowing what the problem was. He reminded himself that a short time ago he had witnessed that his friend and partner had been killed, and now he permitted himself to be irritated because he was stuck in traffic! He defended himself as he was very upset because he had not, in one way or another, been able to help his partner. He was nervous about how this day would develop and the coming days for that matter. Suddenly the car ahead moved and Lars moved forward 12 to 15 car lengths before it was at a full stop again. In a few moments there was movement again, for a short while. This is how he advanced until he saw the problem, a car was stuck in the middle of his traffic lane with the hood open. The owner was looking down at the engine and appeared very frustrated. A private person had taken on the duty of directing the traffic. It was thanks to this man, who stopped the oncoming cars, that the cars on Lars's side were able to drive around the stranded car. When Lars drove around the stranded car in his lane, he heard sirens from a police car that most likely was on its way to solve this traffic problem.

Lars had been thinking about his deceased partner and Sofie while he had been waiting. How was he to handle this sad and difficult task that he had to carry out? Suddenly he came upon a great idea, a matter of course that he had overlooked completely. He would drive via the church and bring along the minister.

Luckily the minister was present and was ready to assist on short notice. He accepted the offer of being driven to Sofie's apartment. On the way there, Lars informed him of the terrible accident that had happened earlier in the day. The minister listened attentively and remained in deep thought after Lars had completed the story. When they arrived, it was Sofie who opened the door, the minister and Lars expressed their condolences. She said that she had been waiting for Lars and they followed her into the living room where the foreman and the shop steward were sitting. These, who had been with Sofie for quite a while, got up, offered their condolences again, and walked toward the exit. Lars followed the men out and was able to say that he would be taking a few days off from work. The men understood and said, "Take as much time as you need," and took their leave.

Lars, who had known Sofie for a long time, could see that she was struggling to not break down. Lars said that he would drive home and change. He would pick up Kari and return as soon as possible. "You will most likely appreciate being left alone for a while," Lars said referring to Sofie and the minister. "When Kari and I return, I will drive the minister back home," he promised.

When Lars returned, Kari embraced the tearful Sofie for a long time and all took a seat. The minister said that he and Sofie had had a good conversation that hopefully would comfort Sofie in her sorrow. The minister was the one to take the initiative to mention some practical matters that had to be arranged. He offered his support and said that several things had to be solved by Sofie herself. "First of all," the minister began, "it will be necessary for you, Sofie, to go to the hospital to identify Andreas. This is demanded of a hospital and you may bring along a friend. But before you go there, you ought to discuss with a funeral home regarding arrangements so that things will be ready as soon as the hospital gets permission to hand over the deceased. You will have to decide how you wish the funeral home to make the arrangements. I would assume that all expenses will be covered by the insurance firm of the construction company. Of course, the church will be able to assist with funeral arrangements and burial if that is what you wish. I want you to know that sending a casket to Norway requires special procedures and is very expensive. Cremation is something that must be considered, and I hope that you and Andreas have talked about this," he said in the direction of Sofie. "Another matter in a case like this, because this concerns itself with a job-related accident, is that the question of guilt will most likely arise. I recommend strongly that you engage a skillful attorney as soon as possible in order for your interests to be taken care of."

Lars said that he would not be going back to work soon and offered to help Sofie in this difficult period, aided by Kari. When the minister left Sofie to be driven home by Lars, the last thing he said to Sofie was that she should not be afraid to call on him for help anytime. "I will gladly assist you," he said as he walked out the door with Lars.

Graduation

Ole Bakken was preoccupied with his final exams. It was a busy and stressful time that consisted of cramming, eating, and sleeping. He was not directly concerned about any of the subjects that he was to be examined in, but naturally he wanted to prepare for his best possible presentations. Today he had completed the test in mathematics. It was customary that the students gathered in groups outside the examination hall to discuss the results. Ole was able to compare most of his answers, but it turned out that he did not find anyone who had come to the same answer as he had on problem number six.

He took the usual route home, but today he did not notice the surroundings. His mind was on problem number six. He remembered the problem, reviewed the procedure that he had selected for the solution, and could not in any way understand how the answer could be arrived at in any other way. He told himself to get these thoughts out of his mind, because tomorrow he had a new problem to tackle.

Tomorrow it was oral English. When he came to the door, it was opened by his aunt, who was waving with a letter. "A letter from your mother," she explained excitedly.

Several weeks had passed since Ole had written his report to his mother on his meeting with Jakob's family. Everyone in the household had from time to time mentioned that they were anxious to learn how the relationship between Jakob and Signe had developed after they received the positive report from Ole. Possibly the letter today contained the answer that they all had been waiting for. Ole put down his school bag, removed his shoes, and hung his outer garments in the hallway. He seated himself comfortably and opened the letter. His eyes swept down the lines, moving rapidly across where it said, "I miss you, hugs, hope you are fine, we are doing fine," and finally he got to what had to do with the report he had sent.

Signe thanked him for the excellent job that Ole had done for her. She had a guilty feeling for a long time for having asked him, she wrote, but now she was happy, indeed very happy. With his report the whole problem had been solved easily. She told him that she was very much in love and that she and Jakob were to get married. Then followed lots of words about how she was hoping Ole understood the situation, that he was not to be disappointed, that he was to be pleased because he had contributed so much to her happiness.

This was big news. Imagine that, his mother was to get married! She was to marry a fellow that he had never met. This was somehow not proper. Ole had seen several pictures of Jakob, which were both well and good, he had heard many praising things about him; however, he was still a stranger. Aunt Irene had kept a little distance, and when she expected that Ole had read the most important part of the content, she could not restrain herself any longer, she had to ask! "What is Signe saying?" Ole got up from the chair slowly and with a smile he handed the letter to his aunt. "Mother is getting married, read the letter yourself."

Uncle Tobias entered the door at that time and Aunt Irene said that he had to hurry up and get in, they had great news. As soon as Uncle Tobias was seated, Aunt Irene started to read the letter aloud. She read it slowly so that every word could be comprehended. When she had finished, Uncle Tobias expressed, after clearing his throat a couple of times, and after he had chewed on what and how he was to get it said, that he considered this to be very good news. He was happy on behalf of Signe, he said, and was of the opinion that they had to come up with a proper way to celebrate this big event.

Uncle Tobias changed the subject and asked Ole how it had turned out for him in school today, and Ole told him of the one problem in math that it did not appear that any other student had come up with the same answer as he had, something that he just could not understand. His Uncle comforted Ole as best he could. "You did your best," he said, and "You cannot do anything to that answer one way or the other now. You have to shelve any thoughts about this for now and concentrate on tomorrow." Ole agreed and said that the next test was oral English. From what he understood, each student would be required to read and explain something in English. Thereafter they were to tell a story of their own choosing. Uncle Tobias suggested that Ole should find his English book after dinner and read something aloud from it, and he advised Ole not to read too fast for the examiners.

The next day the students were called in alphabetically, one at the time. When it became Ole's turn, he knocked on the door and heard a voice inside say: "Come in." The procedure followed more or less what Ole had been led to believe. One of the examiners gave him a book and asked him to read the first chapter on a certain page. Ole thumbed nervously through the pages until he found the proper page and started to read. Once in a while he was interrupted by one of the examiners who wanted to know what the meaning of a word he had read was. When Ole wanted to explain the word in Norwegian, he was reminded that all conversation was to be carried out in English. That made it more difficult, but he still managed quite well, he thought. Next he was asked to tell a little about himself. Ole had thought a little about this the night before, and now he simply wanted to follow his plan.

He explained that almost his entire family lived in Brooklyn. That was his mother, brother, sister, and Uncle, and yesterday he had received a letter from his mother wherein she informed him that she had found a man that she wanted to marry. The examiners clapped, and one of them wanted to know more precisely where they lived in Brooklyn because he had lived there himself for a while. Additional questions followed, and Ole felt quite relaxed as he managed question upon question. One of the examiners glanced at the clock and said "thank you" to Ole, he was free to leave and was asked to send in the next student. This did not take long, Ole thought, and he was actually well satisfied with his performance. As on the other days, he talked with some of the students who had completed the test and with some who were pacing nervously about while waiting their turn.

On his way home, he fell into thoughts about his immediate family and had to force himself to think about the two tests that remained. Luckily he was off the next day, which would help him get calmed down after all that had happened the last few days. In the afternoon he would have time to talk to his cousin about different things, about the letter that he had received, and about the two exams that remained. His cousin had taken the same exams three years ago and could surely provide him with some good suggestions.

According to plan

Lars Tunet had some distant relatives in the Midwest that he had been corresponding with rather infrequently. They had often asked him to take a trip to visit, but somehow he had never found the time. He was really not all that interested, and he had not figured out the details of the family relationships. Lars had also an acquaintance who had settled near Chicago who had indicated in letters to him that he ought to take a trip to visit them. They had written that there was plenty of work to be had in the area and that they were happy there. With everything that had happened of late, Lars decided that if he was ever to take this trip, he would never find a better time than the present to do it. He had told the foreman after the accident with Andreas that he just could not manage to return to the job in the near future. The foreman completely understood this and had asked Lars to take some weeks off. Therefore he had decided rather suddenly to take the trip and had purchased a ticket for the train. He figured that he would be away for about a week and had said his good-byes to Kari two days ago.

Kari was still working at the can factory and visited her friends often while Lars was away. Her friends were about her age and they had lots of things to talk about when they got together. As some of them also came from the same area in Norway as Kari, it was natural that news from there became an important and interesting subject for discussion. They could tell each other about the weather there and who was making plans for traveling to America. They shared news about who had become engaged and married, and who among family and friends had delivered babies.

Once in while Kari thought about the time that Per had seen her lying naked on the sofa. She had wondered how Per really reacted that time and if he had been thinking about the incident since. She was really wondering if Per had been intimate with a woman and she intended to find out more about this. Kari had hatched a plan to get this investigated further, and now with Lars being away she had her chance. If she only dared, she thought.

It was Saturday afternoon when she heard Per come in. He came from the laundry with clean clothing and ironed shirts. Per was dressed comfortably in shorts and a short-sleeve shirt because it was a rather warm afternoon. Kari was standing in the living room doorway when he came up on the landing of the hallway. After a "hello," she said that she had something to show him and ask him about, if he had the time. She invited him for coffee and waffles. Of course, he had time, he only needed to put away the laundry and get straightened out a bit, and promised to drop in after a few minutes.

Per knocked on the half-opened door, and she asked him to come in and take a seat on the sofa. On the small table in front of the sofa she had placed a tray of waffles, a dish of jam, the coffeepot, and creamer. She invited Per to help himself. He thanked her and remarked that the waffles smelled so good, that this would be wonderful. Kari helped herself also, and as soon as Per had tasted the waffles, she asked him how he was doing, if he liked his work, and so on. He explained that he had switched jobs from carpenter to carpet installer and was satisfied with that work, which had certain advantages over his previous job, he explained. He said that he had done well with the carpenter work by having reached full membership in the union, and thereby obtained full pay according to scale. He would not rule out that he would return to that type of work one day. He said that he had explained this to Lars some time ago but he did not know if Lars had remembered to tell her about it.

Kari said that it suited her just fine that he was installing carpets, because that was exactly what she wanted to talk to him about. She pointed to the wall-to-wall carpet in the living room and said that she was not satisfied with it any longer, it was worn, and she felt that the color was rather drab. She had talked to the landlord, but he was not willing to replace the carpet at this time. Kari had heard that Per installed carpets, and she was wondering if he would do a quick estimate for how much a new carpet would cost if she were to pay for it herself. Per did not hesitate in getting the room measured, and while he was doing this, he said he would investigate to see if he could buy a carpet through the firm. He might be able to purchase it for a good price, possibly even wholesale. He thought for sure that one of his friends would help him to install it during a weekend. Kari became enthusiastic when he presented the approximate price he had arrived at. She said that she could afford such a price, and she would contact the owner of the house to seek his permission. Per promised to contact his boss and to bring home some carpet samples for her to select from.

Per took another waffle and noticed that his coffee cup was

empty. Kari offered to put on another pot of coffee, but suggested instead a can of beer, if he liked that. Well, yes, that was probably better he agreed, and Kari went to the kitchen and got a can for each of them. As this was a rather warm day, it did not take long before they were on their second can. They found so many things of common interest to talk about. When Per returned from a quick trip to the toilet, they continued to talk about people known to both of them, of places where they had been, and among other things, Per told the news about his mother. He remarked that at first he had problems with his mother wanting to get married, but after a few days he had become accustomed to the thought, especially since he had become acquainted with her friend. They noticed that it was starting to get darker inside, as the sun was about to set. Kari told about her husband who had traveled to the Midwest to visit family and friends and who would be away for about one week.

"Changing the subject to something different," Kari said, looking directly at Per, "do you remember when you saw me lying naked on this sofa?" Per was shocked and was unable to utter anything understandable. How could she possibly know of that? "Yes," Kari said, "you most certainly thought that I was asleep, but that was not the case. I was very close to it, but I saw you looking at me through the door opening." Per was speechless and embarrassed, and was only able to utter something that sounded like an apology. Kari said never mind, it was not his fault. She had herself to blame for not having assured herself that the door was closed before she had lain down on the sofa. Per was unsure of how he was going to act after this revelation, and considered the situation to be most awkward. Kari wanted to know if he had been thinking about the incident since, and he had to admit "Yes." There was no denying that it had been on his mind. He could not tell her that he had speculated over the episode several times. He had, for example, speculated on what would have happened if he had taken two extra steps toward the door and continued to stare at her for a few seconds longer. He had also been dreaming of her in an intimate way, but that he could not reveal.

Suddenly Kari got up and pulled off the light summer dress over her head. There she was, standing almost naked next to Per saying, ”Have you been dreaming about this?” as she pointed down her body. Per had great difficulty taking his eyes off her as she stood there with her great figure and naked, firm breasts. She noticed that he was letting his glance move down her body and said, “ Oh, yes, I forgot, I did not have these on at that time either,” and pulled off her tiny panties. The last time Per saw her naked, she was lying on the sofa he was sitting on. Now she was standing naked next to him and said that she would not mind if he would like to touch her. This developed like in his dreams, or is this possibly just a continuation of his dream?

Kari could see that Per was completely perplexed and did not know what to think or do. She leaned over him and took his one hand and placed it on one of her breasts. He put his hand barely on her breast, and when he removed it quickly, as if he had been burned, she moved his hand back again. This time she noticed that he was starting to explore ever so carefully. He found her nipple. In her leaning position, she fixed her eyes on his pants and believed she saw a tendency to movement inside. Kari had a plan and knew what the outcome would be. Per was just like a robot; he only listened and looked at Kari.

Kari seated herself on Per’s knees and started to unbutton his shirt and asked Per to feel her crutch. When Per did that, he first felt the hair that he had been starring at that time from the door opening, and then he felt something that was warm and moist. When Kari helped him to enter with a finger, he felt how moist everything there was. Per reacted strongly, and Kari, who had managed to open his belt, did the same. She pulled open his zipper and put a hand down inside his underpants and soon got in touch with his erect member. She stroked it gently and Per got only more excited. He lost his inhibition about touching her and was feeling her all over, and she permitted his probing. Kari had gotten his member in both of her hands and continued to stroke it gently. Suddenly it became too much for Per. He got up partially, moaned something unintelligible, and came in Kari's hands. She was in full control of the situation and knew what to do – now it was her turn to get satisfied. She got up and asked Per to do the same, lay down on the sofa and said to him, "Take me." Again helped by Kari, he got into position and soon got to experience the soft, warm place that he had felt with his finger. He did not need any further instruction now, what he was doing became quite natural. Kari asked him to control his pace, and she was working hard. It did not take too long before she exclaimed a long, "Now," and Per felt her contractions.

They remained lying quietly for some time and again it was Kari who took the initiative and asked Per to lie down beside her. Kari wanted to know if he had any regrets, if he had liked it, if he felt like going to the bathroom, and so on, and Per offered some monosyllabic words like, "Yes, well, OK." This was better than in my dreams, Per thought. "I am going to the bathroom," said Kari, "and I will call on you when you can come in there." She was on her feet quickly and Per was looking at her as she ran naked for the bathroom. Suddenly he was thinking about his clothing that had landed somewhere on the floor. He was naked himself and collected his belongings that he knew contained his seed, and knew that everything needed to be washed. In a short while he heard Kari calling him from the bathroom and he moved to join her there.

As soon as he got inside the bathroom door, he saw Kari silhouetted through the curtain she had pulled in front of the bathtub. She said to Per that he did not have to be embarrassed about taking a pee. This he has to do, and he lined himself up with his back to the shower and heard that Kari had turned on the water. In a little while Kari said, "Come on in here. We can shower together, and you can lather my back." One invitation after the other! And in only a few minutes he was again feeling her all over, with and without the soap. Per could not take much of this before he was reacting and his member was again rigid. Kari smiled and said something like, "Ah ha, so you want more. Okay, I can arrange for that." After turning off the water, she turned to face Per and helped him so that he was soon back into her warm soft place again. This time Per took the lead and while dripping wet from the warm water, they soon satisfied each other completely. After a while they separated with grateful glances at each other, and he turned on the water to give them a quick shower. They found a towel each and were soon standing all dried on the floor looking at each other. What do we do now is the look from both of them, and Per suggested that they get dressed. He explained that he had to go to his room to get fresh clothing, what he had on before had to be washed, he said. Kari understood and offered to take care of the wash for him.

Per went to his room and rummaged in his drawers for some suitable clothing. While he was doing this he had thoughts, like what in the world has he gotten himself into. After all, she is another man's wife. How did this happen? He remembered with certainty that it was she who had started it all. But, I could have run from her when she was standing next to me with her dress off. What do I do now? What do we do? He had no answers. Maybe Kari had answers for this also. He had put on clean clothing and walked into the living room, where he found her seated on the sofa. She had put on a different summer dress and said that she had put on the coffeepot again and that they soon could enjoy a cup with the rest of the waffles. Kari wanted to know if he had liked what they had done, and he admitted that yes, he had. She also wanted to know if this had been better than his dreams about her, and he admitted that was true. Somehow he could not overcome the fact that things had progressed so rapidly, that he had simply not been able to think clearly. He felt that he had been pulled along the entire time and that it was the fact that she was a married woman that bothered him the most. Kari said that she understood him well. She admitted that she was the one who had instigated the whole thing, and that she had done it because she wanted to know if Per had been thinking about her after he had seen her naked on the sofa. She also had problems with the fact that she was married, but that, she said, was after all her problem now. "But," she said, "I do not think that you have done this before, have you?" Per could only admit that he had not. She assured him that she had been taking birth control pills for a long time, so that he had nothing to fear in that direction. Kari continued by saying that this had to be their big secret and she doubted very much if they ever would do it again. But time will tell, she said. They attempted to solve the practical problem with what to do now; they could not really appear together in public. Per got an idea. He suggested that he go to a certain restaurant to have dinner. Kari was to come there in fifteen to twenty minutes. It would look like they had accidentally met there, and they could decide to have dinner together and be able to discuss their predicament further. After all, there was nothing wrong with a tenant having dinner with his landlady.

Regrets

The affair with Kari turned into a major problem for Per. He could not concentrate, and he did not know how to handle the situation that had befallen him. Both had expressed a concern about the future, as long as they lived in the same apartment and especially while her husband was away. They both realized that it might be better if Per moved out. He could possibly move to his mother's apartment. But they did not pursue this possibility further, and he continued to live in his room and saw Kari often. He had attempted to approach her, but she had refused him completely. She asked him to forget the entire episode. It appeared as if she had achieved her goal with Per, and now he was no longer of interest to her. Or, could it be that she was also showing some remorse?

This predicament was not easy for Per to understand. He remained seated at the bar and while he consumed way too much alcohol, he was unable to find an answer to his dilemma. "Why is this so difficult?" he asked himself time after time. "How in the world could Kari get me so totally confused?" In this case he had no one to ask for advice. "Possibly he could talk to Kari." He had to pull himself together, he said to himself – he was forced to find a solution. He tried to tell himself that he simply should look at this as a positive experience. The fact was that he had actually conquered his first woman. However, the problem was that this was not the way it was supposed to be done. One was not to have an intimate relationship with one's landlady, and on top of it all, she was married. And, she was married to a man that he knew well, and he had no intention of hurting his feelings or do anything wrong against him. But now he had done it. Well, she was the one who had taken the initiative, but that was still not an excuse for what he had gotten himself into. There had to be a way out of this, he thought, and that he had to find as soon as possible. Per totally forgot the time as he was sitting in deep concentration, and it was very late when an intoxicated Per came stumbling up the stairs to his room.

When the alarm clock went off the next morning, he was unable to get up. He had a terrible hangover and simply remained in bed. Fortunately his working companions had an agreement that the longest the car would wait for anyone on the designated street corner was five minutes. Per continued to sleep and did not hear when Kari walked down the stairs to go to her job. She, on the other hand, assumed that Per had left for work already, early as usual.

Per woke by lunch time and remained seated in bed for a long time to collect himself. He realized that he was now playing hooky from work for the first time and that he still had a terrible hangover. He had heard that the best medicine for a hangover was to take a couple of drinks, and for that reason he dressed and walked to one of the local bars. Even if the advice sounded repulsive, he told himself that a couple of drinks now was to be considered as medicine. The fact that Per came into the bar in the middle of the day and ordered a double drink was an unusual request for the bartender. Per was served and was soon asked if anything was the matter, and he answered, "Oh now, everything is just fine." The drinks were soon effective. He felt intoxicated after only a couple of drinks and figured that the reason was that he had not eaten anything for a long time. He walked into the restaurant that was connected to the bar and ordered a hamburger and a beer. He had eaten hamburgers there often and had always considered them to be tasty. This hamburger did not taste good for whatever reason. Maybe they have a new cook, he thought, and left most of it on the plate as he walked out of the restaurant.

While standing on the sidewalk, he looked around and asked himself, what do I do now? He meandered down the street that was void of acquaintances at that time of the day, and before he knew it, he was sitting at a bar in an unfamiliar place. He ordered a drink and got into a conversation with some men there who gladly accepted a free drink from Per. He had more drinks, got more intoxicated and became nauseous and experienced stomach cramps. He hurried to the toilet with unsteady steps, and threw up as soon as he got inside, and recognized that he had a terrible headache. He seated himself on the toilet and realized that he had diarrhea. He surmised that he had to get home, and to bed, as soon as possible. On his way out of the bar, he only waved to the bartender when he was asked if he was okay. He had to support himself against anything he could reach – lampposts, traffic signs, and houses – as he was struggling to get to his room. He did not move fast, and after a short while, he could not go on and sought shelter in a doorway. He just had to rest for a little while, he thought, and vomited in some newspaper that had blown against the entry door. He was totally knocked out, everything was spinning, he was unable to continue, and fell asleep. He was awakened by a patrolling policeman, who kicked his feet and ordered him to get on his way immediately or he would be arrested. When Per started to move and moaned something unintelligible, the policeman continued on his rounds.

Per got up eventually and left the place in an unstable condition while supporting himself against the walls of buildings. He understood that he was moving in the direction of his room, and eventually he got there. He got up the stairway somehow and went into the bathroom and was shocked when he saw himself in the mirror. He looked completely miserable. He had lost all sense of timing and did not realize that it was late in the day. While he stood there and splashed cold water in his face, Kari came up the stairs and when she saw Per, she exclaimed, “What in the world, what has happened to you, Per? Are you drunk? You smell terrible. You have vomited all over your clothing. What has happened? Did you not go to work today either?” She was so full of questions.

“Take a bath or shower and tell me what has happened afterward,” Kari said. Per was barely able to stand upright, but he started to undress as best he could and had great difficulty keeping his balance. Kari drew water into the bathtub and said that she would start the coffeepot. Eventually Per got himself seated in the tub. From the door of the bathroom Kari asked Per again what had happened to him today. Per’s behavior was contrary to her opinion of him. She knew him to take a drink or two, but she had never heard of anything like this before. Per moaned that he was so sick and said that he had a terrible headache. Kari promised to find aspirin and coffee, and nagged again from the kitchen to tell what had happened. Eventually he started to talk from his seated position in the bathtub. With his head bent as if in shame and with tears in his eyes he was able to say, “What we did a few days ago has become very difficult for me. I have nobody to talk to about this, except possibly you, so please do not laugh at me, Kari. But I cannot help it, I am only thinking about what happened. Often I am bewildered, I have regrets. I think about the fact that you who are married. I liked what we did, and I would gladly do it again. I do not know what I want, I am confused and cannot think clearly." This was a long statement coming from Per, and she understood that he was in despair. "Per," Kari said, "try to pull yourself together. Get dressed and we will talk over a cup of coffee, which is ready now."

Kari had the coffee ready on the coffee table when he came out of the bathroom with his head bent. He excused himself saying that he had to get to his room and get a set of clean clothing. What he had removed were dirty and smelled terribly. "Have you eaten anything today?" Kari asked when he entered the kitchen, and he had to confess that he had not. Kari found something from the refrigerator and invited him to eat. He drank the poured coffee, took the two aspirin tablets that she had found and tried to eat the sandwich she had prepared. "So, you have been thinking a lot about what happened a few days ago," she said, and he nodded. "I want you to know, Per, that this was something that happened spontaneously," she said, even if she knew very well that this had been her plan that she had carried out that afternoon."You must also know, Per, that I did it, knowing fully what I did, and I admit that it was I who took the lead. What is done is done and we cannot change it. Why can't you just take this as an experience in life and let it go at that? Look at it this way, you were lucky to get the opportunity," she said with a smile. "This is not going to be the first and last time you will be intimate with a woman. Forget about me, and let us remain good friends from now on."

It sounded quite simple when the solution came from Kari who after all had experience being intimate with a man because she was married. Could she possibly have been unfaithful toward her husband before? This was something totally new for Per. He was without experience and had some questions. "Am I to understand that you are not in the least angry with me, Kari? I should not have permitted myself to get involved with you. The truth is that I could not help myself, and I think if the opportunity was open to me again, that the same thing would happen, even though I knew that it would not be proper. I thought that you were unusually beautiful to look at, Kari, and I lost control totally." Kari understood from his look that this was something that was difficult for him to say and that it was something he really meant. "You have surely seen naked girls before?" Kari asked, and Per responded in the affirmative, saying that it had only been some fleeting glances. Never before had he seen a naked woman as he had seen her. "I will never be able to forget you," he said.

The food and the coffee contributed to him starting to feel a little better. Kari could see it, and when he seemed finished with eating, she suggested that he should go to bed. "You need to get a good nights' sleep," Kari said. She reminded him in order to make sure that he got to work the next morning. That would be the best for him, and he also had to remember that absenteeism was something employers did not tolerate. If they also were to learn that he had been drunk in the middle of the day on main the street, the employer surely would not look at this in a favorable way. Per thanked her for the food and said that he would follow her advice. He thanked her for the talk and promised to do his best to put the matter behind him. Kari said, "Forget about me," several times. She reminded him of the girl that he had told her about, and asked if he was still in contact with her. Per confirmed that he was, but that now it would be difficult for him to continue that relationship. Kari assured him that he did not have to reveal anything to her; after all, he did not have a commitment with her. You might want to tell this girl about our affair sometime in the future if you care to. "Carry on as before and forget about me," she said. As he walked down the hallway, she said that they could talk again the following evening, if he wanted to.

When Per finally got to bed, he was suddenly reminded of the elderly couple during the crossing of the Atlantic. Had he now started down the slippery slope that they had warned the rookie travelers about while they were sailing in the middle of the ocean?

New experience

Lars Tunet came home from his trip to the Midwest in a wonderful mood two days after Kari and Per had their talk regarding their relationship. He asked Kari to prepare coffee and something to eat soon after he came into the apartment. Thereafter she had to come and take a seat and listen to him while told her about what he had seen and experienced, he said.

First he told her about the train trip. It had been an experience, and he had seen many fine landscapes, and ridden through several large and small cities and villages. He had eaten excellent food in the dining car of the train, and when night came, the train personnel converted the compartment of the train so that all who had purchased a ticket with a sleeper, got a bed each. He had slept like a prince, he said.

Thereafter he told a little about the extended family he had met. All had been friendly toward him, and some of them were his age.

Other than that, he had seen two childhood friends and had stayed with one of them. They had driven Lars around the small city, and he had accompanied them to a popular bar, where several of the patrons spoke Norwegian.

It turned out that the reason so may spoke Norwegian was that they worked for a firm that was owned by a Norwegian. The firm moved about in the Midwest and erected silos. These large reinforced concrete silos were constructed in a continuous concrete pouring operation. They used something that they referred to as slip forms and the carpenters were making good money. Kari was not interested in how the silos were erected, but Lars was so impressed with this construction method that she let him tell a little about it. It turned out that they could pour continually because they had a method for jacking up the form slowly and uniformly. The concrete appeared under the form as it advanced higher and higher and sufficient time had passed for the concrete to be cured. Steel reinforcing bars were added and concrete was poured continually until the poured cylinder, the silo, had become as high as planned. These silos were completely waterproof and did not leak silage fluids at all. The older silos had big problems with leakage in the seams between the different concrete pours as these had been done at different times and were therefore not continuous.

Lars had a problem concentrating on these details, because he was eager to present a suggestion that he had arrived at. He said that he had been offered a job that paid well by these silo people and he had learned that an apartment was easy to find. After having given this considerable thought, he had simply concluded that they ought to pack up and travel together to the Midwest and try out this possibility. He sincerely hoped that Kari would not oppose his suggestion, he explained. Kari remained seated with a surprised expression. She did not know how to respond. What about her job; she did not know anyone out there, and it was so far away.

"Oh, Lars," she said as she walked toward the kitchen to get something more to eat, "have you thought this suggestion through in sufficient detail? Do you think that it would be possible for me to get a job out there? Or, will this be a job that will require you to be on the move often? If I do not get a job, we will miss that income that has been so welcomed, and the days will be long for me, you know. Do you know if the other fellows there had their wives along?" Kari had several more questions, she said.

A major part of Lars's reasoning was that he could not imagine working on the building where his partner Andreas had the accident. He was sure that the memory of that awful day would not leave him no matter where he worked in this area. Therefore, he thought that a solution was to work in some other type of job in a different location. He did not see any problem with the move, and their belongings would fit in their car. The furniture in the apartment belonged to the owner. All they had to do was to get out of the lease on the apartment and take off.

Kari was thinking about Lars's proposal while she was making arrangements in the kitchen. She dreaded starting in a new place again. She could readily understand that Lars wanted to get away from the work environment here after the accident with Andreas. She was also thinking about her relationship with Per. To continue living here so close to him would not easy, and it could possibly get more difficult with time. Therefore, it might be good for her also to get a new start in a different place. Separation from Per was necessary.

When Kari returned with additional sandwiches and cookies, she said, "You know what Lars, I have given this some thought and have come to the conclusion that I agree with you. Let us try our luck in the

Midwest. And, Lars, if we do not like it there, we can always return to Brooklyn." Kari was one who did not need much time to make a decision.

Lars became so happy that he stormed toward her and gave her a big hug. "Fantastic," said Lars, "let us start to plan as soon as possible. I will talk to my boss here and you give your notice to your superior. You might have to give a certain term of notice. In a couple of days I will call my new silo foreman out West and tell him that we are coming. Do you know something, we are going on a fine and interesting trip. It is going to be like a small vacation. And, that is something we deserve."

The days after Lars returned from the Midwest became very busy for the Tunet couple.

When Per returned from work the day thereafter, he was given the news that they had decided to move to the Midwest before long. Per was offered the apartment and he accepted after he had thought about it overnight. He had already been thinking about getting a larger place, so this suited him perfectly. He needed a place where he could prepare some food and have room for the different things that he had accumulated with time. He also realized that being separated from Kari would be a relief. The owner had no objections with the arrangement, and so it was that Per assumed the lease for the apartment. Per assumed that there was a good possibility of finding a bachelor who was willing to assume half the rent by moving in with him. A renter could use the hall rom as his bedroom, and the rest of the apartment they could share. Per would be getting his own bedroom. He paid Lars the amount he had paid as a deposit on the apartment and thereby the transfer was done.

Lars and Kari were ready early on a Saturday morning to start their trip with a fully loaded car. Per was on the sidewalk to see them off. Handshakes were exchanged between them. When Kari gave Per a polite hug, she was able to whisper into his ear, "Forget me." Per wished them a good trip and good luck in the future. Lars closed the car door, gave it some gas, and they all waved. Soon the car passed around the corner and was out of sight. Lars and Kari were gone.

Shipping firm

Ole was very pleased with the results of his final exam from the science branch of the junior college. He had been a hard-working student the whole time and had really applied himself during the finals. When it was all completed, it was a pleasure for him to relax, and he joined several of his classmates for the festivities after the exams. There had not been too much sleep during the celebrations, but it had been lots of fun and he had exchanged addresses and future plans with many of his friends from the period he had been a student. After a few days with his Uncle and aunt, he decided to travel to the Bakken home to relax, take care of any problems there, and make plans for the future.

It had been strange to get back home to an empty house. As an old habit he somehow expected to meet his mother in one room or another. But he was completely alone, except for a mouse that he could see had ravaged a little and deposited telltale droppings here and there. The mouse, or mice, had eaten parts of an old newspaper and had fallen for a small runner that had been placed under a table lamp. Ole knew that it was customary that such runners were starched with a little sugar water and he thought that was the reason for it being so popular. It was the sweet taste that the mice were after. He knew that he had to get rid of the mouse, or mice, and he had to find the place where they had entered. Ole had a solution for how to locate the mice. He would borrow the neighbor's cat and he was sure that would solve the first part of the problem. To find out where they had entered would be more difficult, and he was hoping to solve that also. When he went to bed the first night, he felt relaxed, but somewhat lonely. He finally fell asleep in the well-known and soothing surroundings, where the only thing he heard was a quiet ripple from the brook.

When he awoke the next morning, he felt fine and well rested. He looked in the different rooms and detected a bad smell when he got close to the pantry. This is where his mother had kept large stacks of *lefse* and flatbread every fall. He looked in and found a dead mouse in the trap that had been placed there. When he got rid of the dried out mouse and got the trap cleaned again, he reminded himself to set up additional traps before he returned to his Uncle and aunt in the city. First of all he wanted to make coffee and help himself from the food he had brought along. Next on the program would be to visit the neighbor, the one who leased their farm, and borrow their cat and bring it back home. Thereafter he would take a walk around the yard, field, and barn.

The field that Per had worked so hard and energetically on a few years ago was in excellent condition. The tenant farmer had taken good care of it and everything else that belonged to the farm. After a quick trip to the various familiar places, Ole seated himself by the living room window with a cup of coffee and a Danish pastry, and looked at the rain that had started a little while ago. He heard how the rain was dripping with regularity from the roof. He had started a fire in the oven and felt comfortable. His thoughts eventually turned toward what had been one of his main reasons for taking this trip, which was to attempt to clarify his plans for the future.

He had been sure of wanting to continue his studies and it had therefore been as a matter of course that he would apply for matriculation at the university for the fall semester. He was unsure of what he wanted to study, somehow he felt that it had to be subjects that were business oriented. His English-language skills had become quite proficient, so possibly studies that were related to international trade would be of interest. Or, he could possibly apply for admission to a business management school.

The next big question was if he should look for employment for a year or so and return to his studies thereafter. Possibly a change with a position in a firm would be good. Sooner or later he would have to apply to enter the workforce. A position would give him two big advantages; he could earn some money and establish a bank account, and he could gain valuable experiences. Maybe after some experience with a job he could get a clearer understanding of what he wanted to study. He was not able to advance these thoughts any further at that time. He knew that no matter what plans he might make, he intended to seek advice from his Uncle and aunt before making a final decision. The rest of the time at the home farm he intended to simply relax and get together with friends and acquaintances. Once in a while he thought of inviting some friends to the farm. It was possible to arrange for overnight stays for several people. But, he scrapped any such plans this time. He had celebrated enough and it was time to relax.

The results from the discussions that followed, with his uncle and aunt, were that Ole had applied to the University and was accepted as an academic citizen of the university.

Thereafter he started to look for a job opening. He looked for vacancies in newspapers and sent letters with his resume to firms that were of interest to him. In only a couple of weeks, he received a response from a large shipping company to the effect that they were interested in him. They wished for him to make contact and arrange for an interview as soon as possible. This was a well-known shipping company and Ole was interested. His Uncle also felt that if Ole were able to get a position there, he would be fortunate.

The interview came off well. The result was that he was offered a position. He accepted and moved into an apartment in the city, where the headquarters for the shipping company was located. With that he had dropped his study plans, in any event for the coming year, and notified the university to this effect.

It was not difficult to move from uncle and aunt, where he had lived for so long. They could easily take the trip in a westerly direction to visit him, or Ole could easily travel to them. This is what Ole did at the beginning, when he had every evening and weekends off. As he gained more experience in the firm, he was given additional assignments with increasing responsibility. He often brought assignments and problems home that he tried to solve for the following day. He became known to many of the personnel, and these acquaintances demanded more and more of his time. The increasing contacts in connection with his job meant that contact with uncle and aunt became less frequent.

As he became better acquainted with the shipping company, he realized that the owner and his son worked on a daily basis in the same building as he did. These two gentlemen knew most of the employees in the office and greeted them by their first names. It took some time before he one day heard a strange voice who said, “Good morning Ole and welcome aboard." This was the big boss himself who said these words and Ole responded to the greeting. The big boss and his son worked long days when they were in their offices, and they traveled quite a bit. Ole gradually got a better understanding of the shipping firm and the nature of its international activities. It was impressive to listen to conversations of where ships were located, how they had achieved their business contacts, the enormous contract sums that were discussed, and how the teletype machines were in touch with contacts all over the world. He heard of plans that the firm had for the construction of huge tankers and how contracts for the construction were negotiated. The firm was also active in the cruise business and owned modern ships. It turned out that the firm had an arrangement whereby employees could get an inexpensive trip on one of the ships, after they had worked in the firm for one year, providing there was space available.

When Ole received the letter wherein it was explained that his mother and Jakob had decided to get married, he was not surprised. This he had suspected from earlier letters, and he had been led to believe that the Torgersen family was of the same understanding. The Torgersen family, through Hulda, had been in contact with Ole quite often, and every time they had invited him back for a visit over a weekend. But it had not been possible for Ole, especially during the exams. Thereafter he had been busy looking for work and a place to live. The distance from his apartment to Hulda's house was greater than when he lived with his uncle and aunt, and it had not been possible to make the trip so far.

The announcement from his mother included an invitation for Ole to participate in the wedding. All he had to do was to decide to travel, and the expenses would be covered by his family "over there." In addition to not having been surprised by the announcement about the wedding, he had not been surprised about the invitation. He had already considered the possibility from time to time, but every time he came to the conclusion that it was impossible. He would have liked to make the trip, but he could not be absent from work for that long a time. He would have to write a letter to his mother and apologize and explain as best he could. He was sure that he would meet his mother and Jakob one day. They would either return home, for a trip or permanently, or Ole would travel to New York with one of the firm's ships when he had accumulated enough time at the firm.

Even though it had not been possible for Ole to travel to Jakob's family for another visit, he had been in regular contact with his family. For the most part it was Hulda who had taken the initiative. She had possibly assumed a kind of motherly role toward Ole, something that he had responded to in a positive manner. With the letter from his mother and after he had made his decision on how to respond to the invitation, it was he who contacted Hulda. As Ole had assumed as a matter of course, they had also heard of the upcoming wedding. Ole had told Hulda that he could not take time off to travel and Hulda told that Jakob's family had come to the same conclusion. They had determined that they would propose that the bride and groom take their honeymoon trip to Norway. The entire family would then be able to arrange for a suitable celebration of the occasion. Ole had said that he thought this was a good idea and had proposed that they ought to present this to the couple. But, as they appreciated how difficult it was for family in Norway to take time off from work for a long time, they assumed that it would be equally difficult for Signe and Jakob, who were both employed, to take a trip to Norway.

Ole was happy with his work. It was demanding, but interesting, and he felt that his efforts were starting to benefit the shipping company. He was pleased about having taken so much English in his education. It was surprising how much that language was used on a daily basis in the firm. He had left the office every day with a satisfactory feeling. His small apartment had been outfitted quite comfortably, and he had a good relationship with many of his age, of both genders, from inside and outside the firm.

He was surprised when he received the notice an hour before closing time on a Thursday. The notice was so unexpected, what could it mean? What could it possibly be that the owner himself wanted to talk to him about at 11 o'clock the next morning? Ole had been to his office before. He had, for example, been asked to follow him in after lunch, or the owner's secretary had come to his desk and asked him to follow her to the owner's office immediately. These visits had been when the owner had been looking for some information from him. This notice was different, and it was so formal. It could not be avoided. He had been anxious and uneasy about what the subject could be this time. He decided to dress neatly the next day. He had to be at the proper place on time, and he had to be well rested.

The next day he reported to the owner's secretary a few minutes before 11 o'clock, after he had been to the bathroom and had taken a last look at himself in the mirror. The secretary greeted him with a, "Good morning," and a friendly smile, which was customary for her. She probably knew what this was all about, but she did not reveal anything either with words or actions. She just asked Ole to follow her. Instead of going to the owner's office, she walked in the direction of the boardroom. She opened the door, indicated a seat for him and asked if he was interested in a cup of coffee. He thanked her, took his seat, received the coffee, and the secretary closed the door behind her and said, "The others will be here soon." The others, Ole thought, and his hand was shaking a little when he put down the coffee cup. He was seated alone by the long, clean polished table of the imposing boardroom. Along one wall there were pictures of board chairmen throughout the years and on the other side pictures of the firm's different ships, a mixture of tankers and cargo ships. A large model of the firm's newest cruise ship had been placed in one end of the room.

It did not take long before "the others" arrived. In addition to the owner, who took his seat at the end of the long table, there were the human resources director and the executive secretary. After the secretary had supplied all with coffee, the owner cleared his throat and started with, "Good morning, Ole." He continued, "I have the pleasure, on behalf of myself and the management, of telling you of plans that we made for you and that we request that you accept. But before I go into details, I want to give you a little background. As you know," he continued, "we have branches in parts of the world where we have our greatest activity. We have branches that are manned with only a couple of people and we have larger branches that can have a dozen or more co-workers." Ole started to really wonder where this was to lead. It was important to stay focused on what was being said. The owner continued after having tasted a little of the coffee. "The personnel at theses branches of ours are often recruited locally, but it happens that we also send personnel from our head office. Such persons often have a better understanding of how we run the shipping company, or wish to run the firm. The director of our activity at the New York branch has for some time informed us that he is shorthanded. We have kept an eye on your progress, Ole," the owner said as he lifted his head and sent a smiling glance toward him. Ole's thoughts reached only as far as "what in the world," before the owner continued, "it is our hope that you will accept a position at this branch that I will explain in greater detail for you."

Ole's thoughts raced fast, "This sounds interesting, please tell me more." The secretary indicated that this was a good time to take a short break while lunch was being served. She had heard that personnel from the cafeteria were approaching in the hallway behind her. It did not take many minutes before a nice lunch was served and the owner said, "Please help yourself, I hope that you will like it." Yes, that he did; it was very tasty and while eating, Ole's thoughts were given an opportunity to slow down from their racing speed. The owner was anxious to continue, and as soon as he had barely tasted the food he said, "I will continue to talk while we are eating if you do not mind." He looked around and saw no objections anywhere. "Our Manhattan office in New York is extremely important to us when it comes to negotiating contracts for our tanker fleet. The traffic across the Atlantic is absolutely our most important investment, but we have to be skillful and be able to compete with several shipping firms from all over the world. You have primarily worked in this area, a part of our plan for you," he said smiling to Ole. "We are of the opinion that you are able to handle this job in New York. If you have questions to ask of us here at headquarters, you know us and whom to direct your questions to. I cannot say all that much more about the position for now. I just want you to know that I do not expect an answer from you here and now. Go home and think it over and inform me of your decision as soon as possible. I will add that we know about your desire to continue your studies and can tell you that in New York you would have many possibilities for doing so, and at excellent universities. We are willing to help with this both financially and by giving you flexible working hours. A well-educated coworker is to our advantage. We are prepared to offer you a good position and a good salary. But this is something I wish to discuss with you if you decide to accept this offer. I also know," he continued, "that you have family in the New York area and that this offer might be attractive to you for that reason. I want you to know that our reason for the offer has nothing to do with the location of your family. We consider you qualified and we strongly believe that you would be an asset to our office there." The owner looked at the human resources director and the secretary as if he was waiting for a signal from them. Somehow they reacted in a way that escaped Ole, such that the owner concluded, "Well, Ole Bakken, it is now up to you. Go home and think it over, we will talk again soon." He got up, and Ole did the same. Ole took the owner's outstretched hand, thanked him for the offer, and promised to return with an answer soon, hopefully by the following Monday. The owner turned in the doorway and said, "I will appreciate a fast answer, and I appreciate that you might want to make contact with your family in New York. Due to these circumstances and to help you arrive at an answer as soon as possible, you have my permission to use our telex machine for personal reasons."

The human resources director and the secretary, who had held back until the owner had left, smiled and congratulated Ole when they separated on their way out of the boardroom. Ole had several matters that he had planned to complete before leaving the office that day. It was not easy to concentrate after what had happened but he would have to his best. Maybe he should send a note to his mother right away? Private use of telephones and telex machines was not permitted in the shipping firm. But the owner had said that it would be acceptable this time, so why not. What was he to say to his mother, sister, brother, and uncle? They would surely be surprised when they read that he had been offered a transfer to the New York office for a demanding and interesting position. He would send a telex to Uncle Tor because he knew that he had such a machine in his office and Ole had recorded the number.

Surprise visit

It was a quiet Sunday morning. Per had arranged himself comfortably in front of the window. He had a freshly brewed cup of coffee in his left hand, a lit cigarette in his right, his feet placed in the windowsill, and the back of the chair leaning slightly backward. The ashtray was placed in the windowsill within reach of his right hand. Per was staring out at the gray sky and the scattered snow flurries that fell infrequently and so carefully. He leaned the chair a little forward, looked down at the street and noticed that the snow did not accumulate. The temperature was still a little too high, but according to the weather forecast it was to get colder. It was expected that the city would be getting between two or three inches of new snow during the day or evening. That much snow would create major problems for the traffic in the morning, Per speculated.

He felt like getting dressed, running down to the corner, and buying the Sunday paper. He weighed the arguments for and against, and decided resolutely. In a few minutes he was on the sidewalk. It had turned sufficiently cold for him to turn up the collar of his jacket. He tossed a rapid glance toward his car and ensured himself that it was locked and that all the windows were shut. If the snow were to accumulate as he had heard from the forecast, it might be several days before he would be able to use his car again. He had no plans for using the car if he had to put on the chains that he had stored in the trunk. Per entered the delicatessen rapidly, greeted the owner, and they exchanged some comments about the snowy weather. He bought some fresh rolls, the large Sunday newspaper, and a pack of cigarettes and started back out again with rapid steps toward his apartment. When he was back in the kitchen, he placed the grocery bag on the kitchen table, found the butter, cut a roll in two and buttered both sides, filled his coffee cup, and took his seat by the window with the newspaper in his lap. He could only enjoy his existence while he sat and looked at winter making its arrival. The apartment owner had started the oil heating system several days ago, and the radiators were now heating the apartment. Once in a while he heard steam escaping from the vents on the radiators with its distinctive whistling sound.

Per had lived in the apartment that he acquired from Lars and Kari for more than one year. With the owner's permission he had made certain improvements here and there. Among other things he had installed new wall-to-wall carpet in the living room and bedroom. He had paid a reasonable price for the carpets, they were leftovers from a hotel installation, and his work buddies had helped him with the installation one weekend. The easy chair he was sitting in was his own, as was miscellaneous equipment in the kitchen. Some of the purchases for the kitchen were made upon the suggestion of Inga, who liked to prepare food. The apartment was very practical for him. He had become acquainted with the vicinity, and had worked up the routines for his daily duties from this address some time ago.

The relationship between Inga and himself was good. They got together often, and after he had purchased the car they had taken several trips to different places outside the city. His dream of purchasing a car had been realized six months ago. He had decided upon a certain price range and type of car. He had gone from salesperson to salesperson, had looked at many cars, driven the most promising, and made his final choice after one week of investigation. When he was ready to make his decision, he had brought Inga along to get her opinion of the used car that he had selected. Inga had been in agreement with his decision, and the car had functioned well in the time he had used it. It had been a pleasure for him as a means of transport to and from work and for private use.

Per mastered the techniques of carpet installations and had seldom had thoughts of returning to the carpenter trade. He looked out at the driving snow and thought to himself that it was indeed well that he had changed his type of work because a day like this was not one for a carpenter who had to work outdoors. He was sure that most carpenters would have to stay home the following day. He did not have any problem getting to work, because he could take the subway if it became too difficult to travel by car.

He leafed through the large Sunday paper and read some articles. After a while he dozed off with his thoughts. Suddenly he was awakened by the entry doorbell. He got up, fixed himself quickly, collected the various sections of newspaper that were spread around the chair into a pile on the floor, and walked toward the stairs. Who in the world can it be who is coming here on a Sunday before noon and in this weather, he thought. He opened the door and there stood a smiling Lars Tunet. Lars removed his cap, shook it, and wiped off the snow from his shoulders before he entered. "This is a pleasant surprise," Per said. "Come in. Are you alone?" Lars thanked him, said he was alone, and that he could visit for only a few minutes. "You have to come upstairs, and we will have a cup of coffee. We can sit in the kitchen where we had coffee on a rainy day long ago," Per said. They walked up the stairs and Per invited Lars to take a seat when they got into the kitchen. "Tell me about your experiences in the Midwest while I fix the coffee," Per said.

"When we left from here about a year ago, Kari and I had decided that we were to take the trip to the Midwest as a vacation," Lars started. "We had a wonderful trip, and saw many interesting places. My how big this country is! Just imagine, when we arrived at our destination, we had driven approximately only half way across the country. We arrived as planned on a Thursday. The place we came to had a small center, a place big enough to have one store of each kind. We called upon the Norwegian foreman for the silo construction. He had found and reserved a furnished apartment for us and explained how we would find it. The house was easy to find and the furnished apartment was fully acceptable to us. We paid the rent to a middle-aged woman and moved in right away with the few possessions we had brought with us in the car. After a short while, we had given the apartment our personal look. The landlady was friendly and explained where we could find different types of shops and restaurants in the center of town, and we drove around for an hour or so in the area to get oriented. You wouldn't believe how flat the country is there and how huge the farms are. The fields are so big that it is not possible to see from one end to the other. We saw a great variety of farm machines and some were very large. It appeared as if a major part of the harvest is corn. There was really a need for silos in that area."

Per could now serve coffee and he had buttered the fresh rolls while Lars had been talking. He asked Lars to continue with his story, and that Lars was eager to do. Per remembered how well Lars liked to talk from the last time they were seated in the kitchen. Lars continued by saying that the following day they had again met with the foreman who had informed them in more detail of the situation. They were told that the construction of a silo for the most part was done with shift work. Just now they were working on the foundation for a large silo and Lars would be participating from the very beginning. He suggested that Lars and Kari orient themselves to the area over the weekend, and that he wished for Lars to be on the job starting Monday morning. The foreman explained that he had eight Norwegians in his work crew, and that three of these had their wives along. "In addition to these three women, my wife is also here," he said. "During the weekend we will be having a picnic at our place and you will be able to meet all of them there. I will see to it that you will be at the right place on time," he said before he drove off.

Lars was so eager in his storytelling that Per only got to nod understandingly and serve more coffee once in a while. Lars continued, "When we met at the arranged picnic it was with a certain excitement. We wondered what kind of people we would meet, their ages, and where they came from. It turned out that all had arrived were Norwegians and just about our ages. Hamburgers and hot dogs were served, as well as corn on the cob that was grown on a farm nearby. Beer and mineral water were available for drinks. A *bløtkake*[17] and a *kringle*[18] were served later with the coffee. The conversations were merry that afternoon, and we, who were the newest of the group, were assured that we would be experiencing many more similar picnics in the future."

Lars was picked up by one of the Norwegians at half past six on Monday morning and driven to the work site. He explained that the area had been cleared and that the forms for the foundations had barely started to come into shape. Lars adjusted quickly to the work and completed the day without difficulty. When Lars wanted to talk more about the special type of form being used, the so-called slip form, Per could not restrain himself any longer. He was dying to get answers to something totally different from the work itself and asked: "Lars, tell me how did Kari adjusted to this move to the Midwest."

"Well, it was not easy for her," Lars started. "Everything was fine during the trip itself, but when we arrived and the work day set in, she changed. She became very quiet, was so full of thoughts, and seldom had a smile or a good laugh. She became moody and could become difficult, even angry once in a while. She did not sleep well at night and sometimes her crying would wake me up. I thought she was homesick and I did my best to cheer her up. She got together with the other Norwegian women, but she appeared indifferent. I was, of course, away for much of the day and she was alone a lot. It was unfortunate that she did not get her driver's license while we were in Brooklyn. That was a shame because the car would remain parked outside the apartment most of the time because I usually got a ride with someone to work. Several times I took her to places where she could practice driving the car. This she agreed to, and you know, Per, Kari is a very fast learner, and it did not take many weeks before she passed the test for a driver's license. I was mistaken when I thought her disposition would improve when she could take the car on a trip alone now and then. This was after all a place where we would be living temporarily. As soon as this silo job was finished, we would pack up, find a new job, or travel to another place on silo construction and follow the same routines again. Kari drove on the country roads thereabouts and often brought things back that she had bought from the farmers. I really thought she was doing her best to settle in where we were. I thought she was longing for Brooklyn and her job there. She admitted as much when I asked her, but once in a while I was told that she was longing for her home at Solbakken and her friends in Norway. I tried to get her interested in pursuing a job in the center, possibly she could master a job as a waitress at the popular diner there."

"Excuse me. Per, I have to go to the toilet," said Lars. Per had been listening intently to what Lars had been saying. Kari, who had acted as if she took their affair so easily before they left, had also developed problems with it, he assumed. Lars returned and continued, "When we had been there for a little more than two months, she told me that she had suffered a miscarriage earlier in the day when I came home from work one afternoon. She had notified the landlady, who had driven her to the hospital to have her checked over just to be sure. The doctors had checked her thoroughly and found everything to be normal. She was to take it easy for a few days and would soon be at full vigor again, she had been told. I was very surprised," Lars said, "because Kari had never indicated anything about being pregnant. So now it was easier for me to understand why she had become so different since we left Brooklyn." He continued by saying that since that day Kari had changed and she had even landed a job in that little diner. They had asked for and received a positive response from the doctors, and they were determined that Kari would become pregnant again when the time was right. But she continued to talk about one thing, namely, that she was homesick for Solbakken. The solution to this became that I promised her that as soon as this job was completed, we would pack up and set course for the old rural district in Norway. This is why we are here. In four days we are sailing on the Bergensfjord. We are looking forward to getting home and being able to spend Christmas with family and friends. Kari is out shopping gifts from morning to night. I am so happy that her good mood has returned."

Lars reminded Per that the silo jobs in the Midwest were seasonal work. These were completed when fall came and started up again in the spring. Those who worked on jobs like that had to secure other work over the winter. "A couple that we spent time with in the Midwest is traveling on the same ship as us, and the two other couples that we spent time with are traveling to Seattle. The men will be trying to get work on fishing boats; they had heard that fishermen hired on boats bound for Alaska could earn good money. The foreman and his wife had family in Chicago and would stay there for the winter. The foreman had worked for the silo construction firm for several years. When spring came, it was his duty to locate workers for a new season."

"You undoubtedly remember the terrible accident when my partner, Andreas Neset, was killed. We have stayed in touch with his widow, Sofie. She is a kind person and has invited us to stay with her the days we will be in Brooklyn. Sofie managed quite well after the accident with many of her friends and neighbors being very helpful, especially in the beginning. It was the loneliness after the funeral, and all the memories and thoughts that had been so difficult, she told us." Per interrupted Lars with, "It has been a long time since I heard something about this Sofie, something to the effect that she was to have received a very favorable court settlement."

"That is correct," Lars continued. "Sofie found a competent attorney who advanced the question of guilt favorably for her. The case was ready to be heard by a court but at the last phase, the construction firm had proposed a compromise that Sofie accepted. The attorney and Sofie are the only ones, aside from the construction firm attorneys, who know details because the agreement prohibited any disclosure of details for ten years. But, it appears as if the agreement must have been advantageous for Sofie. She has only said that she is financially independent and that she has made some favorable investments. She is still working because she does not want to isolate herself, she told us."

Lars continued, "Sofie and some other friends of ours are planning a farewell party for us. It is to be held on Tuesday evening at the local restaurant, and you are, of course, welcome. It was nice to see you again Per, but now I must leave you. I have to make arrangements for shipment of our car and a couple of steamer trunks. Maybe Kari is buying so many gifts that I have to buy another trunk," said a laughing Lars. Per followed him to the entry door and when he opened it, he noticed the cold and he saw that the snow had started to accumulate. When Lars left with, "See you on Tuesday," he made deep imprints in the new snow.

Per walked slowly back up the stairs and in deep thought. Well, what do you know, Kari had suffered a miscarriage. Could it possibly be? No, she had assured him that she was taking birth control pills. Could she have lied? In the time that had passed since the affair, Per had almost been able to put it behind him, thanks to Inga and his work. Now Lars had managed to refresh his memories of that episode again with his stories. Per had to suppress the picture of the affair, do as Kari had said, and "forget it." He was looking forward to being with Inga, who was suppose, to be coming to the apartment in a couple of hours. In the meantime he had to concentrate on getting the apartment tidied up. Inga intended to prepare a wonderful dinner for the two of them.

Per and Inga showed up at the appointed hour at the restaurant on Tuesday evening. Per was anxious to meet with Kari after what Lars had told him about her in their conversation on Sunday. Approximately twenty people had gathered. Some were former friends of Lars from work and some were girls that Kari had worked with in the canning factory. Drinks were served and Inga and Per accepted one each. They soon got into conversation with others, and it appeared as if all enjoyed themselves. It did not take long before Per saw Kari, who was in conversation with two girls that were unknown to him. Suddenly Kari and Per's eyes met, and time stood still for just a very short time for Per. Kari approached, she looked very nice. She came smiling with an outstretched hand and said, "Hello Per, it is really nice to greet my former tenant again." Per introduced Inga and they continued with small talk until they were interrupted by a woman who invited all to be seated. Kari took her seat at the head of the table next to Lars. They smiled at each other and appeared happy. One of the girls who had helped with the arrangements for the evening got up and suggested a "*Skål*[19]" for Kari and Lars, with best wishes for a fine trip to Norway. She continued by saying that dinner would be served momentarily and she extended a "*Vær så god!*" (please help yourself) to everyone.

When the dinner was over, it was already late in the evening. Most had to get up early for work the next morning and found it best to depart. An opportunity for a conversation between Kari and Per alone that evening never materialized. When they separated, Kari said that she wished Per and Inga a good future, and Per and Inga wished Lars and Kari a good trip. "Do not feed the crabs during the crossing! Best of luck in Norway, and we look forward to meeting up with you again somewhere."

Homeward bound

Lars and Kari lived with Sofie Neset before they started on their voyage and they used this time in Brooklyn well to visit friends and to shop. They bought gifts for family and friends in Norway and they purchased a few large items that they knew were difficult to obtain there, or at least they would be very expensive. They bought two refrigerators, one for each pair of their parents, a bathtub including fitting and valves, a kitchen table with four chairs, garments and more garments, and, of course, they were bringing their car. The bathtub was an item that Lars really wanted to bring, even if he was uncertain of where he would install it. His parents would surely like to have a modern bathtub, and he would be able to undertake the installation himself as he felt comfortable working with carpentry and plumbing. Lars and Kari did not have a house of their own to move into, like many other returnees who would often bring furniture, kitchen cabinets, appliances, aluminum screen doors, and tools.

The freight forwarding firm that Lars and Kari had contacted brought the items to its warehouse and would make sure that they were packaged securely. The firm would bring the goods to the dock a couple of days before ship departure and would take care of all necessary documentation. They were told by a company representative that the goods would most likely be packaged into large wooden crates as a consolidated shipment and that the crates would be returned by their representative in Norway. The car would be driven to the dock and it had to be delivered with an empty gas tank and could not contain any nonessential items. All that Lars and Kari had to worry about was paying the bill.

Sofie had offered to drive Lars and Kari to the dock and they filled the luggage compartment of her car with suitcases and bags. Kari was seated in the front and Lars in the back, with one suitcase next to him and a smaller one on his lap. The travel agent in Brooklyn had instructed them to arrive at the dock early, and they saw that the ship, painted in the traditional colors of the Norwegian America Line, was at the dock.

Sofie stopped the car in front of the entrance to the dock and a baggage handler appeared quickly with his dolly. They had decided during the drive that they would have to get help when they arrived because it would be difficult for them to get all of their baggage to the check-in counter by themselves. Sofie was able to park nearby, and with the help from the baggage handler, they were soon in conversation with an agent for the Norwegian America Line. Their tickets were checked and it was confirmed that the luggage tags, which they had received from the travel agent, were securely fastened to all their baggage and that they were properly marked with name and cabin number. It was recommended that they send some of the baggage to the ship storage room because it was advisable to have as little baggage in the cabin as possible. They were told that they would have access to the stored baggage during the voyage if necessary. Lars and Kari discussed this briefly and agreed to let some of their luggage be moved to the on board storage and they were given receipts for these items. This completed the check-in procedures with the Norwegian America Line. They were instructed to proceed to the passport inspection station and from there to the gangways. It was at this point that the travelers had to say their good-byes to their escorts, and Lars glanced at his watch because the passengers had been told that they had to be aboard at least-one half hour before departure. Sofie Neset had been a very kind hostess to Lars and Kari during their time in Brooklyn, and they expressed their gratitude and exchanged hugs. They looked back several times after they left Sofie, waved, and wished each other good luck. Soon they were occupied by some easy questions from the passport inspector. He stamped their passports and asked the next person in line to step forward. Lars and Kari were ready to approach the gangway.

When they came aboard, they had to present themselves to ship personnel who were sitting behind a table. They showed their tickets and were checked off on the passenger list. Cabin keys were handed to them and an escort was offered to locate the cabin. They had enough time to go to their cabin, where they could leave most of their hand baggage, and thereafter look for a deck in the open where they could watch the departure. They saw immediately that this ship had a considerably higher standard than the ship they came over on but even so this ship did not appear as strange and overwhelming as the first ship had appeared. The young man who escorted them pointed to some important places along the way: as the way to the dining room, to the library, to the lounge, and to the swimming pool. They passed a smaller lounge and noticed that coffee and cookies were being served and reasoned that this would probably be a good place for some to wait until departure. However, most of the passengers would surely want to be on an open deck at departure time to take in all of the activities that are connected with such an interesting event.

Their cabin was not large but it was arranged in such a practical manner that they would not have any problem getting their items stored. They were fortunate to have an outside cabin with a small porthole and could see that they were located approximately twelve feet over the water line. They arranged their belongings in a hurry, tossed some of the smaller items onto their bunks, and hung up some clothing in the small closet. There would be ample time to arrange everything properly later. Things would turn out well. They locked the door and walked to the lounge for coffee and cookies. The people that were sitting around the room were talking in positive terms about the upcoming voyage and the conversations were carried out in both English and Norwegian.

The relative quiet in the lounge was suddenly broken by a voice that came over the loudspeaker, "Departure in thirty minutes." This announcement was made twice in Norwegian and in English. Kari looked at Lars and they agreed that as soon as they had finished their coffee, they would move toward an open deck. Most of the passengers had the same idea so that a line formed to get out of the lounge. Lars and Kari found a spot at the railing and were ready for the departure. They saw that the tugboats were at the ready to tow *Bergensfjord* into the East River by the stern. When safely in the river, the ship would be turned so that the bow was pointing in a southern direction. Quite a few people had shown up on the dock to witness the departure, even though this was a working day. They did not expect to find anyone they knew there; the only possibility was if Sofie had decided to wait for the departure. Their searching was not successful. Lars found the colorful paper streamers that he had kept in his pockets that were given to them when they checked in, and he shared the small paper rolls with Kari. They held onto the inner end and tossed out one each. The streamers unrolled and hung down the side of the ship. Lars and Kari tied the inner end to the railing and tossed out some more. Soon the entire side of the ship was decorated with paper streamers of different colors that the passengers had tossed over the side. They exchanged some words with nearby passengers at the railing and everyone was in a good mood. This voyage was to become a memorable experience.

Lars glanced at his watch and said to Kari that the time had come. Not long after, the passengers were startled when the ship's whistle produced three short blasts. They looked down at the dock where the hawsers were removed from the bollards and saw that the ship had started to move ever so slowly from the dock. People at the dock shouted, they waved small flags and pennants, and it was not possible for anyone to hear or understand what anyone was saying among the many who tried to talk at the same time. The shouts from the people on the dock subsided when the ship got into the river and the passengers moved from the port side railing in order to position themselves in different places on the deck to witness the departure and to take in the sights. A dark cloud of smoke came out of the ship's single smokestack when the propellers were engaged to move the ship forward. Soon they saw the tip of Manhattan behind them and the Statue of Liberty ahead on the starboard side. The passengers were looking in every direction and had their own memories of the different sights as the ship moved ahead at a slow speed. When the pilot disembarked by the Ambrose Light House, the ship increased its speed. It became colder for the passengers on the open deck and they started to move toward their cabins or lounges in order to enjoy the view from there. They were on their way.

The voyage had been excellent in the three days they had been on the ship, and they were hoping that the good weather would continue for the rest of the time that remained. The sky was cloud-free and the temperature was such that it was possible to be comfortable under a blanket in a deck chair on the sunny side of the ship. Some passengers had been sitting too long in the sun and had been burned by the strong sun and wind. Lars and Kari had walked several rounds on the promenade deck and had seen nothing but the blue-green color of the ocean and the blue sky. The gusts of wind against them, especially when they were on the shaded side and close to the bow of the ship, were cold and strong enough for them to seek something to hang onto in order to maintain their balance. When they had walked sufficiently, they approached a door that Lars really had to struggle with to get it opened in the strong wind. When inside, they removed their parkas, straightened their hair, and walked toward the lounge. They wanted to relax in comfortable chairs and enjoy a cup of coffee. Kari thought that Lars was somewhat pensive but she did not say anything. She figured that sooner or later he would say something, she knew him well enough.

"Kari," he said after some time, "I have been thinking about something." Kari looked at him and responded with a "What?" Lars continued, "I have tried to analyze what the difference is between this trip and the first sailing. I feel without any doubt different this time. Let me try to express how I feel and you can tell me afterwards how you feel." He seated himself well back in the lounge chair with his coffee cup in his hand and continued. "The first time we departed, everything was so exciting. I was to subject myself to a grand adventure. Everything that I had heard from my contacts in America was positive. They had adapted quickly in new surroundings, had obtained well-paying jobs, had improved their living standard considerably, had been able to purchase clothing and cars, and had even established their own bank accounts. I also wanted some of the good life they described. Do not misunderstand me, there was nothing at home that had upset me or demanded that I leave there. I had work, lived satisfactorily, and did not have any particular hardships. In other words it was not poverty, hunger, and despair that made it necessary for me to leave, as it had been for immigrants at the turn of the century. I wanted to be my own man and would gladly accept a higher reward for my efforts than was the condition at home. It was primarily the spirit of the adventure that made me leave and I figured that this decision could turn into an advantage for us."

"This time my feelings are different. I have a kind of secure feeling in that I am now going home to join family in well-known regions. Let me express it this way, I am homesick and it is going to be wonderful to take in all the old and dear again. I never had the feeling of being in danger in America, but at the same time I felt that I was somewhat of a stranger and had to be observant of my surroundings at all times. Oh my, all in all we had a good life over there and we will surely be remembering many things with longing. But now we are going home, and I feel that whatever I had to be on guard for over there can now be forgotten – I will be able to relax completely. I am only expressing what I feel right now and am fully aware that what I have said might have to be modified later on. The feeling I have now is a good feeling. Well, that is enough from me. What do you think?" he concluded and looked over at Kari.

Kari smiled at him and reminded him that it was she who had first gotten these thoughts of going home and that it was she who had been nagging about it. She was now pleased that he had expressed himself so positively about this decision and about their future. She became so happy that she got up and gave Lars a good hug and said, "Let us go and prepare ourselves before we go to the dining room to share a nice lunch with our new acquaintances."

The captain spoke over the loudspeaker with his daily report this last day at sea, "This is your captain with the daily report." He gave the position of the ship, speed, wave height, and temperature. He continued with what most people were interested in, namely the weather forecast for the next couple of days. This was promising, and the passengers considered themselves lucky for having had such a wonderful voyage. It sounded like the good weather would continue for at least the short time that remained until the end of their trip. The captain said that he expected the Norwegian coast would be coming into view the following morning at breakfast time. Some fog was to be expected toward land but this would dissipate rather quickly. He reminded the passengers that the ship had four ports of calls in Norway. The first call was Bergen, thereafter Stavanger, Kristiansand, and Oslo. After the captain had concluded his report, a different voice was heard over the loudspeaker. It was announced that information on the disembarking procedures for all ports would be given in the dining room at 3 o'clock and it was strongly advised that at least one person from each family should be present.

The days had passed so quickly and Lars and Kari had enjoyed a splendid voyage. They had been active and participated in most of the activities that had been arranged for the passengers in the lounges, in the dining room, and on deck. They had also used the swimming pool almost every day. It was to be the captain's farewell dinner this evening and some time later there was to be a grand evening of dancing. The luggage for disembarking passengers at Bergen had to be placed outside the cabin door by midnight at the latest and for Stavanger passengers no later than 11 o'clock the following morning.

Disembarkation for Bergen passengers was planned for 9 o'clock and for Stavanger later in the afternoon. Lars and Kari had to concentrate on their packing before they started on the evening's busy program. They had plans for getting up early the next morning to witness the approach to the coastline and Bergen.

Early the next morning several of the passengers were gathered forward on the upper deck where they waited anxiously to see the Norwegian coastline. They were well dressed with sweaters and parkas and caps. Directly ahead of the ship there was fog, but most of the passengers yawned and stared. "There," someone pointed as they believed they saw land through the fog that was starting to lift as the sun was coming up. Yes, there was no doubt. They had come considerably closer to land than they believed and they could indeed see the mainland. "The land is revealing itself as it is written in the Norwegian National Anthem," someone said. They saw mountains, fjords, and islands. As soon as the ship came in between some islands and skerries, it gave a long blast with its whistle that resulted in an echo from somewhere. The passengers smiled and laughed; they were happy for this sight. For many this was more than a reunion. It had been a long dream that was finally to be fulfilled. Lars and Kari were also among the spectators and they gave each other a hug. The passengers rushed toward the dining room after this sighting to have a fast breakfast. They wanted to get back to the upper deck in order to see more of the approach and the docking in Bergen. Everyone became so very busy, and they rushed in the corridors and up and down the stairs.

Lars and Kari ate their breakfast and noticed how they were caught up in the excitement. The ship was to remain in Bergen for only a couple of hours before it continued onward, and it would be possible for passengers to go ashore for a short trip after having presented their passports to the authorities. Both Lars and Kari wanted to do this - they could not wait to get Norwegian soil under their feet. First the disembarking passengers would be permitted to the gangway, thereafter the remaining passengers.

Neither Lars nor Kari knew their way around Bergen and they had no plans of straying too far from the dock. They looked about as they walked the streets and remarked how strange it was to hear only Norwegian spoken all around them. They walked into a bakery and bought a piece of a napoleon cake and a wiener bread for sharing with a cup of coffee each. This was something they had been longing for and it tasted as good and as they remembered.

The passengers stayed for the most part on an open deck as the ship continued on a southerly course. The landscape was so beautiful to look at in the beautiful weather. It was green everywhere and the houses appeared well maintained. They passed steamers and fishermen in small boats, and everyone waved and shouted. When it was announced over the loudspeakers that the next port was expected in an hour, Lars and Kari left the open deck for their cabin to make sure that they were ready to disembark. The luggage they had placed outside the cabin had been picked up and all they had left was their hand luggage. They were ready to disembark and had their passports within easy reach. They left the cabin for the last time in order to see the approach to Stavanger. The passengers around them were pointing to familiar places and the feeling among them was high. Lars and Kari recognized several buildings when they got closer to the dock. "I wonder who will be coming to greet us," said Kari.

When it was announced that the disembarkation could start, the passengers who had been waiting for this information in lounges and on various decks stirred. They approached the gangway and proceeded down in a single file. Soon they were on Norwegian soil and they heard the Stavanger dialect being spoken around them. The passport inspection was done quickly and the passengers proceeded to the customs officials. Lars and Kari presented all their baggage, including what they had kept in their cabin and what had been kept in the ship's storage during the crossing. The customs inspector posed a few questions and it appeared that it was most important for him to establish how much liquor and cigarettes they had in their baggage. When this was established, Lars presented documentation for the shipped goods and for the car. They were told that they would have to come back the following day to get the customs inspection for these items. The wooden crates would have to be opened and the items therein had to be sorted and removed from the customs warehouse as quickly as possible. They were told that the most efficient way to do this was to arrive at the customs warehouse with a truck. Their car had to be taken to the automobile examiners for inspection, and taxes and fees would have to be paid before the car could be claimed and registered. After they had received this information, they were ready to meet their families.

The doors from the customs inspection area were opened to let Lars and Kari out to the people that were waiting on the outside, and they struggled to get all their items through the doors. Then the shouts of recognition started, then helpful hands were extended to assist with the luggage, and then they were among their own. These relatives appeared so genuine and solid that they somehow fit into the solid landscape. Lars and Kari were taken in among them. They were home.

Annual meeting

The announcement from Dale Architects and Builders, Inc. explained that the annual meeting would be held at one of the larger local hotels on a Saturday evening. All employees plus special guests were invited. Dress code for the evening was evening dress for women and tuxedo or dark suit for gentlemen. The program for the evening would start with a champagne reception at five o'clock. The doors to the ballroom were to be opened at six o'clock, and dinner would be served at six thirty after a short welcome greeting. The speech for the evening would be given shortly after dinner by the president of the firm, and the program for the evening would continue with fellowship and dancing until midnight.

The guests were welcomed in the lobby of the hotel, where the registration and tables were assigned. The guests were directed onward to a large foyer in front of the ballroom. Two bars were set up there, and a string quartet played classical music from one end of the room.

Champagne and canapés were served by servants who circulated throughout the room. As more and more guests arrived, the noise level in the room increased considerably. The guests were in a good mood, and the discussions flowed freely between the many friends and acquaintances that eventually assembled. Some of the guests had learned that the ballroom could seat up to 200 persons and they knew that the reservation for the evening was for 150.

Precisely at six o'clock the doors to the ballroom were opened and the guests moved in. They were met by a beautifully decorated ballroom. The round tables were covered with white tablecloths and artistically formed blue napkins that were set up on each of the eight place settings. There was a large centerpiece consisting of pink, yellow, and red tulips in the middle of each table. Each place setting had name card and a corsage was available for each woman. The settings had glasses for water, champagne and white and red wine.

At six fifteen a person at the podium requested that there be silence. This person was a well-known radio personality who had been hired to be the master of ceremonies for the evening. He was comfortable and capable in his role and soon had the attention of the guests with some humorous anecdotes. He explained that the musicians of the string quartet that were to play during the dinner were members of the city's symphony orchestra. He would return to the podium after dinner, which was to be served immediately, and he extended a heartfelt *"Vær så god"*[20] on behalf of Dale Architects and Builders, Inc.

The stillness in the room was soon replaced by merry people and the sounds from the many waiters who served one dish after the other with efficiency. A shrimp cocktail was served as appetizer. The main course was a combination of halibut and beef with an assortment of vegetables. Mineral water and wine were served during the meal. The dessert was caramel pudding with sauce and whipped cream. Various cookies were served with the coffee.

All the guests were finished with their dinners after about an hour had passed and were talking while they enjoyed the coffee, and some were smoking. The master of ceremonies took the stage again. He hoped that all were finished with their main course and asked if the meal had been satisfactory. This was responded to with solid applause from the guests. He asked them all to continue with their dessert and coffee while he presented the program for the rest of the evening. He asked the guests to applaud the members of the string quartet for having provided such pleasant music during the reception and dinner. They were packing up their instruments and the members of the dance band were starting to get into their positions. The master of ceremonies announced that he would soon introduce the president of the firm. After the president's speech, the dance band would be making the evening enjoyable with good dance music. Whenever the band took a break, he would be returning with some remarks, and some employees were to be honored for long and loyal service during one of the breaks. He invited the guests to continue to enjoy themselves, dance or just enjoy the music, and he reminded them that the bars would stay open for anyone who might care for refreshments.

"Ladies and gentlemen," the master of ceremonies started about ten minutes later, "It is my great pleasure to introduce the president of Dale Architects and Builders to you. The president is a graduate of New York University with a bachelor of science degree in fine arts and a master of science degree in business. This was followed by a law degree from Columbia University and experience with one of the largest law firms in Manhattan. Ladies and gentlemen, please meet president Helga Bakken Dalen."

An elegant and confident looking young woman stepped in front of the microphone, smiled, and accepted the applause. She tried to say something several times, but was interrupted by applause. When she was finally able to speak, she started by saying, "Ladies and gentlemen, thank you so much for that warm reception. I am delighted to offer some remarks on this occasion and I promise not to carry on too long. First, I take great pleasure in making some personal introductions before I inform you of the firm's accomplishments in the past year. I wish to introduce people in my life who mean everything to me and who each in their own way have made it possible for me to stand here in front of you tonight.

It is necessary that I begin with a little background on the people that I will be introducing to you. A little later you will have an opportunity to meet them all.

Tor Flaten and Anders Dalen came to New York before the second world war. Both had to report before the military draft board when the war started. Anders did not pass the medical tests on account of a knee injury that he had suffered at a young age. Tor was accepted and served in the Pacific region until the war was over. He had a distinguished military career and returned with broad experience in construction. Tor and Anders had made their plans for the firm, which is now called Dale Architects and Builders, Inc., before the war started, but the plans had to be shelved during the war. They started the firm shortly after the war ended.

My father died in Norway during the war, and mother was left with two sons and me on a small farm that was not large enough to support a family. As soon as a family member became of age, he or she had to look for work outside the home. My oldest brother, Per, was the first one to come here after the war, and mother and I followed some time thereafter. Our youngest brother, Ole, who was in the middle of his studies at that time, remained in Norway, under the watchful eyes of our Uncle and aunt there.

Mother got a job in a well-known bakery in the Norwegian section of Brooklyn, and soon she made contact with many people. In due time she became acquainted with a nice man, and after much back and forth it was the heart that decided when she accepted Jakob's proposal of marriage. Mother is now very happy together with her Jakob and we children are happy on her behalf. And we love Jakob.

I started high school as soon as possible after we arrived here, helped by Uncle Tor, and much schooling and many interesting experiences followed. My husband, Arne Dalen, is the son of Anders, and we met while we were students.

After my brother Ole completed his exams in Norway, he would have liked to continue his studies, but for practical reasons he selected employment. His plan was to work for a year or so, and then return to the university. He was employed at the headquarters of a large shipping company in Norway and was later transferred to their offices in Manhattan. So now many members of the Flaten and Bakken families are together again here in the New York area."

Helga accepted the applause and continued, "First, I will introduce my dear mother, Signe Bakken Torgersen, and her husband, Jakob Torgersen." They stood up as they were introduced and accepted the applause. "My two brothers are seated at the same table. There is Per and his wife, Inga, and Ole and his fiancée, Nancy. The remaining man at the same table is my dear husband, Arne Dalen."

When all at that table had been introduced, they remained standing for a while. The family members smiled and accepted the tribute and waved to the guests, after which they seated themselves.

"Wait," said the president with arms lifted. "I have additional introductions. My dear Uncle Tor Flaten is seated at the neighboring table and by his side are my in-laws, Anders Dalen and his wife, Berte.

Tor, is as you know, one of the founders of the firm. He is chairman of the board and president of development and planning. Anders is the other founder of the firm and he is a director with responsibility for the construction department."

Applause from the guests followed, an applause that increased in intensity when Tor and Anders got up and accepted the homage with big smiles and outstretched arms. The two friends smiled and embraced, and blew kisses to Helga at the podium.

When Helga was able to speak again, she continued, "This is an evening when we are to enjoy ourselves, but before I leave the podium, I want to say a little about our plans for the firm. I will give you an overview of the results for the past year, and thereafter I will touch upon some of the plans that we have for the future. I remind you that this is a private firm and the information will not be detailed in the same manner as if the firm were a public corporation.

First of all, last year was outstanding for us. We had considerable growth in our different sectors with improved earnings, and currently we have a record number of orders on hand. The firm's press release contains considerable detail on our activities and copies will be distributed to you after I have concluded my remarks.

Our visions for the firm . . . ."

Postscript

Quite a number of words slipped into the language of an immigrant from Norway that were for the most part words and descriptions for things that were foreign to them in their own language. Immigrants were seldom schooled in English before they arrived and these generated words became part of their daily language. These words were not always recognized by the user when they were seen in print – after all they only knew the phonetic pronunciations as they perceived them. This immigrant language was brought back to Norway, and the ones who had used the language "over there" continued to use it where they lived out their lives. For example:

Immigrant English	-	*English*	-	*Norwegian Bokmål*
apprentise	-	apprentice	-	lærling
badetauel	-	bath towel	-	badehåndkle
baderommæ	-	bathroom	-	baderom
badetobb	-	bath tub	-	badekar
beisbord	-	baseboard	-	fotlist
biims	-	beams	-	dragere
billa	-	bills	-	regninger
bisness laisens	-	business license	-	bevilling
boling allis	-	bowling alleys	-	bowlingbaner
bollsjitta	-	bullshit	-	tullprat
bounsa	-	bounce	-	avvise, som en sjekk
braises	-	braces	-	avstivere
braiset	-	braced	-	avstivet, støttet
brekkfest	-	breakfast	-	frokost
bås	-	boss	-	bas, sjef
båsene	-	the bosses	-	sjefene
digga	-	dig	-	grave
dresser	-	dresser	-	kommode
drinks	-	drinks	-	drikkevare
dørbellen	-	doorbell	-	dørklokke
eit	-	eight	-	åttende
flor	-	floor	-	gulv
florlegger	-	floor layer	-	gulvlegger
florlegging	-	floor laying	-	gulv legging
freimer	-	framer	-	reisverkssnekker
freiming	-	framing	-	reisverk
garbish	-	garbage	-	søppel

hardverståren -	hardware store -	jernvarehandel
hatt dågs -	hot dogs -	pølser med brød
hausingprojekt -	housing project-	bolighus prosjekt
hedders -	headers -	dragere
hålrom -	hall room -	rom på gangen
insurensen -	insurance -	assuranse
isboksen -	icebox -	is skap, is kasse
jekka -	jack up -	bruker jekk
jukboks -	jukebox -	platespiller
jumiditi -	humidity -	relative fuktighet
junien -	union -	fagforening
kannefabrikk -	can factory -	emballasje fabrikk
kar -	car -	bil
kautsj -	couch -	sofa
kidda -	kid, kidding -	spøke, spøker
kjiisburgers -	cheeseburgers -	hamburger med ost
kjekkan -	the checks -	sjekkene
kåloms -	columns -	bæresøyler
kutnail -	cut nail -	flate, butte spiker
kænsla -	to cancel -	å kansellere
laboras -	laborers -	hjelpearbeidere
levil -	level -	vater
loyar -	lawyer -	sakfører
meilboks -	mailbox -	postboks
napp -	nap -	hvil, lur
parloren -	parlor -	stue
pis vørk -	piecework -	akkordarbeid
pleiten -	plate -	vegg markering
plum -	plumb -	loddrett
plummet -	plumbed -	loddet opp

poketbôg	-	pocketbook	-	veske
redikelaust	-	ridiculous	-	dumt, latterlig
relaksa	-	relax	-	koble av
rogg	-	rug	-	gulvteppe
ruffen	-	roof	-	tak
saidvåk	-	sidewalk	-	fortau
sandvish	-	sandwich	-	dobbelt smørbrød
seil	-	sale	-	salg
siling	-	ceiling	-	tak
sinken	-	the sink	-	vasken
sjapp	-	shop	-	forretning, butikk
sjapp stuart	-	shop steward	-	tillitsmann
sjauer	-	shower	-	byge
sjedd	-	shed	-	skur
slippars	-	slippers	-	tøfler
sosjal sekurity	-	social security	-	folke trygd
stimer trunk	-	steamer trunk	-	metall koffert
stor	-	shop	-	forretning
strit	-	street	-	gate
stripper	-	stripper	-	river av former
stritkorner	-	street corner	-	gatehjørne
støddene	-	studs	-	støttene
subkontraktorer	-	subcontractor	-	under leverandør
subvei	-	subway	-	undergrunnsbane
svetter	-	sweater	-	genser
toiletten	-	toilet	-	toalett
tonailet	-	toenailed	-	spikret på skrå
tulboks	-	toolbox	-	verktøykasse
tulboks	-	toolbox	-	verktøykasse
trøkk	-	truck	-	lastebil

trøsta	-	trust	-	ha tiltro til
tu bai fårs	-	two by fours	-	2 x 4 spikerslag
unionhall	-	union-hall	-	fagforeningshall
ævne	-	avenue	-	gate
åffisen	-	office	-	kontor
åverals	-	overall	-	arbeidskittel, overall

End notes

1. House of prayer – *bedehus*
The official religion of Norway is an evangelical Lutheran branch of the Christian church. The church is state sponsored and the king is the constitutional head.
The country has some 600 parishes and 1,600 churches.
Norway has churches of other denominations and synagogues in limited numbers.

Norway has numerous *bedehus* that are managed by locals. Preaching is done by local lay persons and visiting preachers. Most *bedehus* conduct extensive benevolent activities for missionary work inside and outside of Norway.

2. *Flatbrød* and *Lefse*
Flatbrød – main ingredient is flour.
Baked into thin, hard round wafers. Stored in stacks. Will keep well for months when stored in a dry location.

Flatbread is served as is, buttered with toppings or broken up and eaten as a cereal with milk.

Lefse – main ingredient is potato.
Baked into thin, hard round wafers stored in stacks that will keep well for months in a dry location. Sprinkle with water to soften before serving.
Lefse is also available in a soft version that has limited shelf life without refrigeration.
Lefse is served with butter and different toppings depending on regional traditions like: sugar and cinnamon, hard or soft cheeses, egg cheese, jams.

3. Kick sleds
Spark – Metal runner under a chair looking device with the high back serving as a steering device and handle. Propulsion is achieved by standing on one runner and kicking the ground away with the other foot. Very effective on snow and especially on icy roads as it gives the user support.

4. Wooden boxes -- *Tine*
Boxes in different sizes, with locked lids. Used for butter, other foodstuffs, garments, jewelry.

5. Cloudberry
Popular yellow berry called *multe* in Norwegian.

6. Lingonberry
Popular red berry called *tyttebær* in Norwegian.

7. Stew – *Lapskaus*
Stew of meat, potatoes, rutabagas, carrots, onions, cooked to a fine consistency. Served with *flatbrød.*

8. Juice and water
Berries are boiled to make jam, syrup, or juice (*saft).* A popular drink with meals or to quench thirst is made by diluting the juice with water before serving to create *saft og vann.*

9. *Dyne*
Feather quilt.

10. *Stubbslede*
This special sled is made with naturally grown runners of birch tree trunks, shaped as skids, to support the sled frame. The wooden runners are quite durable on grass and snow, and the sleds can support stone and heavy objects over short distances.

11. *Stikkespill – Spille på stikka*
Coin toss at a stick
Any number can participate. Coins are tossed, one at the time from a fixed distance. The owner of the coin placed closest to the stick gets the first opportunity for a share of the pot by tossing all coins into the air and calling out “heads or tails”

before they fall to the ground. The next player in line tosses up the unclaimed coins, and the disbursal continues according to the individual standing until all coins are distributed.

12. Norwegian currency
One *krone* equals one hundred *øre.*
Approximate US equivalent $ 1 = NOK 6

13. *Lutefisk*
Dried cod fish soaked in water and treated with potash lye. The lye is washed out under clean running water before the fish is prepared for consumption.

14. *Kransekake*
Cone-shaped stack of round almond sticks. Glazed and decorated with small flags.

15. *Potetkake*
Main ingredients are boiled potato, flour, salt.
The dough is rolled out thin, cut to an 8 - 10 inch diameter and fried until brown spots appear. Also called *lompe.*

16. *Eggost*
Main ingredients are regular milk, kafir milk, eggs.
Separates when boiled, cheese skimmed off the top. Served with sprinkling of sugar and cinnamon.

17. *Bløtkake*
Large soft layered cake. Can have whipped cream and berries for filling and topping. Also served with marzipan topping.

18. *Kringle*
Coffee ring bread. Butter dough with cardamom, raisins, candied peel, almonds.

19. *Skål*
Bowl or toasting expression. Bowl for toasting is shallow, the word *skål* is expressed when extending a toast.

20. *Vær så god*
Direct translation is not possible.
The meaning is an invitation or precedes an invitation as in, "If you please," – "Be good to," – "Here you are."
Vær så god maten er servert – translates to, "If you please the meal is served."

Index